THE COMPLETE CASES
OF CASH WALE

OTHER BOOKS IN THE DIME DETECTIVE UNIFORM EDITION LIBRARY:

The Complete Cases of Bookie Barnes by Robert Reeves

The Complete Cases of Corpus Delicti Mort, Volume 1 by Julius Long

The Complete Cases of Inspector Allhoff, Volume 3 by D.L. Champion

The Complete Cases of the Jones Brothers by Maxwell Hawkins

The Complete Cases of Steve Midnight, Volume 2 by John K. Butler

THE COMPLETE CASES OF

CASH WALE ™

VOLUME 1

MORTON WOLSON

WRITING AS

PETER PAIGE

INTRODUCTION BY
JOHN WOOLEY

ILLUSTRATIONS BY
ARTHUR RODMAN BOWKER
JOHN FLEMING GOULD
RAFAEL DESOTO

POPULAR PUBLICATIONS • 2021

TABLE OF CONTENTS

PAIGING CASH WALE
BY JOHN WOOLEY

If you read the current magazines… and how can you hope to compete seriously if you don't study your competition?…you will know that many of the private dicks of fiction are almost incredibly hard and ruthless. Take Peter Paige's Cash Wale, for example, or Dale Clark's "High" Price. While the tightwad agency operator Rex Sackler puts Hetty Green [a notoriously stingy, very wealthy businesswoman from America's Gilded Age] to shame with niggardliness. Screwball Max Latin ought to be in a psychopathic ward for observation. The proprietors of these and innumerable other series characters have tagged their heroes with traits too strong to be easily forgotten.

—from "One Childbirth Gives You A Family," by Curtiss T. Gardner, in the January 1941 *Writer's Digest*

ALTHOUGH GARDNER was a prolific '40s pulpster who created the blowhard insurance investigator Bill "Munchausen" Tolliver for the Thrilling Group's *G-Men Detective*, he apparently never cracked Popular Publications, the home of all four of the fictional gumshoes cited in his article. However, he knew quality—and toughness—when he saw it, and it's probably not coincidence that he began his hardboiled quartet of examples with one of the hardest of them all, a diminutive dick by the name of Cash Wale.

Like "High" Price, Wale had debuted in an early '40s *Black Mask* and then settled into *Dime Detective* for the rest of his run. Early on, as you'll see in this collection, he also shrank almost half a foot in the transition from *Black Mask* to *Dime,* downsizing from a self-described 5' 7" to 5' 2".

Maybe Wale's lack of physical stature was one of those "traits too strong to be easily forgotten" that Gardner noted in his writer's-mag piece. But the main quality that jumps out from any of the Wale stories is his ultra-tough, unrelenting character, one that sometimes slops over into casual brutality. If we apply Raymond Chandler's famous dictum about how the detective hero must be "the best man in his world, and a good enough man for any world" to Wale, he might not make the cut.

Then again, Wale's world is chock-full of lowlifes and losers of both sexes who are even more ruthless and cold-blooded than he is, so at least the first part of the Chandler quote works for him. And he does have what passes for a soft spot in his otherwise diamond-hard heart for his partner Albert "Sailor" Duffy, the punch-drunk ex-pugilist.

Wale also has a tendency to speak directly to the reader about his prowess, a convention that dates back more than a century. Notable pulp-fiction purveyors of this bellicosely intimate first-person approach include writer Gordon Young's Don Everhard, who began appearing in *Adventure* in 1917, and Carroll John Daly's pioneering pulp snoop Race Williams, who debuted in the June '23 *Black Mask.* To his credit, Wale doesn't thump his chest nearly as loudly as those two, generally adding a little self-effacing humor to leaven the braggadocio.

It's the kind of conversational style a bouncer or a security guard—someone who's had to make a living dealing with sticky situations and the more unseemly side of human nature—might exhibit, and why not? Not only is Wale working at a combination of both those jobs when we first meet him; his creator also traveled that same side of that street.

PETER PAIGE, author of record for the Cash Wale tales, was actually a man named Morton Wolson, born in 1913 to a Russian-immigrant couple in New York City. His first published work—under the Peter Paige *nom de plume*—appeared in *Black Mask* in 1939, the same year Wolson was cashing checks for his bouncer job in the Cuban Village attraction at the New York World's Fair. That's according to his son, Beverly Hills-based psychoanalyst Dr. Peter Wolson, whose correspondence with Steve Lewis of *Mystery*File* (mysteryfile.com) was excerpted on that website on February 22, 2007.

According to Dr. Wolson, his father "described his job [as] protecting the strippers from overly enthusiastic men and putting wraps on their bodies as they left the stage."

The World's Fair had begun in April, 1939. By September, Wolson, as Paige, had parlayed his Cuban Village job into his first pulp credit, a nonfiction piece provocatively titled "I Guard Nudes." As the title indicates, it centered around some of his backstage experiences with the Cuban entertainers and their audiences.

At the time he sold "I Guard Nudes," Fanny Ellsworth was the editor at *Black Mask*, and apparently she liked the cut of Wolson's jib, because a novel-length story of his ("Swastika Scourge") debuted in the December issue, followed by the first Cash Wale adventure, "Voodoo Frame," in January 1940. (As you'll see in this book, that story also has strong connections to his Cuban Village gig.)

Back in 1981, the well-known pulp aficionado and researcher Walker Martin visited Wolson at the author's then-current place of employment. During the subsequent conversation, Martin recalled, Wolson told him he got into the pulp-writing business "because he was working as a bouncer for $25 a week, and then sold to Fanny Ellsworth—two stories for $170 and he was hooked."

He was so hooked, in fact, that he ended up making a living for years from the pulp magazines, mostly the top-market *Black Mask* and its Popular Publications companion title, *Dime Detective,* which published every Cash Wale yarn but the first two. He was still a Popular Publications mainstay in the early 1950s, as the pulps were crumbling around him; the final issue of Popular's *Detective Tales*, from August 1953, also marks Wolson's last pulpwood sale. That story, which was the only one in the issue with a cover blurb, is worth noting. Titled "Adam and Evil!," it's a weird, sprawling novelette featuring a cave-dwelling doomsday cult, Okies, Mexicans, Nazis, the A-bomb, and his single-name detective character, Kidd.

After that issue, Popular blended *Detective Tales* with another of its pulps, *New Detective,* into a magazine called *15 Detective Stories,* which lasted until June of '55. Essentially, however the demise of *Detective Tales* brought an end to Popular's hardboiled era. (*Dime Detective,* home of Cash Wale, expired the same month as *Detective Tales; Black Mask* had gone by the wayside more than two years earlier.)

Although they weren't nearly as numerous, the smaller sized fiction magazines known as digests (*Ellery Queen's Mystery Magazine, Manhunt, Mike Shayne Mystery Magazine,* etc.) came along in the '50s, offering the same sort of market to veteran crime-fiction storytellers. But it was far more challenging to earn a living solely from those publications. There just weren't enough of them.

Following his pulp career, Wolson did make a couple of *Ellery Queen* appearances, in '54 and '57, both under his own name. One of those stories—"The Attacker," published in January 1954 and centering around a whacko who preyed on blonde women—had some legs. According to *Mystery*File*, editor David C. Cooke included it in his *Best Detective Stories of the Year* collection for '54, with Allen J. Hubin picking it up again for publication in his 1971 anthology *Best of the Best Detective Stories: 25th Anniversary Collection*. Plus, it was the basis of "Prime Suspect," the February 27, 1958 episode of NBC-TV's *Jane Wyman Presents the Fireside Theatre*, featuring an intriguing cast that included William Bendix in the lead, along with Nita Talbot, Claude Akins, Addison Richards, and Robert Mitchum's brother John. Steve Fisher, a *Black Mask* alumnus who'd find steady employment in Hollywood and as a novelist, did the adaptation.

Like Fisher, a lot of writers had managed to jump from the pulps to TV, movies, or the burgeoning paperback-book market. Sadly, though, none of those fields was in the cards for Morton Wolson. The only television/movie credit he earned was for supplying the original story for "Prime Suspect," and while he had one novel published, *The Nightmare Blonde*, by Pocket Books, it came out some 35 years after the demise of the pulps.

With no pulp magazines to sell to, Wolson had to do something else to earn a living. So, by 1970, according to researcher Victor Berch (in a February 19, 2007 *Mystery*-File* blog), Wolson was in the furniture business in New York.

He was still in it on September 5, 1981, when Walker Martin came to visit him.

IT ALL happened because of one of those real-life coincidences that would stretch the credibility of even a second-rate pulp story. Martin had helped an editor,

Herbert Ruhm, with *The Hard-Boiled Detective: Stories from* Black Mask *Magazine,* published in 1977 by Vintage Books. A few years later, Ruhm called Martin, offering to sell him the correspondence he'd had with the pulp writers whose stories were in the collection. Martin passed, but during the conversation, Ruhm mentioned that he had bought some furniture in a Manhattan store, and as he was chatting with the salesman, somehow the *Black Mask* book came up.

The salesman suddenly burst out laughing.

"I *wrote* for *Black Mask,*" he told Ruhm.

"Now what are the odds of *that* happening?" asked Martin with a chuckle in a recent interview. "It's got to be, like, a billion to one. But he gave me the phone number of the furniture store, I called it up right away, and I got Morton Wolson.

"At first, he couldn't believe that someone was interested in him after all the years. But I told him I was a collector, and his stuff was still being read, and he said, 'Well, come on out, and we'll talk about it.'"

As it turned out, Wolson was the owner of the business, called Furn-A-Fit, "like a gigantic warehouse, right in Manhattan, at 453 Park Avenue South," recalled Martin. "A big place, with a *lot* of furniture in it."

Interestingly enough, Martin also remembered that he came in around 10 a.m., they talked for more than an hour, and during that time not a soul came into the store.

"He was an average-sized guy, maybe close to six feet; he looked to be in his sixties," Martin said of Wolson. "And he was super-friendly, not standoffish at all, and really amazed that someone was interested in talking to him about this stuff."

During the course of the conversation, Wolson revealed a number of things to Martin that might otherwise have been lost to the ages. There were, for instance, the writers who'd influenced him. While he said he didn't know any other pulp writers personally, he told Martin that Raymond Chandler, Frederick Nebel, and Roger Torrey had been his favorites. He added that he liked "unusual characters and wise-guy dialogue," and that the Wale novelettes (of around 20,000 words) had brought him about $1,000 each—very good money for the '40s.

Wolson's literary agent had been Joseph T. "Cap" Shaw, the famed *Black Mask* editor from the 1920s and '30s. After being replaced by Fanny Ellsworth—the editor who brought Wolson into *Black Mask*—Shaw had eventually gone to work for the Sydney A. Sanders Literary Agency, with many of his former writers and other pulpsters as clients. Shaw later ran his own agency, and Wolson stayed with him until Shaw's 1952 death.

"I asked him why he stopped writing, and he said it was because the pulps died and he couldn't make the transition to paperback or hardcover novels," remembered Martin. "He *tried* to make the change. He said Joe Shaw was trying to get him to write novels, but he just couldn't do it. I guess maybe the length defeated him. He was used to writing 10 or 20,000-word things, and switching to a 60,000-word paperback meant that you really had to pull it together a lot more as far as plot. He said he could never manage to do that."

One of the things that made an impression on Martin, a Cash Wale fan, was Wolson's thoughts about the Wale stories finding a newer market.

"I mentioned I would like to see them collected in a book," said Martin. "He didn't think that would ever happen."

A couple of years after their visit, recalled Martin, "He wrote me that he'd sold the lease [on his furniture store] and was trying to write a detective novel. He was trying to pick up his career."

That novel may well have been the aforementioned *Nightmare Blonde* from 1988, which was the only Wolson book to see print in his lifetime. He passed away in Laguna Hills, California, in 2003. According to his son's words on the *Mystery*Scene* site, the cause of death was congestive heart failure.

And, yes, Dr. Peter Wolson was named after Peter Paige. That's what Wolson *pere* told Walker Martin.

Was "Peter Paige" the name of a Morton Wolson friend or acquaintance? Did he go to a phone book or some other publication and pick it out? Or did he simply pull it from the air?

Unfortunately, we probably will never know.

Whatever his origin, however, it's good to know that Peter Paige is finally back in print with those two tough-customer creations of his, Cash Wale and Sailor Duffy, ready once again to guide the reader through a take-no-prisoners world of crooks, crumbs, and corruption. It may not be a pretty journey, but for those with an adventurous spirit, it's well worth the price of admission—and then some.

John Wooley
Foyil, Oklahoma
26 October 2021

(Many thanks to Walker Martin, John Locke, John McMahan, John Gunnison, Rob Preston, Tom Roberts, and F. Paul Wilson for their help and encouragement.)

VOODOO FRAME

A MACHETE SWINGS... AND A
HEAD IS OFF! CASH WALE FIGHTS
A GUN-SMUGGLING CREW TO THE
BEAT OF TOM-TOMS....

"**NOW HURRY** just a little," said Conway. "You're in time to see the famous Latin Town Revue, you lucky people! This is where you will see Alita and Dido in that sensational voodoo ritual dance, Nanyego. Hurry just a little to see the major, the most thrilling, the most phenomenal attraction in all Moonglow Amusement Park!"

Conway unwrapped his handkerchief from the mike and leaned down from the spieler's dais. "Rubbernecks," he muttered, indicating the crowds drifting by on the midways. "What do you want, Cash?" he asked me.

Conway was tall, thin, pale and young—a little too smooth to be barking on this honkytonk midway perhaps, but good.

"Don't laugh," I said, "but I lost my badge. Seen it?"

Conway didn't laugh and he hadn't seen it. I wanted the damned thing because Charles Rush, boss man of the Latin Town show, noticed little things like the absence of a badge from the lapel of his "Special." I needed the job and it took very little to make Rush blow his top.

The ticket choppers hadn't seen it and I drifted through the gate into Latin Town.

Latin Town? If you have ever been to mad Moonglow Amusement Park—and what New Yorker hasn't?—you've seen it. A row of adobe structures encircling a large plaza with a raised stage in the center. You've seen it if you delighted in a honkytonk—night club atmosphere and a terpsichorean display of tawny meat.

It was near the raised stage that I walked smack into a pair of arms that couldn't make up their mind to be white or brown. They were both in patches that were also white and brown in patches. This was Dido, head man of the sect that performed the ritual dance. His thick lips trembled.

"Cash, what for you no tells me this things about Monsell before?"

"What things? You seen my badge, Dido?"

"He is marry!" Dido hissed.

"So that's it," I said. "So what?"

"If you are my friends you tell me this things!"

I tried to move out of his grip, but the muscles on his arms stood out like ropes, and you didn't trifle with Dido when he wanted your attention and his lips trembled.

Harry Monsell was the show director. Latin Town had been his idea in the first place. He had induced Charles Rush to angel the venture, then toured half a dozen South American countries to gather a troupe for the show. To the wise guys on the Stem, Monsell was a smart guy who played angles and dames.

Alita, the tawny dancing star of the voodoo number, was up Monsell's alley. But Dido watched over his voodooers like a jealous mother, and was trying to block that alley.

I was making it my business because trouble in Latin Town was my business. Besides, I didn't like Monsell and I liked Dido, and I didn't want the big witch doctor to waste his time doing anything foolish. I said:

"I'm your friend, Dido, but it is all right for Monsell to have a wife. And it's all right for Alita to be nuts about him because there is no law that says it ain't. Forget about it, *amigo*."

"Is a law," scowled Dido. "Is Nanyego law. In Nanyego law, married man who touch maiden lose head!"

Abruptly, he turned and strode off to the dressing room.

I forgot about my badge and stared after him. This was a threat and Dido made a habit of backing his talk that I didn't like. My mind was occupied with this when I happened to look up and catch Monsell scowling down on me.

He stood on a little balcony outside the main office.

"Wale," he called, "the boss wants to see you."

I took my time. The show was due to start in about fifteen minutes. There was a fair crowd drifting through the plaza already. I cleared the stairs leading to the stage and put up chains. I went around and asked more people about my badge. Nobody had seen it.

Rush was getting up steam. I sensed it as soon as I caught the gleam of his imitation teeth. He sat huddled behind a glass-topped desk, his black fedora pulled low over his flabby features. I had no use for him, even if it was his money that had created a job for me.

Harry Monsell sprawled on a lounge in the corner. Monsell had a thin face and wavy blond hair. His bright red tie, green-checked jacket and immaculate flannels made him appear almost as sappy as he really was. I closed the door behind me and asked:

"Want to see me?"

Rush lifted beady eyes from a sheaf of faded press clippings on his desk, then dropped them back again.

It didn't take a crystal ball to show me the score. My face leered up from the top clipping and I whirled on Monsell. "Did *you* dig them up?"

"What difference does it make?" exploded Rush slamming his fist down on the desk. "I hired you with the understanding you were a private detective. Experienced. You gave references. You gave a whole history." He shook the clippings at my face. "With all the bad publicity I'm getting as it is, do you think I can afford to keep a—a gangster in my organization?"

I ignored Rush. I was facing Monsell. I said, "I'm talking to you, Punk. Is this for telling you to lay off riding Dido? Did you dig up those clippings? Why, you poor simp, I was doing you a favor. Fooling around with a guy like Dido, you'll wind up without a head some morning."

Monsell sneered, "Don't waste your breath, Wale. We caught up with you and you're through. Get out. This room is beginning to smell."

A second later he was following his gorgeous red tie up from the lounge. Then he sat down again, starting from where his mouth had met my fist. I am not very big and Monsell topped me by inches and pounds, but there has yet to come a day that I can't take his kind of punk. I didn't release his tie and we had an encore.

Then I had to drop the tie and turn my attention to Rush, who was half-way over his desk and banging away at my back with a telephone receiver. When I finally had Rush unraveled and the receiver back in its cradle, Monsell was gone.

Rush's toad-like hulk crouched behind the desk. The fedora tilted over one ear. His face slowly turned from pink to scarlet.

"Don't say it," I said. "I quit!"

"You're fired!" he managed to croak. "Get out. Turn in your badge. Get out!"

I felt tired and disgusted. I said, "There's still a matter of four days' pay."

"I'll mail it to you. Only get out or I'll have you thrown out!"

"You won't have me thrown out," I said. "Separate yourself from twenty bucks and I'll leave quietly." I reached out and he lurched back, almost toppling from his chair. I scooped up the sheaf of clippings and said, "I'll be hanging around the bar until you make up your mind."

He started to yell something and I snapped, "Some day, Charley, that phoney chin hardware of yours is going to fly out of your mouth and you won't be around to catch it."

Then I left.

BACK IN the plaza again, I stopped to examine the clippings and then Alita crooked a finger at me from the door of the prop room.

The clippings dated back to a time when I peddled lead protection to half a dozen guys named Mike, who are now serving assorted stretches in Alcatraz. Nothing is supposed to be as dead as yesterday's newspaper, yet this stuff was eight years old and alive enough to do me out of a job.

I felt very sore at Monsell as I crossed the plaza to Alita, and speculated whether or not to look him up before I left Latin Town and introduce him to the fist that had been holding his necktie.

Alita backed me up against a skull-shaped altar inside the prop room. Her breasts heaved. Her ebony eyes sizzled. She said, "Hot damn! Hot damn, you one shrimp son of a blankety blank blank, Cash Wale. W'at you tal Dido, hah?"

I sat back on the altar and gently disengaged my lapels from her sepia fingers. Alita had a chronic case of ants. In her short stay in the U.S. she had picked up, besides Monsell, the manners and speech of a Harlem streetwalker.

"I told him," I said deliberately, "that he could do better than lose weight over a couple of tramps."

A minute later I had removed her nails from my eyes and was struggling back through the thickening crowd in the plaza. I was sick and tired of having every punk and his sister make passes at me. I wanted a drink.

The bar was in one of the adobe structures encircling the plaza. A handful of people stood around nursing glasses. A steady stream of others kept entering and leaving. The prices made them leave.

The second rum straight cleared some of the fog from my brain and loosened my spine. I was contemplating looking up Monsell and having it out with him when Sailor Duffy edged up alongside and said:

"Don't drink anymore, Cash. You'll get canned."

"I can't get canned," I said. "I quit."

Sailor looked down at me with eyes that were like ice chips imbedded in a warped billiard ball of a head. He looked down at me because he towered six-three in his socks. Not so long ago he was one of the bigger names in heavyweight circles.

Strange noises in his ears and an urge to break pavements with his skull finally got him. That was the time I decided to go legitimate and, together, we had formed the Cash Wale Detective Agency. These jobs at Latin Town were a last stab to keep the agency going after months of depression. Sailor was Mr. Bounce of the Latin Town bar. He said:

"Then I quit, Cash. I go up to Rush and shove the lousy job—"

"You'll keep your job," I cut in, "if we're going to eat regular. Now get down the other end of the bar and leave me alone. I'll see you tonight."

Three drinks later I decided I wanted to bat Rush around as much as Monsell; more, maybe. I said it out loud:

"I'll push that fat slob around."

"What fat slob?"

Conway stood at my side looking down at me. It is no trick to look down at me. I'm five seven.

"How the hell did you get here?" I inquired.

Conway grinned. He was a nice guy, and a good barker in spite of an eyebrow mustache. We had emptied some bottles together on occasions when life in Moonglow Amusement Park threatened to get us down. He carried the case he used for sound equipment.

"Amplifier went dead. I'm taking time out while the electrician fools around with it. What was that about a fat slob?"

I told him what I thought of Rush. He grinned some more and we had drinks. Sailor Duffy stood down the other end of the bar watching us moodily.

Most of the show passed us by, but, when the voodoo drums started to roll, Conway and I moved over to the door of the bar to watch.

I don't know if you have ever seen a voodoo dance, a *real* voodoo dance. Primitive passions are unleashed and there is a pagan worship of things. A vague mystery is given to symbols and fetishes and, for the moment, you are thrust back into the sorcery of the dark ages. Seven dark-skinned drummers squatted in a semi-circle behind the skull-shaped altar on the platform, beating with dried bones on goat skins stretched over hollowed tree trunks. Each drummer beat out his own peculiar rhythm; all blending in an ebb and flow of compelling drum notes. Then the beat quickened and the drummers struck up a weird, compelling chant.

"I've seen this a hundred times," murmured Conway softly, "and it still gets me."

I did not tell him how much it was getting me. Maybe it was the rum in my gullet. The chant seemed to crawl up my spine.

The drummers grew wilder. The beat speeded until I wanted to jerk away and get another drink. Then Dido spun onto the platform, swinging a black rooster in his left hand and a glistening machete in his right.

I forgot Conway and the hushed crowd pressed up against the platform. I watched, fascinated, as Dido spun closer and closer to the large skull-shaped altar beyond which the drummers bobbed and weaved to their rhythms.

My mind played me a trick and leaped ahead—Dido would spin to a quickening tempo until he was almost on top of the altar. He would flick the machete and the black rooster's head would sail away over the heads of the startled crowd. Dido would fling the bleeding bird from him, strike a triumphant pose and scream something in Nanyego. Smoke would spout from the altar, swirl about, fade—leaving Alita emerge from its midst, clad in a proud smile. She would step daintily from the altar and sweep into a sinewy, pagan dance....

Conway's elbow shifted and I snapped back to earth. Dido was almost on top of the altar. The machete jerked and the black rooster's head flew off into space. Dido screamed in Nanyego and the cloud of smoke swirled up from the altar, faded slowly.

Conway gasped and leaned forward. Somewhere, a woman's voice rose in a prolonged, knife-like scream. I whirled back to the bar, finished my drink, then raced out into the plaza after Conway.

Instead of the sepia form of Alita emerging from the swirl of smoke, there was a figure in a red necktie, green checked jacket, spotless flannels. As I reached the fringe of the startled crowd the figure bowed forward and the tie slipped off. Continuing the motion, the figure dove from the altar and sprawled to the platform, the hacked stump of its neck gleaming at us.

For a moment, only the drummers and Dido and Conway and myself were in motion, then all hell broke loose.

The drum-beats didn't falter. Dido continued to spin and gesture around the stage. A voice rose above the confusion:

"Get that black witch guy! He killed a white man!"

Other voices took up the cry.

Conway yelled something I couldn't make out when I crawled to the stage. He pointed to Dido. I nodded and grabbed one of Dido's oiled arms. He took a few more steps, shivered, stopped. The drum-beats faltered, stopped also.

We had to pass Monsell's headless body to get off the stage and my stomach did a flip flop. Clenched in one of Monsell's outthrust hands was something that glinted silver.

The rum clogged my head and I wanted to stop and think. But the crowd was rapidly turning into a mob. I don't remember exactly how we did it. I recall pushing one dame where she was undoubtedly sensitive. But pushing, yelling, dropping a fist here and there, we managed to get Dido into the prop room and slam the door.

I had good reasons for picking the prop room. It was the handiest refuge. It was where Monsell's body had been hidden in the altar before the stage hands carried the altar to the stage. It was where Alita should be.

And was. A grimy bulb gave the room a vague sort of light. Enough to see a pile of canvas in the corner move. Alita was underneath, bound and gagged. Her eyes bulged in unconcealed terror. Ours bulged, too. On the floor at her side lay a machete with a dripping blade.

Dido lifted it off the floor before I could stop him. He regarded it blankly.

"There go the killer's prints," I said.

Dido turned that blank stare on me. He seemed to be in a trance.

Conway started asking Alita questions but she, also, was staring at me.

I tried to remember where I had last seen my badge. The rum seemed to be oozing into my brain cells and forcing them to relax. I drove myself to think. I knew where it was now, all right. Clenched in Monsell's fist. And there was no chance of getting it. Fists pounded on the door and angry voices called for "That dirty black witch guy!"

A picture was forming in my mind that I didn't like. Rush would be sure to testify how I'd batted Monsell around. The badge in Monsell's hand and my reputation as an unconvicted gangster would all lead to my arrest on suspicion of murder.

Conway gripped Alita's arm.

"What happened, girl?"

"I talk here wit' Harry," she said in a dead tone. "One feelthy so and so come een an' bang Harry on hees nut. Then, bam! He bang me on nut. I go by-by. You ask Harry Monsell, heem tal you. Hot damn!"

"Who was it?" I asked. I had an excellent reason for asking. I was beginning to scent the distinct odor of a frame.

An authoritative rapping on the door cut short her reply. The first to enter was a park guard, green chevrons on the tan jacket of his uniform and a revolver in his belt. He was young, probably just off the police list. Rush waddled in after him, spotted me and flung out an arm.

"That's him!" he yelled. "The guy I told you about, Sergeant. There's your killer!"

The sergeant took a step forward, then blanched and drew back involuntarily. Anyone would blanch at the sight of Dido in costume with a bloody machete in his hand.

"Well," gasped the sergeant, "how about it?"

"Relax," I said.

He looked at Conway, then at Alita and Dido, then back at me. He tried to act hard but a whistle dangling on his chest made a fool of his fingers.

"Don't get tough, you! I mean about the dead guy. You do it?" he asked.

Over his shoulder I glimpsed some of his buddies holding back the crowd. Other of the park cops formed a circle around Monsell's body on the stage. I was glad to see that behind the sergeant and Rush stood Sailor Duffy.

"Rush," I said, "is as screwy as he looks. Sure, I kicked the dead guy around a little before. But nothing serious."

"You ain't answered my question."

"He's stalling!" snapped Rush heatedly. "Can't you see he's stalling? He and that Dido formed a conspiracy. He's a trouble-maker. He told Monsell half an hour ago that Monsell would lose his head. He—"

"How about it?" blurted the sergeant.

I could see he was rattled, working himself up. His fingers dropped the whistle and settled near his gun. Not many of the park cops were armed, and few of these had much experience. I didn't like amateurs with guns. My .32 caliber automatic was flat and didn't bulge the outline of my jacket. I gave Sailor the eye and said:

"Listen, Bud. You look like a nice guy and I'd hate to see you mess things up. Why not wait for the regular Homicide detail to arrive before popping your biscuit? Look, I'm old at this game. I'm a private detective. I got a license. Here, look."

His cheeks burned but he took my bait. His eyes followed my hand and I had my heater out and the safety released before he could reach for his and start anything foolish. Even a would-be cop hero could get that kind of point. In fact everybody got the point and there was a sudden silence.

Conway broke it with a startled whisper.

"Watcha doing, Cash?"

I cleared the doorway with a flick of my wrist.

"I'm not getting railroaded on a frame. I want out!"

Rush looked very sick with my sights lined on his middle chin, and he jerked clumsily out of the doorway. The cops outside were not armed. They stood motionless and looked thoughtful.

A door next to the prop room opened on a passage that led through the spieler's booth and out to the dais from which Conway addressed the crowds on the midway.

As I slipped into this passage, two of the unarmed cops started moving. A police whistle shrilled. Many throats set up shouts at the same time. I caught a glimpse of Sailor Duffy stumbling in front of the two cops, then holding them back to beg their pardons.

Then I was out and lost in the milling throng of visitors on the midway. This was not hard. Charley McCarthy could be lost and unrecognized for hours in a Moonglow Park crowd. And I didn't wear a monocle.

It didn't take long to dawn on me that I had acted like a grade A sap. Maybe it was the rum, but I had let my badge in Monsell's hand and Rush sounding off rattle me into flashing a heater on an officer of the law; a strong enough charge to revoke my gun permit and detective license. And the whole time my alibi was a four star lulu! It must have been the rum.

Rush, Alita, Sailor Duffy and Conway had been with me, one after the other, from the time Monsell left Rush's office until his corpse leaped from the altar. It was air-tight! I had had nothing to worry about except going through a few technicalities. Now I was probably due for an all-around trimming.

I took it all out on five bouncing balls, ten lighted candles and ten clay pipes in a shooting gallery. The attendant's low whistle of respect soothed me somewhat until I noticed I'd been firing a discarded Army rifle. Only one chain of shooting galleries featured that gun. The sign outside confirmed my sudden suspicion: Shoot an Army Rifle! Another Rush Enterprise.

I left the park feeling very glum. It was four-thirty, Friday afternoon, and Rush still owed me twenty bucks. I wanted another drink.

BY THE time I arrived in Times Square I wanted more than that. I wanted a long beard and an airplane and a passport. And half a dozen drinks!

In a little cafeteria off Broadway I sat in a corner and read half a dozen papers about me. They all boiled down to the same thing. There were pictures of Rush and his statement how I had threatened Monsell, then followed him down to the plaza. Alita took up from there and described how I had burst into the prop room with a drawn gun, conked Monsell, then her. Some of the crowd had seen me enter and leave the prop room. This, together with my badge in Monsell's hand, summed up the case against me. It was enough!

Dido was in the clink on a technical charge of suspicion. He had suddenly clammed and that made it worse. They figured I had goaded him to do the actual killing and then arranged Monsell in the altar in Alita's place. Monsell's head and I were still missing. They expected to find both hourly.

Fantastic? That was my reaction until I read the police wanted statement. Cash Wale was wanted for murder. Arrangements were being made to post a reward. He was short and slightly bald and wore natty duds and packed a heater which he had been known to use recklessly in tight places. Their phrase was "gun crazy." There is nothing fantastic about a police wanted statement. And the profile of me on half a dozen front pages wasn't fantastic either. Only unflattering.

I wasn't surprised to see Sailor Duffy come up the stairs on the uptown side of the Forty-Second Street station of the Independent Subway. It was nine o'clock and he was due. He gave no sign of recognition as he passed me and I let a dozen people get between us before following.

He boarded an A train and waited near the door. I remained on the platform. He slipped out again just as the doors closed. I was careful to see that no one else left the train after him before leading the way back to the downtown side. It had taken many hours of practice for Sailor to learn this tailshaking technique.

He slapped a rolled newspaper against his knee and chuckled as soon as we were seated in a downtown local.

"That fooled 'em, hey, Cash?"

"We hope," I said. "Did you get in trouble with those park boy scouts?"

"Nah. They ain't scouts, Cash. Most of 'em's gonna be cops. Rush almost laid an egg when you lammed. Who bumped Monsell, Cash?"

"How the hell should I know? I didn't."

"But you're gonna find out, hey, Cash?"

"Either that or I'll get my pants scorched. How are we fixed for what it takes?"

Sailor had twelve dollars. I took ten.

"Draw some more out of the bank tomorrow, then look us up a furnished room around the east side somewheres. Without bugs. Rush has only our office address so you'll be able to move before they reach the apartment. And don't go back to Latin Town. Quit."

"I quit," said Sailor.

"Think you can remember everything?"

"Aw, nuts, Cash. Didn't I tell you yesterday I don't hear noises so much now? I can remember stuff like that. I even—" His face suddenly screwed into an expression that made an elderly dame sitting across the way move down to the other end of the car. Sailor was just registering excitement. "Look," he blurted, "I even got a clue!"

I unfolded the paper he thrust at me. It was a morning rag filled with stuff about Japs rubbing out Chinks, about ships being submarined, guesses about F.D.R. making it a triple.

"What makes this a clue? Give."

"After you lammed, everybody was running around wild, so I sneaked up to Monsell's office for a gander. I figured that's what you'd 've done if you was there. So I find this and figure like you said, what's so much about a little old paper? So I case the joint good and there's nothing else looks good, so I hang on to the rag anyhow. I want to see what Galento says he'll do to Louis the next time. He's good, that Wop. Remember the time he—"

"So what makes this a clue?" I cut in.

Sailor pulled another Frankenstein with his face and opened the paper to the financial page. And then my features started playing tricks.

In one corner of the page was a ship's news column; lists of vessels coming and going. A penciled arrow picked out one ship: "The *S. S. Mosca,* freight to Perdilla. Leaves 7 A.M. Saturday, North River."

Perdilla, if you remember your recent headlines, is the South American republic where the president, *Señor* Montinez, was assassinated and a slug called *"El Caudillo"* is now running the show. *"El Caudillo"* is the Spanish equivalent for Duce, or Fuhrer, or Public Enemy Number

One, and Americans were quite cut up about the whole business. But that was not what excited me.

Over the penciled arrow, in Harry Monsell's peculiar scrawl, was the notation: *"Sally X. East River. 4 A.M., Saturday."*

"This," I murmured, "is a clue."

I had been wracking my head trying to figure Dido or Rush or Alita as the killer. What had stumped me was a good motive. My badge in Monsell's hand showed it was a planned frame and a planned kill. Passion wasn't enough. There had to be a definite motive. New York was lousy with citizens eager for Monsell's scalp. It was an open secret he played every kind of dirty angle that came his way. But you can't drag an open secret into court.

If Monsell had been interested in this *Sally X* and connected it with a ship headed for South America, I smelled an angle. And maybe a motive. Anyway, it was all I had to go on.

I told Sailor to get off at the next stop and meet me Saturday night at ten in the Times Square Automat. We were pulling into 14th Street. Before leaving, Sailor said, "It's too bad I have to quit bouncing, Cash. Maybe if I hung around I could find some more clues. Maybe I could find the killer, even."

"Maybe," I said.

SOUTH STREET curves around the lower tip of Manhattan and cuts a wide swath up the east side. At ten in the evening traffic dwindles. Clusters of thick-shouldered men loiter before darkened ship supply stores, around the Seaman's Institute, in the dark alleys that jut off from the waterfront. A restless quiet settles over the docks and cobblestones and bridges.

I spent three hours wandering from one all-night dive to the next. I passed out whole packages of cigarettes. Bought every gullet scorcher from canned heat to spiked beer. Listened patiently to hard luck yarns from Singapore and points north, south, east and west. After three hours I was tired and staggering a little and my one question was still unanswered.

It was in a joint called Bombay Mary's, that a fat slob of a seaman with a ravenous thirst bellowed after the third beer, "I heard of 'er. A dinky salt water tub that ain't fit for man or beast. Fisherman. You sure we ain't met some place before? I swear to jeepers I seen you. Calcutta, maybe?"

I slid the tabloid with my picture staring him in the face to one side. "Not Calcutta," I said. "I'm strictly a land hog. Get seasick."

"Then what in blazes you want with the *Sally X?* That tub'd roll and pitch and bounce in the Central Park lake. She'll spill your guts. We still drinkin'?"

I ordered more needle beer. "Got a pal on board," I said. "Where you say she was tied?"

"Didn't. Say, fella, you're O.K. for a lubber.... Can't figure where I seen you."

"On the East River, isn't she?"

"I said she was a fisherman. Around the Fulton Market. Maybe in Veracruz?"

"No," I said. "You didn't see me in Veracruz. Thanks." I threw a bill on the table. "Have a few more on me."

Then I scooped up the tabloid and left him with his bleary eyes cocked in woozy thought. Outside, I chucked the tab in the first ashcan and headed toward the Fulton Market.

As I passed Wall Street a bell intoned the hour. I looked at my watch. It was one-thirty.

It took another half-hour questioning dock watchmen and early workers in the Market to locate the *Sally X*. My fat friend was right. She was a tub; a little larger than a tug, but twice as clumsy. A stubby funnel sent clouds of thick, black smoke rolling up into the night. Oily water slapped at the sides. The odor of fish was terrific.

A truck was backed up alongside. Ice slid down a metal runway to an open hold. There were some figures in the darkness near the truck but they were occupied with loading the ice. I was able to step over the rail to the deck unseen. No place on deck looked good for a hiding place. Near me was something like a tilted manhole cover over a hole. I slid under and felt my way down a ladder.

The fish stink in the dark hold was almost too much and I started back up the ladder. Footsteps sounded on the deck overhead. I dropped down again. Reaching around, I felt nothing but fishes and nets. I gathered some net under me.

A long eternity of seconds passed in that choking blackness. Part of the time I felt like kicking myself for crawling into a strange set-up on a wild hunch. A few times I tensed with my .32 in my fist as footsteps passed over me. Finally, the beer and a reaction to all the excitement numbed my senses to everything but the stink of fish, and I drowsed.

I don't know how long I had been sleeping when something banged nearby and I awoke. I gasped. The *Sally X* was doing just what my fat friend had said it would do. It rolled; it pitched, it bounced. The hold throbbed to the beat of an engine. In the blackness I also did what my fat friend said I would. I became very, very sick.

Footsteps suddenly gathered overhead, then a small square of daylight leaped down on me.

It was a large hold, seemed to run the length of the tub. At one end was the lip of a chute clogged with ice. The hold seemed full, almost to the top, of fish.

I crawled into the darkest corner, drew some net over me and thumbed the safety of my automatic, as another square of daylight appeared overhead. Beyond the growing hole above was a thick-set man with a red beard. He shouted orders, had the hatch covers removed one by one until there was nothing over me but a network of cross-beams. Red Beard wore a grimy officer's cap. He directed the removal of the cross-beams.

The hull of a huge vessel suddenly towered over the opening, then slid out of sight with the tub's roll. I forgot my sickness for a moment. The name on the large vessel's hull had been very distinct: the *S. S. Mosca*, Perdilla!

I had no time to ponder on this. The manhole cover flew back almost directly over my head and a pair of dungareed legs started down the ladder. I drew to one side and kept still.

His shoulders bulged and he was bald. In spite of the fish, he scrambled around the hold efficiently, gathering up ends of a net that apparently ran under the fish. Once, he reached within a foot of me and I almost squeezed the trigger, but he picked up a net end and drew it to the center. There, he fastened the ends together with a big, looping knot.

The engine throb suddenly ceased. We seemed to be gliding forward, then the side of the *S. S. Mosca* slid into view overhead.

Red Beard bellowed down, "All clear, Mack?"

"All clear!" yelled the bald man in the hold.

Red Beard bellowed over his shoulder, "Don't foul those lines, you blithering idiot!" Then, to someone above him, "All clear, *Mosca!* Drop the shackle!"

Minutes later a heavy metal hook swayed into the hold at the end of a cable. Mack dropped the looped net ends over it and called, "Heave 'er aloft, Cap'n!"

The hook started rising and I gulped. I started rising with it. Mack had stepped to one side and stood pressed against the ladder. He got out, "Hey!" as I scrambled down on him. Then my automatic did things behind his ear and he dropped.

For the next minute I ignored him. The net attached to the hook was raising all the fish in the hold. There hadn't been so many after all; just one layer.

The hold was really filled with cases. Long, tightly packed, neatly laid out. One case near me was broken open. Rifle barrels jutted out.

Mack groaned and I let him have a treatment behind the other ear. Then I bound him in net ends, stuffed half his shirt into his mouth, and made him fast to the foot of the ladder.

The hook made a second descent and Red Beard yelled, "Mack!"

"Hah?" I grunted, trying to imitate Mack's voice.

"Get a move on. It's broad daylight and we gotta clear this cargo fast. Clear your slings."

Every four or five cases had a looped rope under them, holding them together. I gathered one pair of loop ends and muffled my voice: "All clear!"

The hook swayed near me and I dropped the ends over it. The swaying didn't help my stomach. "Heave 'er aloft, Cap'n!" I yelled.

I pulled one rifle out of the broken case and became very glad I had sneaked aboard the *Sally X.* It was a U.S. Army rifle, discarded model. From habit I worked the bolt and extracted the lock. It was a peculiar lock, the same model I had used in the shooting gallery, but different. I put the lock in my pocket. I was thinking hard.

For the next hour I wobbled around looping the slings at each trip of the hook, keeping under cover and checking Mack's bonds repeatedly.

Finally, the hold was clear. The tub gave a sudden lurch and the *S.S. Mosca* tilted back out of sight. The engine started up again. A cloud overhead spun around slowly and the crossbeams dropped back into place, one by one.

As the last hatch cover was sliding into place, Red Beard peered through the narrowing crack and shouted: "What the hell, Mack, you gone asleep? Fan your tail aft and give a hand with the lines, blast you!"

The hatch blotted out his face and I was back in darkness.

I went up the ladder.

First I saw water; more water than I ever want to see again. Next I saw Red Beard. His mouth started opening but the muzzle of my .32 closed it. I beckoned with my free hand and conked him out as he came within reach. It was as easy as that. I dragged him down into the hold and bound him next to Mack. I stuffed his officer's hat into his mouth for a gag, then I frisked them both.

I had to get back on deck to examine what I found. No one saw me this time. I could see the back of the helmsman's head on the bridge. We were heading for a pencil line of land on the horizon. The *S.S. Mosca* was just a spiral of smoke in the distance behind us.

There was nothing important from Mack. Red Beard was Captain William Anthony. His wallet gave up an envelope containing five one-hundred-dollar bills and a neatly folded paper that looked like a crossword puzzle. I pocketed the paper and returned the money to the wallet. I had nothing against Anthony, yet.

When steps sounded along the deck, I ducked behind a ventilator funnel. It was like taking candy from a baby. The element of surprise was with me all the way and a few minutes later Mack and Captain Anthony had company.

The captain moved when I returned the wallet to his pocket and I felt over his bonds. They were all secure. I said, "A cute little racket, Anthony. Running guns under fish. And you probably expect to make a catch before going back, just to show. But you're a sucker to risk your neck for only half a grand. Why don't you ask Charley Rush for a raise?"

It was too dark to make out his eyes, but he mumbled something through his hat and I gathered he was telling me to go to hell. I rubbed his beard for luck and mounted the ladder again.

I noticed a new motion to the tub, looked forward and froze. The helmsman's head was no longer visible on the bridge.

A faint, scuffling sound behind whirled me in my tracks. He was built like a house and wore a black patch over one eye. He had made the mistake of reversing his revolver and was bringing it down in a vicious arc. There was only a split second's leeway, but I had made no mistake and had my .32 by the butt. His arm had another foot to go; my finger, the sixteenth of an inch. The black patch couldn't stop lead and he crumpled to the deck, his gun tapping my shoulder gently and sliding off. I didn't feel sorry for him. I was too sorry for me.

There was an added motion to upset my bouncing innards. The tub zigzagged wildly, leaving an erratic trail of foam in its wake. I could hear the grinding sprockets as the wheel on the bridge spun back and forth. I could also hear a peculiar whistling sound on the bridge. That would be the engineer calling up to find out what was wrong.

A little dory trailed behind the tub at the end of a rope. It swung from side to side with each new motion, riding a crest of foam. I was hauling in the rope hand over hand, when steps sounded up forward and a basso voice called, "Cap'n! Mack! Sam! Where the hell are you all? Hey, Cap'n!"

I let the line play out again, took a deep breath and dove off the stern of the *Sally X,* reaching for the line in the middle of its sag.

I got it. The ocean came up and slammed my back. Then everything was wet, green and silent. As I spluttered to the surface, something black loomed up on me and I managed to grab the prow of the dory. For a moment I clung there, gasping for air, then I scrambled on board. My hands were raw, but I was too sick to give a damn.

A grease-smudged face peered down from the stern of the *Sally X* as I cut loose. A bullet whinnied overhead, then a mountain of water bulged up between us. He took more pot shots at me, but he was moving away fast. More watery mountains grew between and then it didn't matter any more. He was out of range and leaving.

It was late afternoon, Saturday. I was about half a mile out and my watch was stopped at five-twenty. I still smelled fish.

MY PAL, Sailor Duffy, was waiting patiently in the Automat when I showed up at ten-thirty.

"You don't look good, Cash. You're clothes is different. Should I get you a tuna fish sandwich?"

I looked around to make sure nobody else was minding our business. I said, "You get me a tuna sandwich and I'll brain you with it. My other duds are discarded permanently in an alley and the first comer can take them and be welcome to them. Only I don't think he will unless he happens to like the smell of fish. Did we move?"

We had. He'd found us a room.

"Good," I said. "Sit still while I figure a few things out... After that we'll call on a lady."

Sailor brightened and I examined the paper from Captain Anthony's wallet. It was a simple box code— ten squares across, ten down. Each square had a message; names of ships, warehouses, dates, amounts of money. Twenty-six were just letters of the alphabet; probably to spell out unforeseen messages. This much was simple.

The key, however, was confusing. Scrawled in pencil, it read: "Key—first two words after NHJAL."

This code was undoubtedly used to give Anthony instructions. The point was to find out who gave the instructions and where Harry Monsell had figured in. And I had an idea.

As we got up to leave, Sailor said, "Why can't it be a couple of dames some time, Cash? When it's only one dame you have all the fun."

YOU COULD have a lot of fun with Blondy Monsell. She was plump where it counted and wore a transparent negligee of eggshell blue that showed you just how much it counted. She had nice eyes, too.

They widened in fright at the sight of me standing in the doorway, and I said, "Hello, Blondy. I want words with you." When she didn't move, I added, "There's nothing to fear, kid. I didn't bump Harry. I'm not even heeled. Look." I showed her the empty holster under my arm. I didn't mention the gun was in the Atlantic some place, or that Sailor Duffy was waiting for me in the street.

She sucked in her breath slowly, then stepped aside for me. Her eyes were still frightened.

"Look," I said when we were seated in a cream and pink living-room, "I'm very sorry for you and I don't want to bother you more than necessary. But right now I'm out to clear myself and the only way to do that is to get the real killer, and the trail, up to this point, leads here."

Blondy's hand reached for mine as she sidled closer on the divan. "I never once believed you did it, Cash."

"Good girl."

"Don't—don't feel sorry for me, please. I was never happy with Harry. Maybe I shouldn't say it now that he's dea— gone, but he was always chasing after someone else. Color, age, nothing meant much to him, only that she wore skirts and didn't balk at passes."

I patted her hand and stood up. "O.K., kid. I'll look around, then ask some questions."

"The police did that last night. They found nothing, Cash."

"I'm different," I said. "I know what I'm looking for."

Blondy's green eyes followed me around the living-room as I cased everything from the pictures to the rugs. She sat tensed on the edge of the divan.

When I made for the hallway leading to the bedroom she snapped erect and whispered, "Cash!"

"There's no dice here," I said. "Monsell must have left it some place. Maybe in the bedroom—"

"Cash!"

"What?"

"I'm lonesome. I'm sick and tired of being alone and lonesome. It was that way all the time with him and now—Cash, can't you look around some other time?"

Her lips were soft and yielding and I thought it would be very nice to keep Blondy from being lonesome, but her eyes were still wide and scared and my insides felt a lot like that. I was wanted for murder.

I whispered, "Later, kid, later," and walked through the hallway into the bedroom. It was dark and I never saw what hit me.

THE SMELL of fish made me retch. Then my eyes opened. Everything was dark, moving. Air rushed against my face and I was jerking from one side to the other. I didn't jerk far. Heavy bodies wedged me on two sides.

It was all very confusing and, for a moment, I sank back into a comfortable drowse. But the fish smell was too strong. I tried making out the faces of my companions. Then I began to swear softly.

Captain William Anthony listened in silence for a few minutes, then said, "Now tell us about yourself, mugg."

I gripped my tongue in a mental vice and tried to think. We were in the back of a moving sedan. Through half-drawn blinds I made out occasional street lamps and a sliding vista of darkened office buildings. We were heading downtown. My head ached.

"He'll talk on the *Sally X*," growled Mack, on my other side.

The captain's beard rubbed against my cheek as he peered close to examine me. "What's the game? Just a plain hold-up, or trying to work a little blackmail?"

"It's blackmail!" Mack exclaimed. "The quicker we get rid of him the better. He's on to Rush and he rode a clear course to the female after leaving the *Sally X.* If we didn't beat him to her he'd of had the whole crew dead to rights. Then it'd been like Monsell all over again. It's blackmail, I tell you!"

"I'm a-minded," grunted Anthony, "that you be spoutin' too much, Mack."

"Leave me be," Mack countered. "It's using my head I am. You seen yourself the love play back there. Him and the widder. It's how he got wind of what was going on. I say we don't have to make him talk. Better to drop him in five fathoms with some anchor chain around his middle. How about you, Sam?"

The driver's turned head revealed my third victim from the *Sally X.* "I'm of a mind with Mack, Cap'n," he said.

"We'll see, we'll see!" growled Captain Anthony in his beard.

More than once on that grim ride I wanted to throw a glance back. After all, Duffy had been stationed outside the house. But each time I thought better of it and kept my eyes fixed forward. My hands were free but that meant little with four hundred pounds of brawn on my flanks.

They were new at this sort of thing. I could tell by the way we rode clear down Broadway without zig-zagging through side streets. And they never looked back. But that didn't keep them from being dangerous. You had only to look at Mack and Anthony to know they were dangerous. I sat still and tried to think until the sedan suddenly lurched to a halt, and I looked out on a familiar corner on South Street.

Mack dragged me after him out of the sedan. The odor of rotting fish, cobblestones underfoot, oily waters slapping against the hull of the *Sally X*—it was all the same.

Captain Anthony slipped a calloused palm over my mouth before I could yell and they lifted me between them, started carrying me bodily out on the pier. They dropped me and made frantic leaps as a taxi lurched off South Street and bore down on us.

The odor of burning rubber blended with fish as the wheels skidded to a halt inches from where I lay.

Mack shouted, "Don't let the runt escape!" He started to shout something else when a human avalanche poured from the driver's seat of the cab and Mack collapsed to the pier like a pricked balloon.

The first slug tore up a streak of splinters in the wood underfoot. I scrambled off my back and Captain Anthony's revolver exploded again when my shoulder struck his knees. The bullet pinged a wild course into the night and he staggered. Before he could recover balance, five knuckles backed by two hundred and forty pounds of meat ruffled his beard and Captain William Anthony lost all interest in current events. He stretched out on the pier for inspection.

I grabbed the revolver from his lax fingers and snuggled the butt in my palm, but Mr. Sam was not having any. He was high-tailing the sedan down South Street into the night. I doubt if he even took time out to look back.

I said, "Thanks, Sailor. You were like the Marines," and made a quick frisk of Anthony's pockets. This time I pocketed the five one-hundred-dollar bills. He owed me that much for the growing lump on my skull. I was not surprised that he now had two identical copies of the box code. I also took back the revolver lock he'd got out of my pocket.

Sailor said, "Cash, I see these monkeys carry you out of Blondy's house. I go over but there's a big crowd and you said for me not to draw cops. Whiskers says to an old lady in the crowd who asks, that you are sick and they are takin' you to a horspital. So I see a empty cab with the key in the ignition, so I tag along. Who are these monkeys, Cash, pals of that dame?"

"Pals of Rush," I said. "If that cab's hot let's scram the hell out of here."

We left Mack and the captain under some canvas on the deck of the *Sally X*. Sailor tooled the cab over to the West Side where we ditched it and took a subway.

FIVE TO ten Sunday morning Sailor awoke me with the theory that Blondy Monsell was implicated in the killing.

"If those monkeys last night was in the bedroom and she let you walk in on 'em cold, she got to be mixed in some-how, huh, Cash? Let's go down later and push her around and make her talk."

Between yawns I said, "She was too scared to let me know they were there. How do we know what they threat-ened to do if she yapped? And don't talk of pushing her around. Anyhow, Rush is our man for the time being."

"I'd like to push Rush around, Cash."

"You'd push your own mother around," I snapped. "Headwork has to solve this. I suspect now that Rush uses his chain of shooting galleries as a cover for his gun running. And I'm sure Monsell horned in for a cut and got smeared. But even if I proved these things I'd still be on the lam."

"I'd still like to push Rush around," growled Sailor.

"Forget it. We're calling on another dame after you find me some breakfast and a paper."

Sailor's idea of a breakfast was wurst, cheese and a quart of beer. The paper was more to my taste. It had interviews with the principals of the "Voodoo Murder" case in Moonglow Park. I was able to find an address in Harlem which I wanted. There was a story about a cab that was stolen, then found on the West Side minus clues. There was no news about a one-eyed corpse on the *Sally X*.

The Board of Estimate had voted to post a reward of five thousand dollars for information leading to the arrest of Cash Wale. Dido was still in the clink, still silent. Monsell's head was still missing with the cops expecting to find both it and me hourly and Latin Town was doing a sudden, terrific business.

"Cash," exclaimed Sailor as we boarded an uptown local in the subway, "Rush is a little guy, almost as little as you. Why don't *you* push him around?"

The lady I wanted to see lived on one of those side streets in lower Harlem that seem sinister and glamorous by night, but shabby and pitiful under the remorseless glare of the sun. It teemed with babies, pushcarts, people of many colors, radios blaring from open windows and the odors that are distinctive of Harlem.

The address I wanted was a dingy basement café wedged between a Chinese laundry and a church. For Sunday morning the café was unusually packed. Every table held a circle of swarthy little men talking heatedly with gestures. The talk died and the gestures froze in midair as I entered. In the rear was a narrow stairway leading up. I didn't use it immediately. A thick-set guy in shirt sleeves blocked the way.

"I want," I said in the mongrel Spanish I'd picked up on the Mexican Border, "to see the miss upstairs. I'm from Latin Town. *Es importante.*"

He had a tic in his left eye which gave him the appearance of continually winking. He looked over his shoulder to a grizzled old patriarch who sat at a table in the corner sipping black coffee from a glass. The old guy nodded and Winky stepped aside.

Half-way up I paused to inspect a green flag on the wall. Crude lettering on it spelled out: *"Perdilla sera libre! Al inferno Fascismo!"* Perdillo will be free! To hell with Fascism!

Alita said, "Hot damn! You?" Then she stepped back from the door. I followed Captain Anthony's revolver in and closed the door behind me. I said:

"Put something on, Alita. I want to talk to you and I don't want to be distracted."

She draped a scarlet shawl over her shoulders. I sat down on a chromium-lined chair and tried to catch my scattering wits.

The room was a knockout. Ultra modernistic even to a Cezanne on the wall. The only places I had ever seen that compared to it were sets in some very tony movies and a couple of the more elegant bars. And here was Alita, only the stripper of a number one honky tonk, with nothing more than a shawl between her and nature, the inhabitant of this streamlined dream!

She lit a cigarette at the end of a long, green holder and started pacing up and down a blue rug that was made for queens or cinematic Garbos. Finally, she whirled on me.

"Why you here? Make more troubles? You tal Dido to keel Harry and now Dido die from the light!" The cigarette waved at the sun-tan lamp. She meant the chair.

I said, "Don't get cocky with me, Tomale. I know the score."

"W'at you say?"

"We both know I didn't conk you in the prop room. I'll tell you something else we both know. Nobody conked you. Someone you know killed Monsell. He put Monsell in the altar in your place and then tied you up to make it look good. Was it Rush?"

The cigarette wavered. Her eyes jiggled. "You crazee!" she hissed.

"Guns to Perdilla aren't crazy. Are they, Alita?"

Holder and cigarette dropped to the rug in a shower of sparks. She stooped for them.

I was prepared for one of her swearing exhibitions. But I was not prepared for the silent fury with which she scooped a short blade from inside the shawl and lunged at me. I was almost taken completely by surprise. Almost. My revolver barrel turned the blade and I flicked a hard uppercut at her oncoming jaw with my left. I didn't like socking a dame, even a she-cat. I didn't want to hang around any more. I'd seen enough. I spread out the shawl to cover her more completely and pinched out the cigarette. That rug was a lulu.

Winky looked up as I came down the stairs but didn't say anything. The hum of many voices stilled again. As I left the café the grizzled old patriarch was still sipping his coffee.

It was a very healthy feeling to step back into the sunlight and look up into Sailor Duffy's battered face.

As we walked down the street back to the subway, Sailor asked, "So now we do what, Cash?"

"We go to the 42nd Street library."

"Why? You find somethin'?"

"I found out Alita is white and she reads good books."

Sailor stopped dead and did things with his eyebrows.

"That chippie, Cash? She's—"

"White," I repeated. "She uses a sun-tan lamp."

"But I seen her plenty, Cash. Plenty of her, I mean."

"Not the way I did," I said. "And she reads good books. And she's guarded by the kind of people who buy guns. So we're going to the library."

"It's like Greek to me," said Sailor Duffy.

We spent the next hour in the newspaper reference room of the library. I read all about how *El Caudillo* became the big shot in Perdilla after Montinez was assassinated. I saw some pictures. I spent a lot of time looking at my knuckles and figuring what and what added up to four.

Then I took Sailor into a corner, slipped him Captain Anthony's revolver and said, "I want you to do two things. First go to Blondy Monsell's house and give her my thanks for not tipping the law I was there. Got any dough?"

"Fifty-five cents."

I gave him a century note from Captain Anthony's roll and stifled his questions. "Get flowers. Orchids. Have the clerk write out a nice note from me but just tell him my initials. Not my name. All that's to kill time so you won't do the second thing too fast."

"What thing?"

"I want you to go to Headquarters after you've seen Blondy and tell them you want the five grand reward for turning in Cash Wale. Then bring them out to Latin Town. I'll be there."

I happened to land next to a cop in the B.M.T. going out to Queens. He gripped my elbow.

"Mister, do you happen to have the time?"

"It's five past two," I said.

"Thanks. I went and bust me wristwatch yesterday."

"That's too bad," I said.

SUNDAY IN Moonglow Park meant a busy mid-way. I filled up on some hot dogs and made a tour of the Rush shooting galleries.

The third one had what I wanted: an attendant cleaning rifles in one corner of the counter. We became old friends when I showed him how to pull a piece of rag through the barrel at the end of a string instead of pushing it through with a ramrod. The locks bothered him more, he said. I had him lay out the parts of half a dozen unassembled locks.

When I was through theorizing I don't think he noticed that enough parts to make up one complete lock were missing. I don't think he noticed because he didn't yell when I walked off with them in my pocket.

I assembled the pieces I had lifted and stowed the result away next to the lock from the *Sally X.* Then I made my way to Latin Town.

Conway was spieling for the first show when I edged into his tip and caught his eye. He was good. Over a hundred people pressed around me but I doubt if a single one caught the tiny flicker in his expression. It as good as said, "Fade to one side, Cash. Be with you in a minute."

He was. The tip rushed for the box offices and he slid off the platform next to me. We gripped hands.

"Nice spiel," I said.

"Don't tell me you're sticking out your neck to hear me bark?"

"Not quite. I need your help, Conway, to slide out of this voodoo frame. But I'm hot merchandise, kid. Helping me would make you an accessory. Think it over."

He didn't hesitate. "What d'you want me to do?"

"Look," I said. "That boy scout cop with the gun, chinning with the cashier, is the one I ran out on, remember?"

"That's right."

"All I want you to do is distract his attention while I sneak through your booth into Latin Town. Then, in about ten minutes, bring him up to Rush's office. Don't tell him I'm there. Just bring him up."

Conway looked at me curiously. "And that'll clear you?"

"That'll clear me."

In the booth I got to my knees and peeked out to see how Conway was doing. He was doing all right. I got in safely and made for Rush's office.

Rush was where I had seen him last, huddled behind the big desk, black fedora pulled low over his flabby face, his synthetic meat choppers gleaming. His face grew apoplectic as I stepped in and slowly shut the door behind me.

"Control yourself, fatty," I said. "I want to have some plain words with you."

"You'll never get away with this," he whispered hoarsely.

"I'll get away with it as long as you peddle artillery all over the map, besides playing boss man of this outfit. You see, we have mutual interests. Do we talk?"

He ran a tongue over trembling lips and nodded.

"Now," I said, "for a starter, who killed Harry Monsell?"

"You did. You or Dido."

He meant it. The funny thing is I knew he meant it. It had to be like that. I knuckled the top of the desk, looked down into his beady eyes and said, "I did not kill Monsell.

We'll try another tack. Latin Town is drawing crowds but it isn't making money. You're losing money. You're a shrewd businessman, could have foreseen it would never return your investment. Why'd you let Monsell talk you into it?"

"He knew." Rush ran a trembling finger around the inside of his collar. "He knew about the guns."

"So he blackmailed you. Only instead of taking cash outright he worked it this way; got a free trip to South America, had the prestige of directing a Moonglow Park show and drew a padded salary. Right?"

"Yes."

I took a deep breath and pretended not to notice his hand inching toward the top drawer of the desk.

"Now, be careful about this one. Who was the agent from Perdilla who negotiated for the guns?"

His shoulders heaved in a shrug. The drawer was sliding open.

"Come on," I said, "we're talking. We're laying our cards on the table now. Who contacted you for those rifles?"

"This stops between you and me, Wale," he pleaded. "There was no agent. Only indirect orders. I was to have the rifles at certain warehouses on specified dates. It all happened by phone. I always collected in advance."

I let him reach into the drawer and said, "You're a smart man, Rush. You wouldn't make blind deals. Who was it? Was it Anthony?"

The automatic he raised from the drawer was heavy and it trembled with his hand.

"So what?" I said.

"So this!" His eyes grew moist with excitement. "You come here to blackmail me and I capture you! This is funny, Wale. All the cops in New York looking for you and I make the capture. And all the time I was telling you the truth. I collect in advance and all my gun deals are blind. For mutual protection. The rifles are left in a warehouse in New York and someone calls for them. And if they don't, I don't care. I'm paid in advance. And if the guns are discovered, why, they're for my galleries. Smart, eh, Wale? Give me your gun. No! Put your hands up! I'll get it!"

His breath wheezed hoarsely. He edged around the desk, backed me against it, took a step forward. His eyes met mine and he stopped. The trembling of his hand became a full fledged shake.

"No," he muttered, "no. Mustn't get too close. Dangerous. Keep 'em up, Wale! Higher! I said *up!*"

My hands remained at shoulder level. Charles Rush was like most business crooks, eager for the big dough but unwilling to take personal risks. I think he was more afraid of the gun in his hand than he was of me.

I said, "Call the cops, mugg. It'll be very interesting. You capture me and I capture you. Maybe we'll both fry."

Then the door behind Rush creaked open and I didn't have to play any more. His head jerked, my hands came down. There was no shot as I wrenched the gun from his fat fingers. He'd neglected to release the safety.

I took care of that detail as Conway and the amusement park cop stepped in the door.

The sergeant looked at me, down at the automatic and flushed. Conway eased to one side. Rush said:

"It's Cash Wale! He was up here trying to hold me up. Arrest him!"

Some people peered in the doorway. I waved the automatic. "Come in, please, and close the door behind you."

Alita entered, followed by a Negro porter. The porter closed the door. Both stood against it, eying the heater in my fist. Everybody was eying it. But me.

"You're wanted for murder," said the sergeant slowly.

"Don't get ideas," I said. "I asked Conway to bring you up here." I turned to Conway. "Right?"

"That's right," said Conway.

Rush looked at me queerly and began rubbing his lips against his imitation teeth.

"So what's the gag?" asked the sergeant.

"It's no gag. I'm going to do some talking. After that I'm turning myself in. To you. But first I'll talk."

The sergeant took another gander at the automatic and nodded.

"Harry Monsell was killed," I said, "because he found out too much about a revolution that's due to pop in a certain South American country. He had learned who was running guns out of America to that country and how and why. But what he didn't learn and what the guy who killed him didn't know was that this particular revolution was doomed to fail."

I could feel the tension seep into the room. I lifted from my pocket the rifle lock I'd taken from the *Sally X.*

"This is from one of those contraband rifles. It's the lock of a discarded Army model. Here, Rush, your galleries use this kind of gun. You tell me why it can't win revolutions."

Rush's fingers fumbled with the bolt. He seemed to grow suddenly very sick. He croaked, "No!" and tried slinging it through a window. It couldn't sling with my hand on his arm and the lock skidded along the floor.

The sergeant picked it up, worked the bolt.

"It's got no firing pin," he stated.

The tension in the room was mounting. I said, "Right! None of the rifles had firing pins because they were not only discarded but decommissioned Army rifles. An added profit for the gun runner two ways. They cost him less and he probably got a rake-off from the present group in power in that South American country. He was selling their enemies guns that wouldn't shoot and when they started their revolution they'd be mowed down."

"Nice business," muttered the sergeant. Even he was beginning to feel the electricity in the air. He shrugged, "And this is supposed to clear you?"

I deliberately let my gun muzzle droop until it pointed to the floor.

"It's a start, sonny," I said. "That lock is part of my proof that I'm just a fall guy. You see, Charley Rush contracted to deliver the same kind of rifles to the revolutionists that he used in his galleries. Here's a lock I just snitched from one of his galleries. You can see it's just like the other except that this one has a firing pin. Rush tried to pull a fast one and—" I didn't complete the thought. I didn't expect to.

Rush started to scream, "I didn't!" Then, "Don't!" His teeth flew forward as his mouth convulsed. He didn't reach for them. He was too busy clutching Alita's hand which clung to the hilt of a short dagger which was imbedded deep in his throat.

His teeth skidded to a stop on the floor and leered up at us.

For one paralyzing moment everyone was too stunned to move. Then a lot of things happened at once. Rush, looking more like a toad than ever, slid off the blade, crumpled to the floor, blood welling from his opened jugular. Alita screamed some Spanish, raised the blade for another thrust.

I let the sergeant thumb his holster safety and draw his revolver. His sights lined on Alita, but his gun was snatched from his grip before he could shoot.

Conway's face was white, deathly white. He said, "Well, Cash, are you going to shoot?" The sergeant's revolver in Conway's hand picked on the top button of my vest.

THIS WAS my big moment but I didn't feel happy. My automatic had a six o'clock bead on Conway's chin. All it took was a faint squeeze and my troubles with the cops were over. But I liked Conway. I didn't want to shoot. I said, "Not yet. You?"

"Not yet," said Conway.

It was a peculiar set up. I knew he was licked. He didn't. The sergeant held up a section of wall, the play beyond him. The porter was frozen against a filing cabinet, his eyes fixed on Rush. Alita's eyes shifted back and forth between the two guns, fascinated.

Conway spoke to her swiftly in Spanish. She passed between us on the way to the door and I could have dropped her. But I didn't. With a hand on the knob she said, in flawless English, "You should have run away, Cash Wale. You don't know the terrible thing you are doing." Then the door was closing behind her.

I said, "I know what I'm doing, Conway."

Conway asked, "Is it true about those rifle locks?"

"It's true. If your men attempted to use them in action they'd have found themselves thoroughly framed. Right now I sympathize with guys who are framed."

"Damn it, I should have examined them. What do you know about Harry Monsell?"

His gun shifted a trifle. He wasn't a gunman, Conway.

I said, "Monsell discovered who you are. Probably heard of you when he toured South America. Maybe he saw a picture and recognized you. I did this afternoon in the Public Library, and it was a very old picture. He put the bee on you. You got Alita to find out how much he knew. He fell for her and she probably found out he'd rifled your apartment and swiped a copy of your code. I know he had a copy because I got it back from Captain Anthony after Anthony found it in Blondy Monsell's."

Rush didn't bleed any more. I was out my twenty bucks back pay. He was dead.

"Go on," said Conway.

"Monsell figured the codes' key because he knew it was your code. The letters, NHJAL, were initials for the tag line in your spiel, 'Now hurry just a little.' The number of letters in each of the next two words indicated which of the hundred code boxes you meant. If you said, 'Now hurry just a little, see Alita—' it meant third box to your right and fifth from the top. And that, in your code, happens to mean 'Get guns in warehouse D.' You used the code to give Anthony instructions without meeting him face to face—in case either of you was being watched. No one would look for a code in a barker's spiel."

"But you did," murmured Conway softly.

"Sure. After I found out who you are. Monsell waited until your code order was for the *Sally X* to deliver a shipment. He came to the spieler's booth and held you up for a piece of change. Right?"

Conway's knuckle whitened a bit on the trigger. Mine did likewise. His face was almost pure white and there was a little twist to his mouth. I could feel his thoughts run ahead of my words.

I said, "The dough he wanted was nothing. But it was too dangerous for that kind of rat to know the score. So you killed him in the spieler's booth."

"That's screwy," said the sergeant. "Monsell was killed in the prop room. Conway never entered it. There were witnesses."

"Only one—Alita. And she would cover him. Didn't he tip his hand when you pulled a bead on her? Ask Conway. He knows it isn't screwy."

"You're sure of all this?" whispered Conway.

"I'm sure. You practically smashed his skull. That's why the head was missing. You didn't want it found because it was supposed to be neatly cut off."

"You're guessing."

"I saw Monsell's smashed skull a few minutes ago," I said. "Once he was dead you tried getting him in your sound apparatus case. The idea was to get him in the prop room without drawing attention. You're always lugging that case around. But Monsell didn't fit and you had to hack off his head with a machete to make him fit. In the prop room Alita helped you place the body in the trick altar, then you bound and gagged her. The body fell out just as Dido swung his machete. It was all planned in advance. It had to be because you had my badge for the frame against me before Monsell was dead."

The porter cleared his throat. "Mistah Wale, suh, what come uv the daid man's haid?"

"It's under the spieler's booth. One board is loose."

Conway seemed to be holding his breath, his lips in a tight smile. "It was very clever of you to figure it all out, Cash."

I calculated the angle of his barrel and said, "Make your play, Conway."

The guns blended in a single roar. I'd let him have the split fraction of a second's edge. But I'd calculated the angle wrong. His slug jerked my shoulder, twitched my shooting arm. My bullet plucked at his sleeve and buried itself in the door jamb.

I watched my automatic drop from nerveless fingers to the floor, where it lay pointing at the porter's trembling feet.

Conway reached behind and opened the door. I had never seen a face so white on a living man. Even his lips were a colorless gash.

"So this is how it must end," he whispered. "I didn't want to frame you, Cash, but there was no one else. I don't want to do this, but I must go on living. There is important work to do."

I didn't watch his knuckle whitening on the trigger again. I said, "You won't be around to do it, Conway."

"Drop that rod or I'll blast you, Conway," growled a heavy voice.

Conway took a long time to turn his eyes.

Sailor Duffy stood in the doorway, Captain Anthony's big revolver in his fist. Conway lurched, triggered his gun. Sailor blasted at the same instant, then he leaned against the door muttering, "Aw, hell. Aw, hell!"

Conway writhed to the floor in slow motion, his own slug expelling a fine trickle of blood from his temple. Sailor's bullet had shattered the top button of Conway's vest.

Conway's eyes were glazing fast. Putting my ear to his lips I barely heard him say: *"Perdilla sera libre."*

A new voice asked, "What'd he say?"

"He said," I said, " 'It'll be a ducky night if it don't rain.'"

Then I realized that half the New York police force was crowding into the office. Talk about your Marines!

CONWAY'S BULLET had nicked my shoulder muscle, leaving two neat holes an inch apart. The M.E. bandaged me. Reporters and flash bulbs popped on all sides. Questions were a dime a gross.

The cops had arrived in time to hear Conway admit he had framed me. They got the sergeant's report, dug up Monsell's head and that's where my interest cooled. Theirs grew hot.

As one police captain put it: "Wale, your story smells. You say you stole in here last night, found this rifle lock in Rush's desk, had a hunch Monsell's head was where it was, found it and figured Conway was your man. Yet you claim you don't know who Conway or Alita were or what country they represented. Do you call that a statement?"

"So help me," I said, "under the present circumstances it is the very best I can do. It came to me like in a dream."

Conway had framed me but I owed him that much. Anyhow, I didn't want to spill any information that might put *El Caudillo,* the Fascist of Perdilla, on guard against an inevitable defeat at the hands of his people. What happened in Perdilla, somehow, had become very personal to me. My dream-hunch story sounded as phoney as it was, but they couldn't pin me to anything. And they had to let me go.

Alita was never caught. No mention was made in the press of a frustrated revolution in Perdilla, so I figured she got news of the decommissioned rifles through to the *S.S. Mosca* before it landed. Rush's connection was never fully traced. He'd been telling the truth. His jobs had been handled blind. I don't think he ever knew that Conway and

Alita were the agents from Perdilla. There was one little item in the papers to the effect that the *Sally X* was found abandoned—with no dead sailor on it.

They let me see Dido when he was released. The hulking witch doctor was still clammed and taking the first boat back to South America. He only opened up enough to tell me, "I tells you Nanyego law is strong. Make Monsell lose head!"

Sailor Duffy was the only person who found out any part of the score from me. It was the night I was turned loose and we were back in the old apartment. I had showered and dressed and was seated before a table piled high with delicatessen and bottles of giggle juice.

"Cash," said Sailor, spearing half a yard of wurst and losing it in his face, "I can't figure it. How'd you connect up that Alita frill with Conway? Nor I can't figure who Conway was or how you found out."

I slipped into my jacket and made for the door. A check for five thousand dollars made out to Sailor Duffy by the Comptroller, and carefully endorsed, was in my pocket. I said, "At the Library I found a rotogravure picture of the family of the assassinated president of Perdilla. Conway and Alita were in that picture, son and daughter respectively. Now do you get it?"

He tilted a bottle on his chin. "Naw. It's still like Greek— Hey, where you goin'?"

"I'm going to find out if Blondy Monsell is not too lonesome to help me cash a check."

THE CORPSE PROMOTER

THE COPS HAD ME DOWN ON THEIR BOOKS AS A KILL CRAZY GUNMAN; MY BEST FRIEND WAS OUT TO MEASURE ME FOR A WOODEN OVERCOAT—AND THE SCREWIEST MURDER SYNDICATE OF ALL TIME HAD MARKED ME FOR THEIR NEXT VICTIM!

CHAPTER ONE
THE PATIENT VANISHES

LITTLE ABIE MILLER stood in the center of my office, his school books between his feet, his hand buried in Sailor Duffy's five-fingered ham. He blinked his eyes so I would not see the tears. Dice has just slipped in the door and was holding up a section of wall, sizing things up. Abie said:

"Pop says they give him the needles all the time. He says you should make them stop, Cash. He says he is going west. Why won't he take me if he's going any place? Why, Cash?"

Dice slithered into a chair without being asked and whistled the first bars of a funeral march. Sailor bristled.

"Lay off, Dice. Lay off the kid, Dice. Ben Miller is our pal and you're a scummy rat. I say lay off, see?"

Dice clammed.

Sailor always spoke like a broken record. He was a little slap-happy from a decade of slug-festing that still had fans talking with gestures. Glowering now at Dice he was not pretty. His head was a swollen billiard ball decorated by a lump of nose, a lump of brow, a lump of jaw and two slabs of red putty for ears. But his eyes were clear chips of grey ice. Sailor was my personnel in the Cash Wale Investigation Agency. And my pal.

I said, "Look, kid. Ben told you to leave everything to me, didn't he? He talked about traveling because he was sick, that's all. What else did he say?"

She lurched forward as the basement rocked from a tremendous explosion....

Abie blotted his eyes with the sleeve of his sweater. He watched Sailor glaring at Dice who was trying to become invisible in the chair and his chest swelled a little.

"I guess it's all right if Sailor and you say it's all right, Cash. Pop just talked about the needles and going west. He said you should make them quit needling him all the time."

I frowned at Abie absently. Irish, freckled and twelve, Ben Miller had picked him off the streets years ago. Ben had adopted the kid and changed his name to avoid future gossip and the arrangement had clicked to the extent of becoming a Broadway legend. Not the gossip column kind; the McCoy.

But now there was something screwy all right. There had been whispers along certain grapevines for weeks that Ben Miller was nosing into a hornet's nest. Ben was sports columnist for the "Chronicle;" one of those old-fashioned newspaper men who went on crusades and couldn't stomach stink. He had lambasted the Boxing Commission for its high-handedness. He had torn into the illegal books like Carrie Nation on a bat and had raised all kinds of hell to install pari-mutuels. He had bucked some pretty powerful syndicates. Now the whispers were out and on Saturday he had been hit with a heart attack. This was Monday.

AS I lifted the phone off my desk it rang. It was Doctor William P. Garse. I said:

"I was just going to ring you, Doc. About Ben."

"That is why I am calling you, Cash. It is what he talks about. I want you to come over to the hospital and hear for yourself."

"Now?"

"If you can make it."

"I can make it," I said. I meant it. Doc wouldn't call me if it was not serious. Dice spoke as I pronged the receiver:

"That Doc Garse?"

Looking at Dice was like chewing a lemon. Emaciated, a monotone in grey from his hair to his socks, he could have been anywhere between thirty and sixty. I didn't give a damn. Once I had saved his life by plugging a rat who had him on a spot marked X. It was in the line of business in a case that had nothing to do with Dice but he had been useful since. In my racket, stools lead to results more than clues. I looked at Sailor and said:

"What do you want here, Dice?"

His expression retained the query but he got the idea and moved toward the door.

"Scram, Dice," said Sailor. "Scram! Cash wants you to scram!"

With his hand on the door Dice asked, "Heard from Major Strong yet?"

Sailor said, "Get out, Dice. G'wan, shoo!"

Abie stuck out his chin. "You heard Sailor. Scat!"

Dice scat.

I told Sailor to meet me at the hospital after he took the kid home.

"Hokey doke," said Sailor.

The kid followed him out with an expression that was generally reserved for Ben Miller.

The telegram arrived as I was preparing to leave.

"Cash Wale stop have uncovered serious irregularity re last hospital fund match stop see me at once stop usual retainer stop Major Strong."

I jammed it into my pocket and locked the office. This was business but it could wait. As Chairman of the Boxing Commission the Major had used my services a few times in the past. A little hardheaded, he was prone to yell, "Wolf!" Even pretended to smell mice in Ben Miller's attacks. This was business and I was called Cash for a damn good reason. But it could wait. Ben Miller was in trouble and Ben was my pal.

THE GOOD DEED HOSPITAL was a small build-
ing on the East Side in the Seventies that still managed to
be imposing. It was a ten minute walk from the subway. I
made it in five.

I found Doc Garse in his office on the top floor. He rose
to shake my hand as I came in. His palm was moist, which
startled me.

"You don't know how glad I am, Cash. Maybe you can
understand what Ben is getting at."

"I'll try, Doc."

He nodded.

"Both of us. But I don't think you realize how dangerous
it is. He must be stopped before it is too late!"

"Dangerous!"

He nodded again. Head man in the hospital, he generally had the sort of poise that flicker smoothies strain to
imitate. For years Doc, Ben and I made a point of reserving
a table in a local flesh pot once a week and chewing a very
entertaining rag; the doc drawing on his background as a
surgeon with a battalion of sappers during the Big Bout.
Ben dishing out the sporting dirt and my memories dating
back to when I peddled lead protection to half a dozen
guys named Mike who are now doing assorted stretches
in Alcatraz. A picture of this flashed in the back of my
mind as Doc stood there without any poise and with a
moist palm and told me I had to stop Ben from something
dangerous before it was too late. Which was why my nerves
jumped when the public address voice called the doc to the
desk on the main floor before he had a chance to elaborate.

To kill time I started filling my pipe and trying to recall
to mind the recent whisper about Ben.

"So you're Cash Wale!"

I wheeled and saw her for the first time, lounging on a window seat in a dark corner of the office with a cigarette balanced in her fingers.

"I'm Cash Wale," I said.

"Gun crazy." She tilted her head appraisingly. "Ex-gangster."

"You read the wrong papers," I said.

"Why—you are so small! And so skinny!"

I let it pass and said, "That's the first time I've known Doc to fall down on an introduction." Then my eyes really concentrated and I said, "But it makes sense."

Even the hospital uniform could not hide the long, delicate curve of her thigh. Her hair was a halo of speckled gold framing a copper glance that sparkled with amusement. She laughed and there were bells in her voice.

"Maybe you are not nice people?" Then, as my face tightened, she said, "Oh, I'm sorry, Cash Wale. I didn't mean that, really. Doctor Garse has been nervous ever since Mr. Miller arrived. He even neglected to order new linen. Which is why I am here now. I'm Miss Stevens, the Nurse in Charge."

When the wall phone rang she answered, then nodded to me.

I took the receiver, discovering that she came up to my eyes, which was nice, and that she used a very provocative perfume, which was nicer. It was Doc:

"Cash? The damndest thing just happened. An ambulance was stolen. That is what I said, stolen! All the drivers are accounted for and one ambulance is gone."

"Maybe an interne just took a practice spin around the block?" I suggested.

"No. I even checked that."

"Well, is there any way I can help?"

"No—yes—I mean after you have seen Ben. He has only about one week left to live and it is a damned shame this thing preys on his mind."

I had a quick vision of little Abie holding back tears in my office and bellowed, "What? One week?"

"Have Miss Stevens take you to him, Cash. I didn't have the heart to break it to you earlier. Make her explain. Look, I must trace that ambulance. Excuse—"

I stood there a full minute with the receiver to my ear after the phone clicked dead. Miss Stevens fingered my elbow.

"Is something wrong?"

"Take me to Ben Miller," I said. And as I said it a nurse crashed in the door crying:

"Miss Stevens! Doctor Garse!" Her eyes swept the room as if the doc might be hiding in it. "He's gone!" she exclaimed. "After all his wild talk, he's gone!"

Miss Stevens clinched her cigarette then took the nurse by the shoulder and shook hard. "Who is gone, Clair?"

Clair made a face as if she was going to sneeze, then broke down and slobbered in Miss Stevens' arms. She was the sort of woman who looked over-ripe. Her curves bulged at the seams. Mascara smeared down a dark complexioned face that might have been pretty had Miss Stevens been absent. After a few seconds she subsided and blurted:

"Mr. Miller. I left him for a minute. When I returned he was gone!"

I said. "Why did you leave the room if he talked wild?"

"Sometimes," said Miss Stevens bitingly, "even a nurse must leave a room!"

I left it at that. Leaving Clair in the office, we raced down the corridor to the elevator, hearing, as we went, the metallic voice from the P.A. speaker announce:

"Mr. Miller is missing from Ward Five—"

IN WARD FIVE an orderly was saying: "He passed me going down the hall. With another man. He had his bathrobe on. It seemed all right."

Doctor Hendrick, a big man with thick-rimmed glasses, nodded to me curtly. "Hello, Wale." He said to the orderly, "Don't you know patients on this floor are not allowed out of their wards?"

The orderly shuffled his feet uneasily.

"Yes, sir. But this was Mr. Miller, Dr. Garse's friend. I thought—"

"You had no right to think!" stormed Doctor Hendrick suddenly. "This is your last week here, Niles. Saturday you're through!"

Niles shuffled out of the ward backwards, his face turning pale as paste leaving only the scar on his lip livid. He muttered something just as he slipped out of the door.

Hendrick mopped his brow with a handkerchief.

"Miss Stevens," he murmured, "Major Strong must be notified at once."

"What's this about Major Strong?" I asked.

"Ben Miller has sworn to kill him," said the doctor. "I thought you knew. Isn't that why Doctor Garse sent for you?"

"Mr. Wale hasn't been told yet," interrupted Miss Stevens hastily.

I said, "Wait a minute, both of you! First Garse tells me over the phone that Ben has only a week to live and now you're saying Ben is out to croak Strong. Doc Garse knows his business, but I think you're screwy. Now dish it to me from the beginning this time. Without double talk!"

Miss Stevens gasped a little and plumped down on the messed-up cot that had been Ben's. Doctor Hendrick took off his glasses, stared at them a moment as if he had never seen them before, then put them on again. He cleared his throat and spoke slowly:

"Mr. Miller's heart had developed a strong murmur. To keep it going we had to inject adrenalin continuously. Doctor Garse attended to the injections personally. There was delirium and Mr. Miller spoke wildly. It is all down on the nurse's reports if you care to see them."

"Hang the nurse's reports!" I said. "What the hell are you stalling for?"

Miss Stevens gripped my arm.

"He seemed obsessed with the idea of killing Major Strong and exposing a graft. Something about the money from the Hospital Fund Match last week," she explained.

"Hah!" I said. "It comes out! You're all afraid the stink of such an exposure will cut into this hospital's share of the gate. Is that it?"

Doctor Hendrick balled his fists and there was a quiet moment. Then he relaxed and strode from the ward without a word.

"Okay, tough guy!" said Miss Stevens with angry sparks flashing from her eyes. "I didn't tell you earlier because of your Damon-Pythias act about Ben Miller. He raved we were all in a weird plot to kill him. He said Major Strong was a thick-headed tyrant who should be removed. And he said he would attend to that little thing. We had your Ben Miller in a strait-jacket all last night because, delirium and all, he insisted on rushing through the corridors and shouting for a gun. Now he's missing. I would say if you really cared so much about him you would rush over to Major Strong's house and stop a murder. And, Mr. Gun Crazy, if you could manage to get in front of a bullet while you're about it you would—you would—oh, go to the devil, Cash Wale!"

The swing of her hips as she strode from the ward took some of the edge off her words.

But I finally had what I wanted. Ben Miller was in a very nasty kind of trouble. That mad killer stuff was malarkey. Ben would step aside for a mosquito if it came to a showdown. But getting to Major Strong was an idea. The wire in my pocket mentioned an irregularity about the recent bout. Ben babbled about a graft in connection with the same bout. If there was any lead it was this. And besides, the wire mentioned a retainer.

Sailor Duffy nearly walked over me at the door. He picked me up and brushed me off and for a few terrifying seconds I felt like a punching bag. Then he said:

"Hokey-doke now, Cash. I slapped the kid into dreamland. Hokey-doke?"

"Hokey-doke," I said. "Now you've got me doing it! Come on. We've got a job!"

CHAPTER TWO

MURDER MANIAC

MAJOR STRONG'S residence was almost as much of a New York landmark as was Major Strong himself. It lay in the center of an entire block on lower Riverside Drive; a neat colonial edifice completely surrounded by giant oaks and, as we approached, buried in darkness. Once the proud showplace of earlier Strongs, now it was tenanted only by the Major and his all-around man, McGinnis, a hangover from the war.

I left Sailor in the driveway just in case Ben Miller should show. There was a wrought iron knocker. I banged it once and got set for McGinnis with a no to the prospect of seeing the Major. A few minutes passed with no other sound coming through the darkness than the smooth drone of autos passing along the Drive, an occasional boat whistle from the river. I banged again.

More silence from the house.

I pushed and the door swung open. Light from a room above streamed down the curved stairway to a large-bellied hall. Silence lay thickly over everything.

Cautiously, I ascended the stairway and entered the room from whence came the light. I had never been upstairs before. It was a small bedroom, monk-like in its simplicity. The furniture formed nothing but right angles. Even the Major's clothes folded neatly over the back of a chair and his riding boots standing by the bed fitted into right angles.

The Major's gargantuan paunch billowed a spotless white sheet impressively. His pink cheeks formed smooth curves under the precise grey tips of his mustache. Light from the single lamp sparkled from the thin trickle of blood that oozed from a blackish hole over his right eyebrow and grew on the pillow in a dull red clot.

I unlimbered the .32 Colt automatic in my shoulder harness. Not that I expected anything just then. Silence hung over the house like a shroud. It was more like inviting something to happen. I was burning up. The Major had wired me on business and now I was out a fee. Besides, I had liked the guy. And finally there was Ben. The layout was too cute. First, out of a clear sky, he raved about killing the Major. Then a stranger walked him out of the hospital. And now the Major was dead. It was too cute.

I went to the door and barked:

"McGinnis!"

An echo barked back from the hall. Nothing else. I hesitated a moment about searching for him, then decided I had to work fast and find Ben. McGinnis could wait. I re-entered the room.

From the size of the wound and the powder burn, it had been a large calibred weapon held close. The Major had obviously been asleep when it happened. No crime of passion, this. It was cold-blooded murder. And recent, if the running blood was an indication. Perhaps just before I had arrived.

I scouted around the room, opened drawers, searched the closets. There were odds and ends, nothing pertinent. Then I kicked over a riding boot and the notebook fell out. It had only one page with writing; four names listed under each other: Ben Miller, D. Jonas, Clair Ashodran and Sam Hagarian. The last had a Brooklyn address next to it. Under these names was the notation: "$50,000 grafted by the scum!" That was the Major's style.

STEALTHY FOOTSTEPS in the hall downstairs made me pocket the book and slip to the door. I stooped low enough to avoid casting a shadow and edged to the top of the stairway.

There are ways of doing things. My way is to move fast and jump the other guy. Holding the gun easily in front of my face, I stood up abruptly and lined the sights. And looked down into the glazed eyes of Ben Miller.

He stood at the foot of the stairs, clearly outlined in the light from the room behind me. A shabby bathrobe was thrown hastily over his hospital pajamas. He was alone.

"Cash," he said, "they told me I'd find you here." His voice sounded tired and low as if it took an effort to speak.

I lowered my gun and started down the stairs.

"Ben, you've got to scram out of here quick. It's a frame and you're it. Who brought you—"

"Cash," he cut in with the same dead voice, "they told me to give you this." He lifted something from the pocket of his bathrobe and held it out although I was still a good fifteen feet up the stairs.

An orange flash leaped from his hand and a steel fist hammered into my side.

"Don't, Ben!" I yelled. I dived against the wall and jerked up my Colt. The gun in his hand exploded again and something hot tugged at my sleeve.

"They told me to do it," he said. "I didn't like it, Cash. But they told me." The dull tones were sinister now, and maddening. My sights lined on his chest and I made half a dozen convulsive tugs on the trigger. Pal or no pal, nobody makes me into a target! But something about his blank expression stopped me each time.

Ben Miller suddenly dropped the gun, turned and strode toward the rear of the hall.

"Ben!" I yelled at the top of my lungs. "Listen to me! Who are *they?*" But he just floated through a layer of shadow out the back door as if he was a marionette at the end of a string. And I was too stunned for a moment to follow.

When I did get to my feet, Sailor Duffy crashed in through the front door. "Cash," he said, "I heard shooting."

My side was numb. I found I could walk down the stairs all right. I said to the Sailor:

"Ben just went out the back. Go get him, Sailor. Watch out for his gun. I don't think he'd use it on you, but watch out."

Sailor jabbed the air viciously with his left, ducked gracefully for all his two hundred and forty pounds, shifted balance from left foot to right and sent a right hook whistling in a shallow arc. He said, "Hokey doke," and jogged easily out the back door. I holstered my Colt, stooped over and picked up by the barrel the gun Ben Miller had dropped.

That was the moment Detective Lieutenant Larry O'Toole swept in the front door with half a dozen men!

O'Toole saw me and his lanky frame stiffened. Tomato eyebrows narrowed and what showed of his thick, red mane seemed to bristle. He said, "Hah! If it isn't the murder midget himself!"

"Save it for the press, copper," I snarled. I waited while he posted a man at the door and sent the others to search through the house. Then I said, "Major Strong is upstairs in that room with the light. He's dead."

"So?" said O'Toole gently plucking Ben's weapon from my hand with a handkerchief to keep fingerprints intact. "Finnigan," he ordered the man at the door, "take a gander upstairs."

AS FINNIGAN reached the landing on top I plucked Ben's weapon back not so gently and managed to palm the butt in doing it. "Listen, rattlebrain," I said, "don't make accusing actions before you're wise to the layout. The Major wired me and I'm here legitimate. And this doodad is not mine. So lay off me, see?" And as I said this I was rubbing

Ben's gun clean of any fingerprints Ben might have left behind.

O'Toole held out his hand and there was ice in his eyes. He said, "The gun, Wale!"

I gave it to him.

He said, "That's the last crazy stunt you pull on me, shrimp. Now give me your gun. I'm going to break you and run you out of town for destroying evidence in a murder case. But first I'm going to hold you as an accessory."

There was something about the dry way he said it that made me believe he intended to do just that. I gave him my Colt automatic. He emptied the chamber and magazine, put the cartridge clip in one pocket and the gun in another. I did not offer him the .25 Walther automatic that lay snugly against my calf inside my trouser leg; the unregistered one.

I said, "Talk big, copper, but don't start something you can't finish. My picking a gun off the floor and handing it to you doesn't make me an accessory to anything. If only my prints are on the gun it's just too damn bad. It happens that pacifier plopped a slug in my gut and if I am anxious to examine it before you make it into a picture star, it is merely nerves. Shock, you might call it. And no jury in the world would think different. Now get me a doctor."

O'Toole was quick on the uptake. I had to hand it to him. His face relaxed into a smile that neglected to include his eyes. He said, "Who shot you, Wale?"

"It was dark," I said. "But I think it was a little old man with a long green beard. One knee bent in and the other out. He didn't tell me his name. Now how about that doctor?"

Finnigan came to the head of the landing and called down, "It's murder all right, Lieutenant. Major Strong.

Plugged through the head by a gun held close. Never had a chance."

O'Toole waved him back. "Look things over, Finnigan. I'll be up in a minute. Don't fall over anything." Then he turned to me and purred, "Okay, shrimp. I'll send out your description. Only the lady next door neglected to mention the guy you describe. She only saw a human gorilla and a boy walk into the house without being asked. Then she heard a shot and called us."

Finnigan appeared on the landing again. "This room has already been cased!" he called down excitedly.

"All right, all right," replied O'Toole, waving him back. "Look around for what they overlooked. They always slip."

"How about that doctor?" I repeated. Pain was pushing through the numbness in my side.

O'Toole was about to reply but his eyes suddenly lifted over my shoulder and widened. I turned to see a plain-clothesman enter the hall from the back door with Sailor Duffy in tow.

"Look, Chief. I found this guy shadow-boxing out on the back porch. There is also a very dead stiff outside on the driveway leading to West End. Banged on the head and run over a couple of times by a car. He's got a face like chewed leather."

Sailor Duffy's features danced in excitement. He brushed the plainclothesman aside and came over to me blurting before I could stop him, "Ben went in the ambulance, Cash. I yelled, 'Why you shoot Cash. Ben?' But he got in the back of the ambulance and didn't talk. And the damn thing lams before I can get my hooks on the door and I see it run over McGinnis. And McGinnis is our pal. So I give 'em the old left. I jab, I hook, I cut 'em to pieces. I scramble 'em, Cash, with the old left!"

The plainclothes dick's eyes widened. "Chief, this gorilla's crazy as a coot. He smeared nobody. He just stood out on the porch there shadow-boxing!"

O'TOOLE WASN'T listening. "It comes daylight," he murmured. "That would be Ben Miller, wouldn't it, shrimp? A missing persons call went out for him half an hour ago. And for an ambulance. Both from the hospital run by your pal, Doc Garse." He was looking at me and there was something in his expression I had never seen before. He said softly, "A little old guy with a green beard, eh? Listen, shrimp, the Medical Examiner is a quack for my dough. You better go some place where they know how to de-slug a gut. Then get in touch with me. I'll want a statement. And take your double-talking sidekick along with you."

"How about my gun?"

I felt chilled inside. I had reasons. If Ben had entered the back of the ambulance as Sailor said, someone else was driving. And that someone else probably slugged and ran over McGinnis who was a damn good egg. Then, according to O'Toole, a female had phoned that she had seen Sailor and me enter the Major's residence. After which she heard one shot and then phoned. But how could any neighbor see who went in or out of the Major's house when it was completely hidden by oaks and night. O'Toole arrived in a tenth the time it would have taken had he been summoned after the two shots had been fired. There was probably a man out now checking on the call but I knew what he would find; an empty booth in a store far removed from the scene of the crime. The set-up stank. And I wanted all the artillery I could get.

O'Toole shook his head with his eyes clinging to mine. "It'll have to be checked at ballistics first."

"Nuts," I said. "Smell it. The rod hasn't been fired in a week."

"Routine, shrimp. I'll have to keep it."

I said, "Come on, Sailor. This place is giving me the creeps. Let's get the hell out of here."

Just as we reached the darkness on the front porch the pain really arrived in my side and I sagged to one knee. Sailor gripped me under the arm and for a moment he almost looked human.

"What'll I do, Cash?"

I said, "Get me back to the hospital. To Doc Garse. Quick!"

Then I passed out.

CHAPTER THREE
KILLER AT LARGE!

"NO," SAID Doc Garse for the fourteenth time, "it is not serious, Cash. Not enough to keep you off your feet. But I would advise rest, anyhow."

We were in the doc's office at the hospital. I was stretched out on the window seat and Miss Stevens was slapping the last layer of plaster around my middle. Sailor Duffy watched, fascinated. Doc Garse sat behind his desk. His hair was dishevelled, even to the grey dashes on his temples and he was dragging on a cigarette as if it was his last. I had never seen him that nervous before.

My head ached and I felt hot. And I itched. I scratched, but Miss Stevens kept slapping my hand away.

Doc explained the anti-tetanus injection had given me a slight fever and was responsible for the itch. Both would wear off by morning.

"How about Ben?" I asked.

He seemed to age ten years at the question. "Out there some place." He waved at the night through the window. "We heard a news broadcast that he was wanted for the murder of Major Strong and McGinnis. I can't understand it, Cash. A bad heart doesn't affect a man that way.... What will they do to him?"

I threw off Miss Stevens' restraining hand and struggled to my feet. Slipping into my shirt, I said, "That depends on who gets to him first. If it's me, I've got angles. I think he can be cleared. If it's the cops, God alone knows...." I could feel the doctor wince. I winced, too, inside.

I didn't mention the Major's notebook because holding back evidence in a murder rap is a serious offense.

"Can I see Miss Ashodran?" I asked casually.

"She's off duty now," said Stevens.

"That would be Clair, the nurse who made out those reports on Ben?"

Garse looked interested.

"Why do you ask, Cash?"

"A hunch. Can I borrow those reports?"

Doc sent for them. It was after midnight and I was very hot and tired. When the reports came I said, "Come on, Sailor, let's go pound our ears."

Miss Stevens caught my arm at the door. "Take care of yourself, Cash Wale. That cute little pistol strapped to your leg nearly shot an orderly when we stripped you. I wouldn't be rash."

"I won't," I said, grabbing a handful of that speckled sunlight and bringing her face up firmly under mine. Her lips were like rubber for a moment, then melted into a hot moist circle, then turned back to rubber again. Sailor caught her fist at the deep end of her hook and twisted it gently down to her side.

"Don't hit Cash," he rumbled. "He may get shot."

We left on that.

DICE'S SQUEAKY voice calling my name awoke us in the morning. Sailor was sprawled over three chairs and I was draped over the desk. My side was very stiff as I rolled to my feet. I hid the sheaf of reports I had studied before going to sleep, then Sailor opened the door.

Dice slid in and made a feeble crack about whether we had a home.

"What do you want, Dice?" I yawned, not bothering to explain. Nobody with any self-respect explained to Dice.

He spread out a morning tabloid on the desk and sleep dropped from me like a lead weight. The headline was: "Killer At Large!" Under it were two pictures. One was Ben Miller with the caption, "Did doomed writer kill in the madness of delirium or—" The dash carried over to the other picture, me at my worst, and a caption: "—did Cash Wale, the gangster with the detective license, add one more victim to his bloody list?"

A second page editorial elaborated:

"Why do authorities continue to allow a known criminal to remain at large? Why don't they at least deprive him of his license and gun? Police say they are convinced Cash Wale had no hand in the murders at the Strong residence. But he was at the scene of the crime when the police arrived WITH THE MURDER GUN IN HIS HAND!" Then followed the usual threats and insinuations, stuff which my lawyer, Harry Goldfarb, would make the most of if I emerged clean. It was old stuff. I was used to it.

I found a bottle in a desk drawer and passed it to Sailor for breakfast. He took a long drag, then handed it back managing to keep it out of Dice's reach. I did my duty and returned what was left to the drawer.

"So what, Dice?" I said.

Dice shrugged and eyed me through narrow slits. "Maybe we could do business," he suggested. "I know some of the score. You're in a hole and you can't get out. You're pretty good at figuring the score from nothing, Cash. I know. But this time you got a blank."

He was fishing but I wouldn't take the bait. "I got a blank," I agreed. "How much?"

"It'll take dough, Cash. I'm sticking my neck out."

This was interesting. Dice was a runner for bookies and a peddler of dope. Information dribbled to him from a thousand different sources and he peddled squeal as a side-line. Maybe he had something. And maybe he had what seemed like something. I did not consider the third alternative then. I repeated:

"How much, Dice?"

"One grand."

My insides tightened into a knot. Sailor caught my look and edged up behind the rat. Dice had been holding out and I don't like guys who hold out. Particularly when a pal's on a spot. But before I could get started, Little Abie Miller almost tore down the door to get in.

Abie was not carrying a tabloid but I could see headlines in his eyes. His freckles were streaming wet.

"Cash! The kids at school say Pop's a killer! They say I should be in a reformatory! I ran away from school, Cash. I'm never going back; never! Never!"

Sailor said, "Aw, hell!" He patted the kid's head awkwardly. "The punks are lyin'. Don't bother about the punks, pal. The dirty damned punks!"

What is a guy supposed to do with a crying kid? Abie was giving with all he had. I felt uncomfortable as hell and killed time fumbling with my pipe until the sobs subsided. Then I said:

"They're lying, Abie. Sailor is right. The cops are stuck and trying to make Ben into a goat." I filled the pipe, lit it and took a long drag. I said, "I'll tell you something just between you and me. I'm not stuck. I know Ben did not do it. I'm going to find the guy who did and plug him three times through the belly. I'm going to clear Ben, kid."

I wished I felt as sure as I sounded. I had myself to clear as well as Ben.

Abie wiped his eyes and nose in one stroke. "I knew Sailor and you'd fix it," he said, then added: "Yesterday I forgot about this. Ben asked me to find it and give it to you."

I looked at the first page of the notebook Abie handed me for a full minute before I remembered. Most of it was shorthand scrawl which was so much Greek to me. But scattered around among the hen scratches were three names written in longhand: D. Jonas, Claire Ashodran and Sam Hagarian. Again there was an address next to the last name. Except for the omission of Ben's name this was an exact duplicate of the list in the Major's notebook!

I knew Clair Ashodran. There was something familiar about the other names. I said:

"Dice, do you know—"

Sailor interrupted, "Dice lammed, Cash."

I told Sailor to take the kid over to the hospital and wait for me there. After they left I compared the two lists of names and smoked out the pipe. Then I took another cut out of the bottle and left the office.

IT WAS one of a score of brownstone buildings that stretched down the block. A shabby sign in a first floor window advertised a double room with private bath and kitchenette, reasonable. The address checked with that in the Major's notebook so I ascended the short flight of steps and fingered the bell.

When the door opened I smiled and asked, "Is Sam Hagarian home?" Then I drew back and gasped for air.

She had purple bags under her eyes and a faint mustache. A pink dressing gown that had seen better days lay unevenly over a mush-melon bosom. It was fastened together in front by a large safety pin. She reeked of garlic.

She said, "He ain't been here for two days. If you're his friend tell him to catch up on his rent or he'll find all his junk out on the sidewalk." Her gaze slithered down my crumpled trousers and her eyes hardened.

I put one foot where it would keep the door from slamming.

"Rent?" I asked. "That is probably what Sam meant when he wrote me he needed money fast." My wallet appeared and I allowed green to show.

She opened the door wide again, her gaze settling on the wad. "I can't understand why he should need to ask for it," she said. "After earning so much from that last big job—but I ain't being perlite. Come in."

I held my breath passing through the door. She pressed too close. Her hand guided my elbow through a dark hallway to a drab little office in the rear. Her fingers lingered a little longer than necessary and sent signals. "Ten roomers," she sighed, "and not a decent paying guest in the lot. Would you be looking for a room?"

I slipped the wallet back into my pocket before her eyes could grow hooks and said, "You mean that job Sam got with the Milligan Company?" This was a bluff. There was no Milligan Company. But it made no difference.

"I don't know what company," she shrugged. "Are you a C.P.A., also?"

"No. Sam borrowed my camera over the week-end. Didn't he tell you about it? That's why I'm here."

"And the rent money."

"Maybe," I said before she could dwell on that angle, "I might take a room here at that. If it had a bath and a kitchenette. And it was close to Sam's."

She gasped delightedly and I nearly passed out. "Why I have just that!" she exclaimed. "Across the hall from Mr. Hagarian. Of course, the rent—"

"That would be swell. Didn't Sam tell you about my camera? It's pretty valuable."

"Do you really want a room?"

"Sure. If it's reasonable," I said.

She took a key off a wall hook and beckoned me to follow. On the stairs I gripped her bare arm. I said, "Let's look in Sam's room while we're up there. He might have left my camera around with a note." This time my fingers signalled.

Her hand dropped over mine. "I go in there once a day, honey, to clean. There ain't no note. What did you say your name was?" Her hand was greasy.

"Becker. Let's try anyhow."

ON THE second landing she stopped to catch her breath. I tried to get windward of the garlic but she leaned against me heavily. "I can look again if you want," she breathed. "What's your first name?" She wore nothing under the robe, but I didn't get excited.

"Jim," I said.

She bumped hips with me up another flight and led me to the back of the hall under a grimy skylight. She fumbled a little with her key, then straightened up and wigwagged with her eyes. I was getting very sick of garlic. I took the key from her and unlocked the door.

At first I thought it was still the garlic. Then I got another thought and looked sharply at the landlady. But she only looked disappointed.

The room was as interesting as an old shoe. A narrow bed that sagged in the middle. An ice box dresser. A chair. Light struggled through the dirt smudged window and settled on a silver framed picture resting on top of the dresser. There was no camera. I didn't expect any.

I was using my nose and, despite the garlic, it was easy. An odor that seemed to come from a hundred rotten eggs permeated the room. Only I knew there were no rotten eggs.

"Smell anything?" I asked the landlady. Her mustache quivered slightly as she glanced around the room.

"No."

"Of course not," I muttered. "The whole world must smell like garlic to you."

She said, "What?"

I said, "I said that camera ought to be around someplace."

It was not difficult to trace the smell. I kicked aside the chair and opened the door to a small closet.

Sam Hagarian had a hooked nose. He was short and swarthy and looked slightly familiar although it would have been impossible to say exactly what he looked like. The flesh of his neck was swollen blue and parted by a thin rubber strap that held him suspended from a clothes hook high on the back wall of the closet. He was nude.

I could tell he had been dead a couple of days by his bloated feet and hands where the blood had settled and by his blue color. And the smell. The rest of the closet was completely bare.

The door was open only a few seconds, but the landlady had been looking over my shoulder. She made a clucking sound deep in her throat, bent sideways and did things with her breakfast. Then she leaned back and screamed.

I STEPPED over her breakfast and said, "Damn it, shut up! Do you want this place to be crawling with coppers?" I was sorry as soon as the words left my mouth. There had been a brief picture etched in my mind of the editor of the morning tabloid howling for my scalp.

Her pupils dilated in terror. Instinctively, she drew the wrap tighter around her. "You knew he was there all the time!" she gasped.

"You're crazy!" I said going through the dresser drawers in no seconds flat. They were all empty.

"No I'm not!"

"Use your head," I urged. "Why'd I return here if I knew?" I tore the picture of Clare Ashodran from the silver picture frame on the dresser and stuffed it in my pocket.

"The money!" she mumbled. "You came back for the money. You didn't find it when you killed him and now you came back for the money!" Her throat swelled and she let out another scream.

I slapped her face and the screams choked in her throat. There was a white imprint where my hand had struck on the scarlet of her cheek. She said:

"I know you now. You're Cash Wale, the gangster! You killed Major Strong! And you killed Mr. Hagarian too!" She whirled and streaked for the door.

I got there first.

"I'm Cash Wale," I said. "So what? If you didn't stink so much from garlic, you'd have found him two days ago. Do you know what it'll mean to your rooming house license when it comes out there's been a stiff here two days? Do you know Article Five, Section Seven, Paragraph C of Habeas Corpus on rooming houses? Do you know what the Health Department will do to you on that?"

I didn't know myself but it held her long enough for me to reach around the door and feel the key still in the lock.

I reached out and gave her a firm shove, then I slipped into the hall, locked the door, pocketed the key and started down the stairs four at a time.

It was not until I was on the second landing that I heard her pounding the door and yelling for help. In the street, I pitched the key down the first sewer I passed, then zigzagged around half a dozen blocks.

I wanted to think. Up to now there had been nothing but loose ends. Now they were beginning to meet. Sam Hagarian's murder was linked to Major Strong's by the Major's notebook. He had been killed on the heels of completing a big job for which he had received a pile of dough. The killer had left the room bare of any possible identification. Why? To conceal the identity of that job. It was beginning to add.

THE CORPSE PROMOTER 81

There was a way of finding out what that job had been but it meant selling the idea to a lot of officials to whom I was marked lousy. Anyhow, I had no time to fool around with red tape. But there was another possibility. One that tied in with Ben Miller.

I ducked into the nearest subway entrance as a police car streaked past me at about forty miles an hour, siren screaming.

CHAPTER FOUR
ARMENIAN JOE
TAKES A HAND

AT THE hospital I found Sailor Duffy in the middle of a crowd of convalescents telling his fistic saga, with gestures. Little Abie ran over to me. I said:

"Tell Sailor to meet me outside in front of the hospital in about ten minutes. You stay here."

The convalescents were getting a great kick out of the Sailor. The big fellow had a knack of winning people to his side. Nurse Stevens stood at the edge of the group taking it all in. Doctor Hendrick stood by her side, smiling. The smile froze and he moved off when I approached.

"Such popularity," murmured Miss Stevens. "I think it can be traced to your obvious sense of inferiority."

"That's dandy," I said, "but I'm allergic to psychology and right now I'm in a hurry. Where can I find Miss Claire Ashodran?"

Her eyes twinkled.

"Think she'll be more receptive to your technique?"

"You can go to—cut the comedy," I said. I produced Ben's notebook. "They told me at the desk that Doc Garse is out. Could you give him this when he returns? Ask him to translate it for me. I can't savvy shorthand. Now, where's Clair?"

"Down in the basement, in the laundry. I—"

"Thanks," I interrupted thrusting the book in her hand. I rumpled Abie's hair and sped to the elevator.

Green arrows on the walls guided me through the basement corridors to the laundry. It was a large concrete walled room filled with piles of towels, sheets, pyjamas. At one end a slippery metal chute ran up into the street letting in the only natural light through a grating. I had to round a huge pillar before sighting Miss Ashodran.

She was stooped over a pile of soiled linen checking it off from a list in her hand. I came up softly from behind and tapped lightly on a plump shoulder.

She straightened out very slowly. The mascara was all in place now making her face darkly alluring. Penciled brows lifted a trifle at sight of me, "Mr. Wale!"

"You wrote some very interesting things about Ben Miller in your reports, Miss Ashodran. But you neglected to mention what Ben said about your boy friend, Sam Hagarian."

CLAIR ASHODRAN'S breath hissed inward and for an instant she resembled a Maltese Cat arching its back. Then she let out her breath and spoke carefully.

"I wrote exactly what he said, Mr. Wale. Every single thing he said is on the reports."

"Even what he said about Sam Hagarian's big job and the fifty thousand dollars graft?"

I lifted the .25 caliber Walther automatic from my side pocket as she tossed a head full of black locks at me and started for the door.

"Don't leave now," I said.

She turned to see the muzzle settled on her ear and a smirk twisted her lips. "You can't bluff me, Cash Wale," she said. "You wouldn't dare use that!" Then she looked into my eyes and the smirk evaporated leaving her face full and a trifle flabby.

"I never give a crook an even break," I whispered.

"You're crazy if you think I had anything to do with it! I just work here!" Her tone was defiant. But her eyes were not.

I allowed a sneer to linger on my face for a full minute while I let my newspaper reputation work for me. It was easy to follow the progress of her thoughts. When they reached utter despair, I said:

"Who killed Sam Hagarian?"

The effect was startling. No act, this. She was too frightened. Her hands fluttered. She tried to say something, licked her lips to get it out but could only manage a hoarse whisper:

"Sam?"

I nodded. "Strangled to death with a hospital tourniquet and left to hang high and dry in a dinky closet in a Brooklyn boarding house."

"He killed him!" she gasped. "He killed Sam!"

"Who killed Sam?"

"He'll kill me next!"

I gripped her shoulders and shook until her teeth rattled. When some of the terror left her eyes I said:

"Once there were three guys named Moe. What do you think of that!"

Her eyes were blank for a moment, then a foolish chuckle caught in her throat. "I'm sorry," she said.

"Good. Now tell me about it."

She drew close. I knew a lot of tricks and kept my Walther automatic pressed into her middle.

"He made me do it!" she exclaimed. "There was so much money. It was a chance for Sam and me to get married. But then something went wrong and he had to kill Major Strong. Sam wasn't the last. You don't know how brutal he is. There will be others if you don't stop him. He is—" She lurched forward as the basement rocked from a tremendous explosion.

Her eyes twisted. Her mouth opened once and a cascade of blood welled out. I leaped back out of the way letting her pitch forward to the floor.

My automatic barked once at the edge of the pillar near the door where a wisp of heavy smoke still lingered. A bit of plaster chipped off from my bullet. I chipped some more plaster on the other side of the pillar with a second shot. By the sound of the detonation and the dime-sized hole in the nurse's back where she lay sprawled on the floor I knew my .25 automatic was up against a more powerful weapon.

I squeezed two more shots on either side of the pillar to keep the killer's head behind it. The only other way out of the basement room was the chute leading up to the sidewalk.

Keeping the pillar edges alive with flying plaster, I got on the chute backwards, pressed my shoes against the sides and slowly worked myself up. I had an idea of coming back through the front of the hospital fast and surprising the killer from behind.

Near the top of the chute my feet slipped and I went into reverse. Twisting about, I flung out my hands and managed to stop sliding. But the automatic clattered on the cement floor below.

The basement echoed to another terrific explosion as I scrambled back up and a hole appeared in the sheet iron near my hand. Sheer desperation inspired my movements as another shot lifted a strand of my hair and the third creased my left shoe alongside the heel. Then I was over the top, through the grating which swung back on a hinge and diving out into the street. I did not bother to look back.

SAILOR DUFFY was entrenched before the hospital entrance when I sprinted around the corner. The two strangers who were with him seemed absorbed in what the Sailor was saying.

Sailor saw me and called, "Hey, Cash! C'mere and meet some pals. Palsy-walsies. They wanna take us in their cab. They gotta cab. I like to ride in cabs."

It sickened me to realize that the street was deserted as one of the strangers, a wiry lug with green eyes, stepped forward and pressed a side pocket in my direction.

"Cash likes to ride in cabs, too," he announced. "Don't you, Cash?"

The side pocket was eloquent. We crossed to a cab parked at the curb. The thug behind Sailor was dumpy and he wore glasses. He also pressed a pocket. He said:

"Ride up front with me, heavyweight. The scenery is better."

Sailor was all enthusiasm. "That's good! That's good! But let Cash see the scenery. Cash's my pal!"

Green Eyes said, "No. Cash wants to sit in back and talk to me; don't you, palsy-walsy?"

I said, "I'll sit in back, Sailor."

The cab wound around a few streets, then headed up Madison Avenue. At every red light Green Eyes pressed that thing into my side and asked:

"Wanna gab with the traffic cop, palsy?"

I scarcely noticed him. They wouldn't risk pulling anything raw in the middle of the city. What bothered me was their angle. Up to now the killings all had a certain amateur slant to them. These guys were pros. If they tied in to what had happened to Major Strong and Hagarian and Ben Miller I wanted to hang around for some answers. If it was a side issue from another case it was a waste of time and I wanted to get out. In the meantime all I could do was sit and wait. I am a sucker for lead eloquence.

The garage was deep in the east side of Harlem; a multi-floored affair that elbowed aside scores of dilapidated tenements. The cab drove into a large elevator in the rear. Heavy metal doors clanged behind us and the elevator began to rise. About fifteen feet up it stopped. We had not reached the second floor yet.

Green Eyes motioned us out of the cab.

"That was a short ride, fellers," Sailor said. "I like rides in the country, where there's grass."

"That'll come by and by," smirked Dumpy. "Now we're gonna play games."

Sailor said, "I like games. That's—"

"Shut up, Sailor," I said. "These guys are rats."

"Rats? I'll scramble 'em, Cash! I'll give 'em the old left."

Green Eyes took his hand from his pocket and there was a gun sticking to it. He slanted it up under Sailor's eyes. "We don't scramble easy," he said.

He opened a small side door and waved us through with the gun. When the door closed I could hear the elevator renew its ascent.

It was a low ceilinged room sandwiched between two garage floors. At the far end was a mahogany desk with a few piles of papers, a telephone and a fresh newspaper spread out. Behind the desk sat a man I was not surprised to see.

ARMENIAN JOE was fast becoming important in the boxing game. His Hospital Charity Bouts were luring million buck gates in a new era of sporting prosperity. His small, over-dressed figure was a landmark in certain circles. What was not generally known was that Armenian Joe ran one of the biggest horse racing books in the business. He sat now behind the desk wearing a navy colored derby and fingering a long blue cigarette holder.

Dumpy said, "We pick these monkeys up easy, Joe."

The promoter motioned the thugs to chairs. There was no one else in the room. I said:

"Your hospitality stinks, Joe. A wire would have been more polite if you wanted to see me."

Joe lifted a pair of ebony eyes that said they hated my guts. "You no like?" he purred softly, tapping the desk with the cigarette holder.

"No, I no like!" I didn't like his eyes.

"That's good, Cash Wale. Because I no keep you long. You and the screwball here." He snapped the paper around on the desk. It was an afternoon rag and no tabloid. My face leered up at me from a box in the middle of the first page under a scarehead that screamed:

WALE KILLS C.P.A.!

There was a smaller picture of the amorous landlady. My eyes widened as they skipped down the column. Apparently I had forced her up to the dead man's room at gun point and demanded his money. When she couldn't produce I had violated her person and boasted of killing everyone from the Lindbergh baby to Major Strong.

A front page editorial crowded the war news to the side columns proclaiming that the police were launching the greatest manhunt in history. It begged any armed citizen who spotted me to shoot me down like a mad dog. There was a lot more but I had the idea. Armenian Joe's eyes were singeing my hair. I looked up and said:

"I don't get it, Joe. This stuff is malarkey. But why should you shill for the cops?"

"My name," said Armenian Joe, "is Joe Hagarian. Sam was kid brother."

There were death-heads in the gambler's eyes.

"Wait, Joe," I said. "Think! Why should I bump your brother? I swear I found him strangled in that closet. I'm working on the Major Strong case and I found Sam's name and address in the Major's notebook. I was just checking up. That landlady was on the make. I gave her the chill and she burned. She's sex slappy. I swear that's straight, Joe!"

The Armenian motioned to the thugs. "Sure you work on Strong case," he hissed. "Is how you find Sam has twenty-five grand in his room. But you no fool me, Wale. You kill Sam all right."

Something *thunked* behind me and I whirled to see Sailor Duffy sag slowly to the floor. Green Eyes stood to one side with his gun held by the barrel. As I started for him Dumpy jabbed his gun muzzle into my wound and I howled. Dumpy cracked me across the jaw tightly. "Clam up!" he barked.

"I got the Major's book in my pocket, Joe," I said earnestly, turning back to the promoter. I said to Dumpy, "In the right hand pocket of my jacket." I was not making any moves with my hands that might be misunderstood.

Dumpy snagged the book and tossed it on the desk. Armenian Joe riffled the pages, then looked up and I knew I had missed.

"Sure," he said, "sure. It is all here. Where Sam lived and the fifty grand graft. Now Sam is dead and no dough. You kill Sam all right, Wale!"

There was a knock on the door followed by two more before I could reply. Green Eyes undid the latch, then stepped back resting his gun easily.

"Dice!" I said.

The little grey stool saw me from the doorway and blanched. He looked over at Sailor sprawled on the floor and grew even greyer. He said, "I came, Joe. Like you asked."

"Not now, Dice," said Armenian Joe. "Make it eight o'clock tonight in Time's Square subway, uptown side— you know where. Okay?"

Dice's eyes flew in circles. "Okay," he said backing out slowly, "I got it."

"And, Dice!" Armenian Joe waved the blue cigarette holder significantly. "You see nothing here, no?"

"Sure. Sure. I ain't no rat, Joe!"

I started to yell as Dice slinked through the door but a house fell on my head and I forgot what I was going to say. I forgot everything.

CHAPTER FIVE
AN AMBULANCE CASE

IT WAS the heel of a shoe. Hairs stuck to a reddish clot on the edge. The heel came down again and my head seemed to snap inside. There was a salty taste of blood in my mouth.

Green Eyes' voice pierced the ringing in my ears. "Not here, Joe. We can do all this in Yonkers. If he croaks here, we'll be hot."

The heel wavered over my eyes, started down again. I wrenched to one side and sharp pain stabbed me in a dozen places up and down my body. But the heel skidded in a pool of blood next to my head and someone tumbled down on me. I looked up into the hate-laden gaze of Armenian Joe.

"Not here any more, Joe," pleaded the voice of Green Eyes. Armenian Joe rose slowly to his feet, kicked my side. The shirt over my wound was scarlet.

Then the phone rang.

"Throw water on the ——" The promoter picked up the phone. He had removed his jacket. Perspiration splotched his blue shirt, soaking even into his blue suspenders.

"Hello?" he said. "You? I wait long time for you. Yeah. We got 'em!"

A stream of water smashed into my face feeling as if they had neglected to remove the pail.

"Listen," said Armenian Joe into the phone, "I don't forget favors. I close books on you, complete. Yeah, I know I lose twenty-five grand but getting this monkey where I can do him good is like a million bucks to me. You betcha! I finish him good in Yonkers."

THE CORPSE PROMOTER 91

I heard more water swish and turned to see Sailor Duffy splutter up to a sitting position.

The gambler was still talking. "What you mean sure? You got Joe's promise, see? That's plenty good. And to show I deal square I tell you something. I know you bumped Strong. No, wait. It's all right by me. If he nose around it make good business. But I handle Cash Wale all myself. You'll what? That's good! I wait."

Sailor Duffy looked at me and his expression was startled. "What they done to you, Cash? You got blood. All over it's blood!"

"Shut up!" growled Dumpy, coming over and kicking Sailor in the ribs. Sailor reached and Dumpy produced a gun and Sailor subsided.

"Don't try playing rough, palsy-walsy, or papa'll spank. Didn't I tell you we play games?"

Sailor rumbled deep in his throat. I said, "Take it easy, Sailor. For the time being we're on ice."

"For the time being?" Armenian Joe laughed harshly. "You one tough guy, Wale. But Joe is tough guy, tougher than you. I keep you on ice for a week. Maybe more. I kill you ten times a day. After a while you beg Joe to bump you for keeps. But I tell you about Sam, what a nice guy is Sam, how I give big dough to Sam to make him set for all his life and then he got to get bumped by a —— like you. You gonna wish he bumped you, Wale. You gonna wish it when I break all the little bone in hand and feet and make you to bleed slow from hundred little cuts. Then I burn out one eye. Then…" For what seemed like a year the blood crazed Armenian described what he would do to me down to the last gory detail, kicking my raw wound every now and then to hold my attention. Sailor Duffy had to be clouted out five times during the recital before the same signal was repeated at the door; a single knock followed by two.

Green Eyes undid the latch again with his pacifier poised. Shocks were coming thick and fast now. I yelled:

"Ben! Watch out!"

Dumpy slammed a foot into my mouth and I toppled backwards.

Ben Miller still wore the same pyjamas and hospital robe under a trench coat. There was a stubble of beard all over his face. He said:

"Come on. I am ready." The same dead tone as in the Major's house!

DUMPY PRODDED me to my feet and Green Eyes got his shoulders under Sailor who was still out from the last clout. Armenian Joe lead us out into the elevator where a Good Deed Hospital ambulance was waiting. A glance at the license plate showed me this was not the missing ambulance. But I had no chance to think it over.

Armenian Joe looked at his watch as all except Ben got into the back. Ben stepped into the driver's seat without a word. "Four on the dot!" exclaimed the gambler. "Plenty smart to work with guy what knows his onions!"

Green Eyes asked, "Joe, can that monkey up front be trusted?"

"You betcha," Joe snickered. "That what I mean by guy what know his onions."

I felt sick and dazed as the elevator descended and we rolled out into the street. Armenian Joe pulled the blinds and settled back on the foot of the stretcher. Green Eyes sat opposite him on the end of the bench. I sat halfway down the bench between him and Dumpy. Sailor lay sprawled on the floor.

Dumpy called to Joe, "Does this guy up front know where he's going?"

Joe snickered again. "You betcha!"

"Then what happens to him?"

"He gets bumped. I make favor for friend."

I said, "Joe, you're making a mistake about me. The guy who killed Major Strong killed your brother and copped the twenty-five grand."

Joe looked at Green Eyes who swiped at my head with the butt of his gun. I leaned sideways and the butt smashed into a metal brace. Something pinched my ankle but I didn't look down.

"You'll be sorry for this as long as you live, Joe," I said.

Joe said, "Don't talk, Wale, or you find out quick how to be sorry. Before we get to Yonkers."

I scarcely heard him. This was my chance to look down and for an instant I looked into one of Sailor's slightly parted eyes. It closed in a slow wink and remained shut.

The ambulance lurched around a curve and Green Eyes leveled his gun at my chest.

"Don't get any ideas, pal."

Looking around, I saw Dumpy hold another roscoe aimed at my back. My foot pressed gently against Sailor's outstretched hand. He pinched it again. I looked at Dumpy significantly and repeated the business with my foot.

I said, "Joe, do you know Clair Ashodran was killed this afternoon? By the same guy that killed Strong and your brother."

The promoter's face was blank for a moment. I could see he did not know Clair from the back end of a truck. Then his eyes grew nasty and he said, "I tell you no talking, Wale!" I let my eyes drop again and caught Sailor's closing in another slow wink. It was hard to tell whether he caught on. Sailor lived in a child's world. But in times of danger he sometimes had relapses of intelligence.

The ambulance lurched around another curve. I noticed from the sound that Ben took his foot off the accelerator just a second before a turn.

We rode on in silence for about twenty minutes with me repeating the play with Sailor and noticing how Ben always slowed down before a curve. It was a driving habit. He slowed down at other times but the way he did it before a curve was distinctively gradual.

Armenian Joe looked at his watch. "We be there quick now," he announced. His gaze fastened on me and I could see him mentally lick his lips. I had never seen such concentrated hate in a man's eyes before.

I pressed my foot hard against Sailor's hand and said, "Joe, you're a sucker. The guy driving this bus is Ben Miller, my pal. He's out there alone with no one to check on his direction. Did you notice we made two left hand turns? Is that the way to Yonkers, Joe?"

Doubt flickered across the Armenian's face.

"Clam the ——!" said the gambler.

At the same moment I heard Ben's foot let up slow on the accelerator and knew it had to be now or never. Green Eyes was reversing his gun and bending my way. Joe was lifting a corner of the blind to look out. I said:

"Sailor, now!"

OUT OF a corner of my eye I saw Sailor Duffy uncoil from the floor like a steel spring snapping at Dumpy. Green Eyes swung the gun just as the ambulance lurched around the curve and I caught the butt as he shifted off balance.

The interior of the ambulance trembled to a roar as something hot sizzled past my ear. There was a second roar when I squeezed the trigger on Green Eyes' reversed gun and a hole leaped into his cheek.

Armenian Joe was twisting around, clawing at his shoulder holster. My second bullet twanged harmlessly through the roof as Dumpy came hurtling over my shoulder.

Joe's gun barked and the slug twitched Dumpy's body still in the air before my face. Before I could line my sights again two hundred pounds of conditioned sinew swept the length of the ambulance. A knotted fist zinged past and snapped full into the startled Armenian's face. His head cracked back against the door and the door swung open. I yelled:

"Ben Miller, stop! Stop the ambulance!"

Through the open door was a rapidly receding vista of trees, grass, a rider on horseback looking at us, startled. Another horse was streaking in the opposite direction, riderless.

Sailor cracked the promoter again. I pounded on the partition that separated us from Ben Miller and shouted as loud as I could:

"Snap out of it, Ben! It's Sailor and Cash!"

But the ambulance sped on without slowing. There was no way of reaching Ben from the back. I motioned to Sailor and he nodded.

"Hokey doke, Cash. I get it. I get it, keed!"

We backed down to the hanging step behind the ambulance. Green Eyes and Dumpy could do Ben no harm at his destination but Armenian Joe was only unconscious. I reached in and dragged the gambler out feet first. Deliberately, I let him drop.

There was a dull plop and he was lying spread eagled on the road rapidly slipping behind us.

Sailor and I leaped together, working our legs fast. But it was impossible to work them fast enough. The pavement smashed up to meet us and my sleeves shredded into raw streaks of flesh under my arms. Sailor took it better, curling as he fell and rolling over on his shoulder like a football player retrieving a fumbled ball.

The ambulance, way up ahead now, suddenly swerved, rocked, then disappeared in a cloud of smoke. A deafening explosion knocked us off our feet.

Something sailed into the branches of a tree overhead: part of a steering wheel.

Sailor cried, "Cash, the ambulance exploded! It blew up! Boom!"

With my teeth gripped firmly in my heart I started toward the smoking heap. Sailor passed me on the run.

The ambulance was a twisted mass of metal. Green Eyes lay across the road in three separate pieces. Dumpy was out of sight. Ben Miller was on his face in the bridle path that ran alongside the road. I rolled him over. His head, drained of color, moved from side to side weakly.

After a while his lids fluttered open and I saw his eyes were no longer glazed. He whispered:

"Cash—doped injections… knew what I did. I killed… couldn't help… doped… Where's Abie?" His face grew still again.

"We're taking care of Abie, Ben," said Sailor huskily. "Me and Cash. Me and Cash and Abie."

Ben smiled faintly. His wrist pulse was weak but steady. A fat man with red jowls and expensive pants drew up on a large black horse.

"Had an accident?"

My nerves jangled. I said, "What the hell do you think we had, a game of potsy?" I said, "You fan that nanny's tail to the nearest cop or phone and get help. This man needs medical aid at once!" I got to my feet as he lashed the horse into a gallop. "Sailor, you stay here with Ben. I'm going after that gun I dropped back down the road and then plant three slugs in a rat's belly. I wish I knew where we were!"

"It's Van Cortlandt Park, Cash," said Sailor. "I trained here plenty when I was a prelim punk. Road work. I know this place like a book. A book."

I found Green Eyes' gun near Armenian Joe. The promoter's face was swollen and discolored. His legs were snapped under him unnaturally. He was breathing but unconscious. A couple of fellows in union suits with numbers on their backs were standing around gawking. I waved the gun.

"Are you heel-and-toe monkeys gonna stand there all day? This guy's hurt. Go get help, quick!"

They went.

CHAPTER SIX
RED TRAIL'S END

THE TAXI driver looked at my mangled face. His eyes traveled down the welts on my arms to my blood soaked shirt and he made as if to say something. I wasn't having any. I let the gun precede me into the cab.

"Don't get ideas, chum. I am in no mood to argue. Get this heap to the Good Deed Hospital. Catch on?" He had a thin face and a drooping mouth and he looked as if he caught on.

The gun was a Smith and Wesson automatic, a little to the heavy side. I did not like heavy guns but this was no time to be particular. There was a dull, murderous ache inside my chest that demanded satisfaction.

I said, "Turn on the radio, chum."

There was no music on the station to which he dialed, only a man's voice talking in excitement:

"We interrupt this program of Filch's Liver Tablets to forward a police warning to all citizens living in the vicinity of New York City. Within the last twenty-four hours Cash Wale, the notorious private detective with a reputed blood lust, has murdered three men and a woman in cold blood. His latest victim was Miss Clair Ashodran, a nurse at the Good Deed Hospital. She was killed in the hospital basement, probably after a criminal attack. The medical examination has not been completed as yet. Wale was last seen escaping from the scene of the crime. He is dangerous and armed. His description follows...."

I watched the cabby's eyes study me in his rear view mirror. His right hand dropped off the wheel.

"Don't reach for that wrench, chum. I am dangerous and armed."

His right hand returned to the wheel.

I ENTERED the hospital with the cab driver's cap draped low over my eyes. The driver was trussed up in the back of his cab which was parked in a side street. But it had been a rush job. I had to work fast. The nurse at the desk took one look at my arms and shirt and said:

"Don't tell me. You had an accident! Go to emergency, third door to your left down the hall."

I mumbled a question.

She said, "Probably in the laundry. But first go to emergency. Wounds like those can't wait."

I entered the fourth door to the right which led to the laundry. There was no need to follow the arrows on the walls this time.

Nearing the door to the laundry, I suddenly felt weak and washed out. My wound ached. My head was splitting and my arms felt like lead weights.

No sound came from the laundry.

I took a deep breath, crashed into the door. It was unlocked and I went spinning through, staggered past the wide pillar and landed on one knee.

The scene that greeted me was one that will live forever in my memory. But I was not sightseeing. My gun was in my hand and cocked. The element of surprise gave me the necessary instant to get set. Then I shot Doctor William P. Garse three times through the belly.

He had been leaning over a large canvas case with a wicked black Luger pressed into a pillow when I entered. Now he bowed down in a slow, twisting motion, sagged to the floor pulling the pillow into his stomach. The Luger clattered by his side. He was dead by the time he landed.

It took but a few seconds to cut Abie and Miss Stevens and Doctor Hendrick loose from their bonds and gags and get them out of the large canvas case which I recognized as the kind used for soiled linen.

They all started talking at once. I said, "Shut up, all of you! Abie, Ben's all right, a few bones broken maybe, but all right. Now go lock that door. There's gonna be hell to pay soon as a cabby gets loose from his suspenders, and I've got things to do."

As Abie went, I turned to the others. "Well, are you gonna stand there and watch me fall to pieces? Fix me up so I can move around in the street without attracting too much attention."

Doc Hendrick came out of his trance fast. "Had you all wrong, Wale," he mumbled. Then, in a clipped voice he said, "Stevens! Bring me the works!"

The blonde angel's eyes marked me lousy as she dragged me to a wash basin in a corner of the laundry and drowned my arms. Which was an unpleasant surprise. I expected orchids.

"You hot-headed numbskull!" she cracked. "All this bloodshed could have been avoided had you waited long enough for me to tell you I could read shorthand!" She caught my disappointment and the N.G. backflipped out of her eyes leaving a gentle smile that said O.K. "I'm sorry, Cash."

"Skip it," I snapped. "What gave out from the short-hand?"

"The reason Doctor Garse stole all the money. It started when Miller was trying to prove the Boxing Commission to be a fraud. He traced the gate receipts from the last charity fight and discovered that the money this hospital received was accounted for in books which had been certified by a public accountant but was not accounted for in tangible improvements.

"He checked up on Doctor Garse who handled the funds and found that he secretly bet large sums of money on horses. Garse bet through a mysterious individual, a D. Jonas, who couldn't be traced. But Ben Miller did trace the C.P.A. who audited the books and discovered he was the brother of Armenian Joe."

"So," I cut in as they began doing things to my face, "Ben must have sent this information to Major Strong who, knowing he had to proceed cautiously, wired me to get proof enough to make a case. Then Ben probably faced Doc Garse with what he had uncovered, being a very impulsive sort of guy. And Garse, seeing his soft cush and position in life hanging in the balance, probably doctored a drink or something and put Ben on ice in the hospital here with that fake heart rap. And used Sam Hagarian's girl, Clair, to be Ben's nurse and keep him hopped up on dope."

DOC HENDRICK slapped some liquid fire on my arms and said: "When Miss Stevens told me what was in that notebook I searched Miss Ashodran's room and found a small bottle labelled Adrenalin Serum. But a lab test showed it to be a cocaine mixture strong enough to make even the most powerful mind succumb to criminal suggestion and hypnosis."

"I figured as much," I said. "Garse had to act fast. He went about covering up his trail in the same cool, deliberate manner he would mix a drink.

"He killed Strong, or had Strong killed, because that was a leak that could be plugged no other way. McGinnis just happened to blunder in at the wrong time. He killed Sam Hagarian who was the only valid witness to his misappropriation of charity funds. Claire got it when she was about to spill the works to me. He managed to have Ben and me around to draw suspicion away from himself.

"Then, when Ben had served his purpose, he planned his *coup de grace.* He arranged for Ben and Armenian Joe and me to be in an ambulance in the middle of Van Cortlandt Park at four-thirty this afternoon. Armenian Joe, because the gambler knew of his bets and had been taking a fifty-fifty cut in every graft through his brother, Sam. There was a bomb concealed in the ambulance to go off at four-thirty; a little knack he'd picked up as a surgeon with a battalion of sappers during the war. And, if it hadn't been for Sailor Duffy who is too unpredictable to fit into anybody's plans, Garse would be sitting pretty right now. Doc, what time is it?"

"Almost seven-thirty," said Hendrick.

Abie tugged at my trousers.

"Cash, what about us? He was gonna kill us, Cash. Dr. Garse made us walk down here all together from the office and he said he'd blow my head off if Miss Stevens or Mr. Hendrick did anything. Then he said he'd put us with the dead people the school kids cut up for practice. He said it was too bad we was all together when Mr. Hendrick told him we knew he was a killer and was gonna call the cops. I was scared stiff, Cash."

Miss Stevens gave a finishing tap to a new bandage on my wound and a similar tap on Abie's chest and said, "You were grand, Abie." Then, to me. "Now you can go out and get banged around some more."

"Maybe," I grinned. "There's one guy Garse trusted enough not to bump. We may have an argument. And, Abie, it's *Doctor* Hendrick and *Mister* Garse. You've got to learn how to distinguish between a front and the real thing."

Doc Hendrick's face grew even redder.

Just as I was buttoning up an ambulance driver's uniform, the voices I had been expecting sounded outside the door. O'Toole's was loudest.

"Wale! I know you're in there. I know you're holding Doc Garse. But it won't do you any good, you gun-crazy shrimp! I'll give you five minutes. If you're not out by then I'll blast a hole in the door and drop in a tear gas grenade, so help me! Wale! Do you hear me?"

My fingers on his arm stopped Doc Hendrick from answering. I motioned toward the laundry chute. "Lift me up that," I whispered, "then wait a minute before

letting him in. Talk first, or he'll shoot through the door."
Out loud I said, "I'd hear you in Canarsie, you redheaded
monkey. But it'll take about four minutes for your strange
words to make sense."

At the foot of the chute Miss Stevens grabbed my ear
and whispered angrily, "Stay here and let us explain. He
won't shoot with all of us standing around you."

"He wouldn't shoot at me standing alone," I whispered
back. "O'Toole is a very peculiar guy. Look, Steve, you're
pale as a ghost. What you need is a drink." Then I had my
hooks in blonde sunlight for a second time and my lips did
things. This time she did not swing.

I was crawling through the grating into the street as
O'Toole's voice started in again in the basement below. It
was then I realized I had left the big Smith and Wessen
automatic behind. But it was too late to return for it. A
prowl car was rounding the corner and I had to lose myself
in a group of pedestrians.

IT WAS exactly eight o'clock when I entered the uptown
station of the Interborough Subway at Times Square. The
usual after-work crowd had thinned out a bit but there
was still enough of a jam left to fill the station with an
even tempo of bustling commotion. In my buff trousers
and jacket I was inconspicuous enough to get where I
wanted—which was a few inches behind Dice.

He was standing next to an iron railing at the edge of
the platform, close to the opening as if he was waiting
for a train. I said: "Armenian Joe couldn't make it, Dice. I
came instead."

He turned slowly, as if it took an effort. I do not know
what he saw in my face but the corners of his mouth trem-

bled. I gripped the pipe in my pocket and pressed it into his side. There was something hard there.

"Aren't you glad to see an old friend, Dice? I saved your life once. You always said you was my friend."

"Cash," he whispered hoarsely, "my hands were tied, honest! I can help you with the cops, Cash. I got angles that'll put you out in the clear. I won't even take a cut. For free, I'll do it. Like you said, friends, Cash."

A Seventh Avenue Express roared into the station like a huge, mechanical snake. People crowded all around us. I kept my pipe pressed into Dice as three sprinters in a row caught the soft rubber edge of the door just before it met the narrower edge of the train and wriggled in. I waited for the train to move on before speaking.

I said, "What is your name, Dice?"

He looked puzzled. "Dice," he said.

"No. I mean your complete name."

"Dice Jonas."

I had known this for half a day now but I wanted to hear him verify it. It was all I could do to keep from blowing my top right there and then. I said:

"You ran bets from Garse to Armenian Joe."

"That was business, Cash."

"Slimy business. More, you knew Major Strong was going to call me in on a case but kept your mouth shut. You drove Ben in the ambulance when he killed Major Strong, then you slugged and ran over McGinnis who was a right guy. It had to be you. Garse was at police headquarters making a play about wanting the ambulance back and every one else was accounted for. Except you."

The whites of Dice's eyes showed.

"You can't prove that!" he said. He said it a little too loudly. I pressed the pipe harder and his voice dropped back to a low whine. "Garse forced me all the way, Cash. He made me do it, just like he made Ben. You don't know Garse."

"I *knew* Garse," I said.

I ALLOWED the implication to sink in as a Lenox Avenue local pulled in at the other side of the platform, disgorged, and swallowed its loads of people, then moved on. Dice whispered: "Cash, get that crazy look out of your eyes, please. What you gonna do? I'll spill what I know to the cops. I'll—"

"I never give a crook an even break, Dice. You know that."

"But you can't, Cash!" Terror was in full possession of him. "Not here!"

"I'm a marked guy already, Dice. I took you out of the way of death once. Now I'm simply putting you back."

"I'll pay you, Cash. Dough. I got plenty. Don't look at me like that!"

My pipe went around the hard object once again I said: "How much?"

Color flushed back into his cheeks. His hand trembled as he pulled the object from his pocket, a stuffed wallet. I could hear another express in the distance as the bills emptied into my free hand. A brief thumb riffle showed they were all hundreds! I dropped them into my pocket. The train was almost at the station now. A fresh gang of people were crowding around us. I whispered:

"Scram out of here, Dice Jonas."

His slight grey form moved eagerly. Somehow, his foot caught under mine. My elbow pressed into his chest as I turned to go the other way, forcing him back, back. His arms flayed wildly.

The crowd surged forward and my foot lifted as the Van Cortlandt Express roared by the platform. A woman screamed as if her lungs would burst.

Hundreds of voices took up the scream. I pushed back through a bedlam of surging arms, legs, flushed faces. Vaguely, I was aware the express had hissed to a stop short of its destination.

In a minute I was deep in the milling throng. The news speeded by me from mouth to mouth and changed complexion in a few brief seconds.

"A drunk man fell under the train."

"No, he jumped! He yelled, 'Down with the system' and jumped!"

"A girl was with him. It was a suicide pact!"

A beetle-browed man with a package under his arm looked over my shoulder and gave out like a punctured balloon. I stepped over him gingerly and into the waiting arms of Detective Lieutenant Larry O'Toole.

FOR WHAT amounted to a minute but seemed like a week we stood there looking into each other's eyes. Then he reached into my pocket and pulled out my pipe. He stood staring at it as if he had never seen one before. Then he waved it at the edge of the platform.

"That was Dice," he said.

A man I recognized as Finnigan came up and tapped O'Toole's shoulder.

"There's no identification on him, Chief. Gawd, he's a mess! It'll take an acetylene torch to get him out."

When Finnigan left I said, "So now I'll get booked on all those screwy charges. But I've got the whole business cleared, O'Toole."

O'Toole said, "Not those charges, Wale." I did not like the implication. He said, "That was taken care of at the hospital. Armenian Joe and your pal, Miller, spilled enough to give you an all around out—almost."

"That was fast work."

"We work fast," said O'Toole. "We even learned how Dice Jonas figured in, and a pickup order is being broadcast right now. We learned everything except how you found out it was Garse."

We were getting buried under an avalanche of elbows as more people kept streaming into the station. O'Toole signalled a man where he was going, then led me upstairs and into the little room marked "Men."

I said, "When Ben told me the injections were doped I remembered Garse had made a point of handling them personally. But how did you know Dice's name was Jonas?"

"He's got a record."

In spite of the spot I was on, I burned.

"Why the hell didn't you tell me?"

"Why the hell didn't you ask?"

Finnigan burst in with Dice's wallet. "Found this in the stiff's pocket. Picked clean!"

O'Toole took the wallet. A damp red streak ran down the middle.

"Stand by below until the emergency crew arrives," he ordered Finnigan.

We waited until Finnigan concluded some business and left.

O'Toole's jaw tightened as he turned to me. "I wonder how this happened?" he asked. "Dice always carried his roll."

I could see by his eyes that he did not really wonder.

I said, "Maybe he got an attack of conscience, O'Toole. The guy who got socked hardest from the whole mess was Ben Miller's kid, Abie. The poor little sucker got run out of school by a pack of headline-drunk squirts. I figured Dice felt he was responsible for everything, having been in a position to wise us up from the start, and figured maybe he could make it up to Abie. Leave him a cush to get through college maybe."

O'Toole looked at me for another generation. Then he said, "And you think he might have left it in some bank under the kid's name?"

I took a deep breath and said, "Maybe in the Road Savings Bank. I dunno. Dice liked that bank. Took sunbaths against the wall. It was like an office to Dice. Maybe you'll find the dough in the kid's name there. If you drop around tomorrow."

His face couldn't seem to make up its mind to relax or stiffen. It remained blank, framing wise eyes.

"Maybe," he said slowly. "It's too bad there's never a reliable witness when someone goes over during the rush hour. A hundred people see a hundred different things; like little old men with long green beards brushing rats off the platform, for instance. Drop around headquarters tomorrow for your gun. Do it after you check up if Dice really did leave his roll in the kid's name. And forget what I said about breaking you. I was excited." Then he turned and walked erectly out of that room marked "Men," without once looking back.

A peculiar guy, O'Toole; but right.

SAILOR AND Abie and someone else were in my office when I arrived.

"I've got it fixed for you to go to college when you grow up, Abie," I said. "You can be a real doctor if you want. Like Doc Hendrick."

"Nuts!" Abie exclaimed. "I ain't gonna be no sawbones. I'm gonna be a champ. Like Sailor Duffy!"

Sailor blurted, "Everything's hokey doke now, Cash. I got Ben to a hospital and the gut stitcher said he'll pull through fine. And the phone's been going like mad. Abie answered 'em. Little Abie, can you imagine? He knows how to gas over a phone."

"They was shysters and editors, Cash," said Abie. "The editors was afraid you'd give 'em liberal suits or something. They said they wrote bad mistakes about you. I said they was damn tootin'. They want to settle out of court. The shysters wanted to make suits for you. I said they should call up tomorrow. Then there was a tough looking guy Sailor knowed who brought that letter on your desk and said it was thanks from Armenian Joe for doing him a favor. I guess that's all, Cash."

"Not on your life," I said sternly. And then Sailor Duffy lifted Abie by the seat of his pants and lugged him home for an all night flop!

The envelope from Armenian Joe contained an interesting amount of greenbacks which I did not hesitate to pocket. After all, I rated something for all the shellacking I received.

Miss Stevens took her dainty number fours off the edge of my desk and sat upright. "I'm waitin' for that drink, Cash Wale," she said. And, as I filled two glasses from what was left out of the bottle, she asked, "Why do they call you Cash?"

"That's how I deal," I explained, handing her a glass. "I owe nobody. And expect others not to owe me. Now you, for instance. I have a distinct recollection of loaning you a pair of kisses in the last twenty-four hours."

We were both very tired but she had enough left on the ball to flood her face with sunlight.

"I always pay my debts, Cash."

And she did. With interest.

LOTTA HAD A HUSBAND

INTRODUCING CASH WALE—THE
TOWN'S TOUGHEST PRIVATE
OP—AND HIS SIDEKICK, SAILOR
DUFFY, WHO HAD NOISES IN HIS
BALD HEAD BUT KNEW THAT HE
HADN'T MURDERED THREE GIRLS
IN CENTRAL PARK, EVEN IF HE
WAS A GORILLA MAN AND SKIRT-
CRAZY TO BOOT.

CHAPTER ONE
DEAD ALIBI

HER FACE looked like something out of a meat chopper although the rest of her outlined under a white sheet looked all right. Plump, but all right. A tag dangling from one exposed ankle said: *Unidentified. Beaten to death in Central Park by unknown assailant. No. 5673.*

I forced myself to look back at the mashed face. The police artist who had reconstructed on paper what might have been her features had caught an elusive resemblance to someone I had once seen but couldn't remember, despite the two excellent reasons in my pocket that urged me to.

The attendant cleared his throat. "This your sister?"

"I'm afraid not."

He slid her back into the ice-box. A cute place, the morgue. But not on a full stomach and in the heat of an August morning. I said: "Someone didn't like her."

He was tall, stooped and bored and I could see he was straining a gut to talk. "What made you think she might be your sister?" he offered.

"The crack she made before cashing in," I said.

"You mean about somebody's husband doing it?"

"She didn't say that. I read in the paper how, when they found her, she was mumbling, 'Husband—the tramp was high—husband—' And then she died. She was knocked to pieces and hysterical and, under the circumstances, the words could mean anything."

"Like something about your sister, for instance?"

I shrugged and his interest shifted into high.

"You wanna see the other, Mr.—er—Mr.—"

There were two more. Found on successive nights after a cop saw the first dumped out of a car. All three had been found near the Columbus Circle gate to Central Park. Beaten to death—by hand, according to the M.E. Not a stitch of identification on any of them, not even labels. And laundry marks had been cut from their clothes.

The attendant pulled out the two others on sliding shelves and I shook my head. I didn't know them.

Welts on their throats showed purple against the yellowish pallor of embalmed flesh and didn't help my lunch. Neither did the hysterical dame at the

"You're a punk," I said and jammed the muzzle at Kid Apollo. "Back away and forget it."

far end of the room who was getting violently sick over a
male stiff who had been dragged from the East River.

At the door the attendant said: "If you leave me your name and address and a description of your sister, I could let you know if she turns up, Mr.—er—Mr.—"

"Mr. X," I told him and walked out.

I had no sister.

THE DEEVER GYM, on Eighth Avenue near Forty-second, was another kind of morgue, where the "unidentified" could still move and talk and breathe—and not much else. It was known in the fistic world as Punch-drunk Haven. Vince Deever made a pretty penny supplying human punching bags to dive for Names on the way Up.

His office was grimy with thick rolls of dust piled in the corners, tattered pictures on the walls, a dog-eared desk and a pinhole that made believe it was a window.

The same adjectives go for Vince Deever—grimy, tattered shirt, a dog-eared expression and pin-holes for eyes.

"Hey, Wale!" he called, beckoning with an inch of cigar when I looked in the door. "I wanna see you."

"Make it fast," I said, stepping inside.

"Only a minute, Cash, only a minute," he whined. "It ain't *my* idea, y'understand. What's been talked around. So, to pertect myself, I gotta ast ya, see?"

"Ask me what?" I said.

He flinched at my tone. Vince Deever would flinch before a mosquito that looked him in the eye.

"Now don't get sore, Cash," he pleaded. "Some of the boys seen you hanging around the cops a lot lately. You know how talk spreads an' how the boys get jittery. *I* don't believe none of it, Cash. Why, I tell the boys, 'Cash Wale, he's not the kind—'"

"What's on your mind, Deever?" I cut in.

"Well you *have* been seen," he said.

"I've a job to turn up a missing dame. That calls for canvassing jails, morgues and hospitals among other places," I said.

"Sure, sure! You fix that with the boys. Me, I'm told I'll lose business with you an' the Sailor around. So I gotta ast you to take Sailor Duffy outta here. See my predictament?"

His eyes were fastened so unwaveringly on the bulge under my left lapel that they watered. I could have pressed the point and found out who was passing the word that I had turned pigeon. Deever would take little pressing.

But other things were on my mind and I let it ride. Questions lay in my mind like icicles. My slap-happy pal, Sailor Duffy, could answer some of them. I turned to enter the gym proper.

And almost knocked over Hymie the Ham, who appeared in the doorway.

Hymie the Ham was something out of a barber shop. Perfume hung about him like a cloud and you couldn't tell whether it came from his sleek black hair or the handkerchief exposed under one immaculate lapel. He managed Name fighters by way of an obscure past that made cops look twice when he passed and ordinary citizens hold their wallets when he was around. The "Ham" part of his name referred to his penchant for mugging.

Right now his eyes settled on the bulge in my jacket and he said: "H'lo, Wale. Wanted to see you."

"Everybody wants to see me. What's from you?" He exhaled on a set of manicured fingers and tried a win-friends-and-influence-people smile.

"How about matching the Sailor with Kid Apollo in Philly? Five hundred for ten rounds."

"The Sailor is retired with his head noises and me." I said and started past.

His fingers gripped my arm. "Wait a minute, Cash. Ain't it about time you collected on that slug-happy bum inside?"

That's when his fingers left my arm and he stepped back with a grunt. I didn't touch him. My hat floats five feet and two inches off the floor and I'm built accordingly while Hymie the Ham, was all of five, eleven. I just undid the button of my jacket and looked at him.

My reputation did the rest.

I walked unmolested into the gym proper and then I understood why Hymie the Ham had buttonholed me.

THERE WERE maybe a dozen of Deever's has-beens gathered around a ring in the center of the floor yelling their fool heads off. They were shapeless caricatures and their heads were full of strange noises, but they howled in glee while Kid Apollo, the latest "find" of Hymie the Ham, pounded a carbon copy of themselves in the ring.

All I knew about the Kid was from the papers. He was young, plenty of snap to his punch, strong legs, a string of one-round kayos lay behind him and a shot at the light-heavy title lay ahead.

He had box-office appeal, the profile of a chorus boy with curly blond hair to set it off. The skirts went for him and he returned the compliment in spades. He looked good in the ring.

The man he was pounding kept bearing in with a stiff-legged shuffle and tried to bring massive shoulders behind occasional hooks. His ribs were pink from Apollo's fists. He wore no headguard and his scalp gleamed nude under the lights.

He caught sight of me, waved, "Hiya, Cash!" Kid Apollo unleashed a wicked left hook and Sailor Duffy went down to his hands and knees, a dumb, hurt look creeping over his face.

I said: "That's enough. Come down, Sailor."

Apollo leaned on the ropes and grinned down at me. "S'matter, shrimp, can't see a guy take it?"

"I left orders around to lay off the Sailor," I said.

"*You* left orders!"

"Kid!" came Hymie the Ham's voice from behind me. "Kid, I want you to meet Mr. Wale. Mr. *Cash* Wale."

Sailor Duffy was crawling through the ropes. I said: "Get dressed."

He nodded, jigged around a little. "Hokay, Cash. But first I shower, *hagh?*"

"Skip the shower," I said.

"Hokay." He trotted out to the locker-room.

Kid Apollo was looking question marks over my shoulder at his manager. I whirled and grabbed a handful of Hymie the Ham's jacket.

"You know Sailor just comes here for a workout," I said.

Hymie nodded vigorously. "Sure, sure, Cash. But the Sailor *asked* for a chance. The Kid was just stringing him along. He didn't mean—"

That was when the muzzle of my Colt put a bright red streak on the cheek of Hymie the Ham, and I turned fast, jabbed the wet muzzle into Kid Apollo who had just scrambled through the ropes.

"You're a punk," I said. "Back away and forget about it."

He backed, his Adam's apple commuting between his chin and collar bone.

A throaty female voice giggled: "My, my, but isn't the little man tough!"

She sat on a bench against the wall, toying with a small dumb-bell. She had blazing red hair, and a hat with a green feather and a check suit and dark Hollywood sunglasses.

I pegged her for one of Apollo's bimboes and turned back to the others. They all stood motionless. It was strange how none of them moved—the dozen stumble-bums, Kid Apollo, Hymie and Vince Deever who had appeared in the doorway.

The Colt was back in its holster and, all together, they could have ruined me. But the only movement was Hymie the Ham's handkerchief swabbing the blood from his cheek.

My reputation again.

We stood like that, inhaling the smell of sweat and liniment, until Sailor trotted back in, togged in dungarees and a blue work-shirt. Vince Deever hopped out of our way as we left. That redhead's voice sailed after us.

"My, my, but are all you big strong mans afraid of that little bad man!" And wound up in a hysterical giggle.

IT'S FUNNY how the Sailor and me hung together. Was a time he had the boxing world agog as he slugged his way into a chance for the heavyweight crown. Only you can't slug without getting slugged and, after dropping a ten-round decision to the champ that still has fans panting, the noises came to his head.

He slipped fast.

We met in a breadline argument where he backed my play. You've got it, brother. Repeal had shot my racket to hell and I was on the bottom, too. After that, when I tried going legitimate, he hung around. It was like that through half a dozen odd jobs until I hit a stake and opened the Cash Wale Investigation Agency.

Citizens tagged us as a couple of tramps. To avoid. We made out regardless.

But now my slap-happy pal was in line for the Ossining squat and that was the headache that had sent me from the morgue into Deever's gym after him.

Walking along Eighth, he kept shadow-boxing at my side and mumbling: "See how I had that punk backin', Cash? See my left catch him every time?" Jab. Hook. Counter. "I'm taperin' out, Cash. How's for me to come back, Cash?"

I said: "How's the noises?"

He stopped shadow-boxing and turned a shade whiter. Sailor had bad dreams about bug-houses. I steered him into a cafeteria. It was only ten in the morning. The place was half empty. We brought iced coffee and slices of pie to a corner table and I sat watching him eat for a while.

Then I shoved the clipping from my pocket across the table.

He had to frame the words with his lips. I knew them by heart. A headline—

CLUE TO "GORILLA MAN" SLAYER!

And my headache—

Police disclosed today the existence of a witness who described a man leaving the scene of the latest "fiend" slaying in Central Park late last night.

Inspector J. Quinn told reporters today that he is convinced the three women who were victims of fatal attacks on successive nights were all slain by the same hand.

"He is a tall, powerfully built man with the battered features of a prize-fighter," stated the inspector. "He was seen leaving the crime scene in the early hours of the morning. Other identifications were his rough 'working-man' clothes and his habit of mumbling and shadow-boxing as he walked...."

What got me more than anything else was the start of the final paragraph—

The police are maintaining the strictest secrecy concerning the identity of the witness and expect to make an important arrest hourly....

Sailor finished reading this, started to lift his glass, then set it down again as his stubby features twisted into an expression of sick dismay.

"Go on, drink!" I whispered. "Act natural. Was that you in the park?"

"*Nagh*, Cash! Not me! I don't do things like that, Cash!"

"When I returned from Harlem this morning you'd just gotten in. Tanked. Your eyes are bleary from no sleep now."

"Sure, Cash. I was over to Pappas' Grill. Some guys bought me drinks for showin' 'em how I put the champ down twice."

"What guys?"

"In Tony Pappas' back room. I never seen 'em before. Fans."

We sat staring at each other and I found myself believing him. Don't ask me why. He had a normal appetite for skirts and they avoided him like old age. And there were times when he was batty as a bed-bug. But he had never lied to me.

At least, until then, never.

"Let's check," I said.

TONY PAPPAS' Grill was on Fortieth between Eighth and Ninth. Greek Broadway. There are garages and office buildings around but mainly Greek clubs and cafés. At any time of the day or night you can find small groups of swarthy, thick-set men holding down the corners and keeping their eyes open.

That's their business.

Pappas' Grill wasn't much to look at. A bar, screened alcoves along the walls, some tables in the middle where you could usually find a score or more of Greeks sipping coffee and puffing smelly fags.

In back were small rooms where you could buy a wager on a horse, a packet of "snow," the address of a blonde or a couple of thugs to break your mother-in-law's leg.

Tony Pappas was a shock of dirty white hair over a weather-beaten face. We'd had dealing during prohibition and his hand dropped out of sight behind the bar when Sailor and I walked in. No one else was around.

I kept my hands in sight, said: "Pappas, the Sailor tells me he lost a ring in here last night. You find?"

Pappas had a trick of not blinking. "Sailor, he no wasa here las' night, Wale."

Sailor Duffy leaned over the bar. "Tony, don't you remember? Me! Them guys blowed me to beers. Didn't you tell 'em how you saw me put down the champ two times with a straight left? *Hagh*, Tony?"

Pappas shook his head very slow—too slow. "I'da know if Sailor, him here, Wale."

"How about your bartender?"

Pappas called: "Nick, you come-a here!"

Nick wore his black hair cropped to a stubble and his left eye was completely white—no pupil. A little barrel-chested guy, he came in from the back, looked down at Tony Pappas' hand behind the bar, then up at me. "I ain't seen the Sailor here last night, Mr. Wale," he said.

I laid a hand on Duffy as he began to tremble.

Pappas was talking again. "Looka, Wales. Thees ain't not *my* weeshes, bot the boys, dey ask me tella you you talks too plenty wit' the cops to come-a here no more. So I'm tella you."

I had to stop Sailor from launching a *blitzkrieg* with a bottle he'd grabbed by the neck. I dragged him to the door. There I turned on Tony Pappas, who still concealed his hand behind the bar.

"For that crack, Pappas," I said, "I am going to return some day soon and deal with you personal."

Walking back to Eighth, Sailor urged: "Why'ncha let me take 'em, Cash. I coulda massacreed them two—"

"Go home," I said, "and change out of those work clothes. Then register at the Sloan House Y as Mr. Kenneth Hammond of Chicago. Buy yourself an armload of magazines and stick to your room until I call."

Sailor blinked at me. "You believe what I told you, Cash? About me bein' there last night?"

"Whether I believe you or not, it's a dead alibi now. Kenneth Hammond—and stick to that room."

"Hokay, Cash, hokay. Kenneth Hammond."

I flagged a passing hack as he started for the subway. I gave the hackie a Wall Street address. I didn't enjoy that ride.

CHAPTER TWO
PENNY ANTE

F.K. WINTHROP was (and is) a very important citizen. To crash his Wall Street office you have to be O.K.'d by three secretaries and a bodyguard. When I entered the plush-and-chrome ante-room, there were two bankers, a Western congressman and half a dozen other Bigs ahead of me.

They were behind me when secretary number one gave me the eye to go in. The bodyguard, an ex-wrestler named Hogan, didn't play for my heater this time. His knuckles still wore a scar from the first time he tried.

In my racket you jump the other guy or get jumped. Hogan nodded and I passed through a ticking door.

It was a small office taken up mainly by a thousand bucks' worth of desk. The man sitting behind it looked like Elmer of the World's Fair posters—wisps of gray hair, round soft face, pudgy build.

The tale of his rise from a barn to this Wall Street throne-room could be told by an army of sharpies who took him at his face value and got took, in turn, by F.K. Winthrop.

He tipped the key of a box on his desk, said: "I am not to be interrupted, Lucille." He tipped the key back, said: "Have you made any progress, Wale?"

"A little," I said, sinking into five-hundred dollars' worth of chair and snagging a two-buck cigar from the desk humidor.

"That is not satisfactory, Wale," said F.K.

I said: "Look, pal. I told you I'd find her if she was in the city. I've got some leads. Not many. But leads. If you think

I'm faking, turn it over to a regular agency. I didn't ask for the job. *You* called me in."

He didn't like that, F.K. No, he didn't like to be told off by a guy he could buy and sell a couple of thousand times. The color drained from his cheeks.

"They warned me about you, Wale!" he whispered. "You know damn well why I can't trust an agency. The commissioner, himself, told me you would eat your mother's heart for a dollar. You—"

I carefully set my lighted match down on the mahogany veneer where it blackened a circle the size of a dime and gave up the smell of polish.

"Don't ever crack like that again," I said very slow. "We settled the financial end last week. I'm called Cash for a damn good reason, but don't ever crack like that again unless you want to see how far I'll go for free."

He swiveled in his chair and stared out the window at New York harbor basking in the glare of an eleven-o'clock sun. For a few moments it was just the sound of his breathing and occasional boat whistles from the bay. When he turned back, the lines were smoothed out of his face and the color was back in his cheeks.

He had it, Winthrop. Control.

"I spoke hastily, Wale," he said stiffly. "What did you want to see me about?"

"You read about those three dames they found murdered in Central Park?"

Only his whitening knuckles gave away the fear my words must have struck in his heart.

"There is an unnamed witness," I continued. "I want you to find out who that witness is and give me the name and address. I'll be home waiting for the dope."

He licked his lips. I could see he was afraid to ask me a direct question. "Wale," he said, "you'll do everything in your power to find my daughter?"

"Everything," I told him. I put another match to the tip of the cigar.

"I will get that name for you," he said. "Only, for God's sake, please bring my girl home!"

"If she's around," I said, getting up.

The assorted Bigs still held down chairs in the anteroom as I walked through.

GOING DOWN in the elevator, I didn't feel so good. I had a billionaire eating out of my palm and two bucks worth of smoke drifting through my lungs. But I felt bad.

In my pocket was the snapshot of a blond slinky female with eyes a couple of sizes too large for the rest of her face. Maida Winthrop, the one and only offspring of F.K.

Her picture should have appeared hundreds of times in the scandal sheets, but didn't. Winthrop *gelt* killed news stories, quashed pictures. The pride of F.K. and his fear of kidnapers was responsible.

From his own lips I had gathered Maida Winthrop was an oversexed, thrill-seeking bimbo who sampled everything from dope to dopes. Two marriages had been secretly annulled—one to a barber, the other to a Filipino bus boy.

It was like that.

Now this cute kid turned up missing.

F.K. offered me five hundred to find her. I raised it to double or nothing and he agreed. I figured it a snap. Before Repeal I made out by peddling my heater to the highest bidders—most of them on ice now—and what I do not know about Gotham's shadier side, simply isn't.

I figured it a cinch and, for a week now, I'd been casing hop-joints, bordellos, bistros, hospitals, jails and every nook and cranny a thrill-seeking blonde with a roll might be clipped. I had only that one snapshot to go by—but slinky blondes with eyes that size come rare.

I had traced her to a "slave" party in Harlem the night she disappeared. The trouble was, "slave" parties in Harlem are as exclusive as the subway at five P.M. and I couldn't get a line on who else attended that particular shindig—or even exactly where it was held.

And there hadn't been a whisper concerning Maida Winthrop since.

So, going down in the elevator, I felt bad all around. Fooling with a guy like F.K. was deadlier than gun play. My asking him to check that "unnamed" witness had nothing to do with his missing Maida.

It had to do with the frame settling over Sailor Duffy.

I believed the Sailor had been to Pappas' Grill and that his description in the papers was a plant and if they ever caught up with him, he was that slap-nutty, he'd talk himself right into that Sing-Sing jolt.

I felt so bad when I reached the sidewalk, I tossed that two-buck cigar into the gutter.

SAILOR AND I live in a furnished apartment between West End and Riverside Drive, the kind of block that changes complexion weekly and minds its own business. We could move around the corner and never be traced in a hundred years.

I didn't relish the prospect of sitting around alone, waiting for Winthrop to phone, but there was nothing else to do.

Then I keyed open my door and found out I wasn't going to be alone.

Inspector Jack Quinn, of Homicide, said: "Come in, Cash, come in."

Bushy gray eyebrows were the first things you saw on Quinn. After that you noticed his sleepy eyes and the sharp lines slanting down to his jaw. We didn't take to each other. But he was a square cop.

I said: "Warrant?"

He said: "O.K., Sam. It's Wale."

A beefy-faced plainclothesman with a scar on the back of his neck stepped from behind the door at my elbow and holstered his gun. He tried to close the door. My shoe was in the way.

"How about a warrant?" I said.

Quinn showed it to me and I let Sam close the door. It was made out for Albert Duffy. That's Sailor. He was wanted for suspicion of murder. We went inside together, settled around in chairs, me next to the phone. I didn't like the play at all.

"What's with the Sailor?" I asked.

"Where was he last night?" Sam countered in a high voice.

"I wasn't home."

Sam regarded me owlishly. "He was here just a few minutes before we arrived. Changed clothes and skipped. Don't you think that peculiar?"

I spread out my palms and lifted my shoulders, French style.

Quinn waved a finger at me. "How's your sister, Wale?"

"I have no sister."

"I know that," he said.

"That business at the morgue," I explained carefully, "had to do with a legitimate case I'm on—if you Hawkshaws want to know."

"We want to know," nodded Quinn emphatically. "What case?"

"*My* name isn't on that warrant." I said.

"That can be arranged," said Quinn.

"Try it," I grinned.

He shrugged. "O.K., Wale, you win. There was a warrant. The D.A. quashed it. There's pressure behind you."

"That's how it is," I said and picked up the receiver as the phone began to trill.

Both Inspector Quinn and Sam started for the phone, then stopped. Neither of them expected my play. I did. That's how I was able to cover them clean with my Colt before either of them could draw.

"Sit down and play ball," I said, motioning with the heater. They sat. "Not you!" I said into the phone. "Give it to me again. Slow."

F.K. Winthrop's voice calmed a bit. "That witness is a woman, Wale. Miss Penny Gay. She lives in room 812 in the Fenner Hotel on Fifty-eighth Street. She was in the park last night near where that girl was found—"

"Skip that!" I cut in. "Don't call me back. I'll get in touch with you."

I hung up and dialed the first number that came to my head. A man's voice answered and I hung up again. That was to befuddle a tracer. Only the last call can be checked on a dial phone. And, even then it takes doing.

Quinn and his beefy aide, Sam, sat like a couple of wooden Indians. They weren't even *thinking* of making a break.

My reputation once more.

I left them cuffed to the shower in the bathroom and dropped their rods in a garbage pail on the way out.

THE FENNER HOTEL had two admirals under a sidewalk canopy and about a dozen generals shoving their brass buttons around the air-conditioned lobby. The sprinkle of dames holding down plush furniture wore real ice and those bored expressions that pass for hot stuff in café society.

That was all right. My pants were creased.

I entered an elevator and stared the glamor boy down. "Six," I said.

His eyes dropped a notch and we rose in silence. At the sixth I walked out as if I knew where I was going until I heard the door of his cage slam shut. Then I mounted stairs to the eighth floor.

812 was in a corner, which was a break. A dame's voice sang out, "Ye-es?" when I knocked.

"It's me, Penny," I said.

You generally open a door to someone who calls you by your first name.

She did.

I pushed her inside and shut the door behind me. She was larger than me. But right. A tight-fitting purple dress and black net hose left no doubt about that. I'm a sucker for black silk on a shapely calf. And for soft brown eyes, ivory skin and waves of honey-colored hair.

"I don't know you," she said in a musical voice.

"You will, babe," I grinned at her, "you most certainly will!"

She wasn't even rattled. I watched those soft brown orbs inventory my clothes. The price tags must have been right.

Her shoulders lifted a trifle. A smile came from behind her eyes and she said, "O.K., hots, you're in," and turned her back to me and calmly led the way into her suite.

No mistake about it, brother. Men were this fluff's business. But strictly.

I waded through ankle-deep rug and settled in a hip-deep chair while she lifted a bottle of scotch from where it held open its pages of a confession mag and set up another ruby glass next to the one already out.

"Straight?" she said, making a complete turn so I would miss nothing.

"Straight." I said, missing nothing.

She handed me a glass and dropped her lashes. "O.K., hots, who steered you?"

It was good scotch. I unbuttoned my jacket and watched her eyes glisten. "The guy who sent me," I said, "is a tall, powerfully built pug with a habit of shadow-boxing and mumbling as he walks."

I could see Penny Gay was not too bright. In her groove she knew the answers. This threw her off stride.

"Why, I thought you—"

"Some other time, babe, some other time," I said and watched understanding pull a mask over her face.

"*That!*" she whispered huskily.

"Yeah. That. And before you blow a tube, hear me out, babe. The guy I mentioned is a special pal of mine and I'm helping him off that frame you're helping him on. The name, babe, is Wale. Cash Wale."

It didn't register. That was O.K. Until Winthrop's call, I'd never heard of Penny Gay.

"I will even," I went on, "go so far as to buy my pal off that frame."

That registered! We were back in the groove. Her brows puckered.

"How'd you find me, hots?"

"Cash can do a lot," I said. I was telling *her* something! She actually licked her lips. She was on the make, this frail, no kidding.

But then worry drew the mask back to her face and her head shook slowly. "You're too late," she whispered. "I can't back down now. They'd—" Her lips clamped.

"Me, too," I said, letting my jacket slide all the way open. It was tough on her. She was in the middle.

It was tougher on the Sailor.

"Will cash buy a name?" I asked.

The violent shake of her head sent the tawny waves flying. I liked that.

"An address maybe?"

Another shake.

"Look, babe," I cautioned, "this can't go on. A dead witness is no witness and that ends the frame. Only I don't want it to end with you. You're in the middle and I'm getting fonder of you by the minute. It's the lugs on the other side, I want them."

The open jacket got her. Lines came to her eyes. "*You* look," she said in a low voice. "This goes back to something big and, like you say, *I'm* in the middle. You remember that first girl who was found—Lotta?"

"Sure. Lotta. So what?"

"Lotta had a husband, hots, and the husband played the field. There was a red-headed tramp on a jag and some words and Lotta and this redhead scrapped. The redhead passed out before it was over."

"We playing Guess Who?" I said.

"Stay in your pants, hots. Lois and Barbara and Penny were on the sidelines—and some sharpies—it was that kind of party Lotta stepped into. Those other two girls found dead in the park—after Lotta—you remember them?"

I nodded.

"Lois and Barbara. *They were in the middle also!*"

"So the red-headed tramp was on a jag," I said, "and passed out. Lotta, who was somebody's wife, was still alive. But Lotta is now morgue meat and Penny is buying out of a squeeze by framing my pal who shadow-boxes and mumbles when he walks. It's coming clear. But not enough, babe."

Her soft eyes slid from the butt of my revolver to my pants crease and grew wise.

"You'll buy an address that ties in, hots? The address of the party? And leave me out?"

"I'll buy," I said.

Penny Gay stood up and smoothed the purple satin around her hips. "That calls for another drink," she said. She headed for the bottle, still bearing herself so that I wouldn't miss a thing.

I didn't. Not even when she brought the scotch in only one ruby glass and fed it to me from my lap with one soft arm around my neck.

CHAPTER THREE
GREEK TO GREEK

I LEFT room 812 of the Fenner Hotel maybe an hour later. I didn't have the name of Lotta's husband. I didn't have the hundred and fifty smackers that had constituted my roll until then. I did have an address on Fortieth Street and maybe a quart of scotch inside me and some newly acquired memories. But positively!

Perhaps it was more than a quart searing my gullet. In the swank lobby, I don't recall objecting when a general in brass buttons steered my arm.

There was a door. But no admirals under a sidewalk canopy outside. There was an alley instead, deep between brick walls that towered so high that the alley was lost in dank shadow. I remember yelling, "Hey!" and reaching for Brass Buttons.

He wasn't there.

A pair of punch-battered heads jutting from massive sweatshirts were there. A fist exploded on my left ear and a thick voice mumbled: "Haryah, Cash, old kid, old kid, old kid!"

A second fist paralyzed the right side of me from my neck, where it struck, down.

In that first moment I was falling, I remember clawing inside my jacket for the Colt and my fist coming up with air instead of blue steel.

The cement floor flew up and stunned me.

"How's it feel to be a hard guy, Wale?" mumbled that thick voice. Then I was rolling away from a heel slamming down—

And turned flush into a leather toe coming up!

There was more. The world turned blood red in my eyes. Sobs I couldn't help burst from my lips. Steel claws seemed to be lifting me up at intervals and mallets seemed to be knocking me down again.

And that thick voice. "It's fer pokin' around where ya ain't wanted, hard-guy Wale!"

Then a red-knuckled fist was growing in my vision and I remember that one didn't hurt—just a buzz between my ears.

I remember a strange voice screaming: *"Hard-guy, Wale! Hard-guy Wale, with a dozen bullet-riddled stiffs waiting in hell for a crack back at you! And you had to lose your heater to a quart of scotch and an armful of purple satin curves with a night-court pedigree! How's the reputation, hard-guy Wale!"*

And then I realized it was nobody's voice screaming. Just hot thought burning through my brain. I opened my eyes and looked at a world that wasn't blood red any more. I was staring up between blank high walls at a gossamer fringe of white cloud drifting under a slice of bright blue sky.

It was over. I was alone.

For a while I lay there, then I crawled to my knees and sobbed out that quart or more of scotch.

I have mentioned my reputation. Without it, I would starve. It brings me cases that are too hot for the regular agencies to handle. I have not committed one tenth the shenanigans that fall to my blame—but that's O.K. A reputation is one tenth fact, the rest, rumor.

It works in reverse twice as fast. Let the story of my brush-off get around generally and I would be marked down from a killer to a clown—my racket would be shot to hell.

This was searing through my head when I rose to my feet and something white scuffed away from my shoe. I picked it up and a sound burst from my throat like the sound a condemned man must utter when they unstrap him from the chair and hand him a pardon.

It was a grimy little card—DEEVER'S GYMNASIUM—WHERE THE *CHAMPS* TRAIN!

It must have dropped from the pocket of one of my attackers. It was going to salvage my reputation, that card. Make no mistake, brother, my reputation was my living and the story of my brush-off was slated for oblivion—if it meant slating Vince Deever and two of his stumble-bums for oblivion along with it.

Only I had things to do first. By this time Inspector Quinn and his beefy sidekick, Sam, had probably worked loose from my bathroom and had been paging me via police radio and other means.

The other end of the alley was a corrugated iron door which opened on a parking lot. I straightened up a little in a Turkish Bath, some more in a tailor's, then killed the taste of scotch with an automat lunch consisting mainly of tomato juice and chartered a hack for Wall Street, considerably refreshed.

It was two thirty and hot as blazes.

THE PLUSH-AND-CHROME ante-room was still inhabited by Bigs, some of whom I recognized from my earlier visit. My name still drew the first nod from secretary number one. Hogan, the bodyguard, touched a button, the door ticked me in and then I knew it was not like the morning.

F.K. Winthrop still looked like Elmer. But a sad Elmer. I mean S-A-D as in purple bags under red-lidded eyes and sweaty palms and papers from that thousand-buck desk strewn all over the floor—some with shoeprints where there had been a lot of pacing.

He waved me to a chair and turned to stare out at New York harbor—simmering now under the post-noonday heat.

When the pause began to sag, I said: "O.K. What gives?"

He swiveled without meeting my eyes or even cracking about the strips of plaster on my face.

He shoved a check across the desk at me.

He said: "Get out. Drop everything. Don't ask questions."

The check was for one grand and made out to me. I shoved it back.

"Call in the G-boys," I said. "It's up their alley. But you might as well give me the details."

I watched the check move back towards me and the tight clamp to his lips. "Look, pal," I said as gently as I knew how, "this is your office. There can't be dictaphones planted or anything like that. Maybe they saw me come in. They'll see me leave no matter what happens. But will they know you talked? See what I mean?"

He saw.

"They promised not to harm Maida if I played along, Wale," he intoned, his words coming heavy. "If not—" Another pause began to sag in the middle, then he wet his lips and continued: "It started shortly after I phoned you this morning. My number is unlisted. But a stranger called, asked me if I would like to hear from my daughter. I should admit a Mr. Ransom—get that, Wale, *Ransom*—to my office if I did."

"You did," I urged.

"Well, he was an ugly little closemouthed—"

"Animal," I said.

"All he said was that I should sit by my phone and assent to whatever was asked me over it. He spoke with an accent, this—animal!" The last word spat out of Winthrop's mouth.

"And you were phoned?"

"By the vice-president of my bank—my own bank, Wale! A stranger had presented a draft for ten thousand dollars signed by Maida and made out to, 'Cash.' Should the bank honor it, he asked. I said the bank should and that man just sat there and leered at me.

"Then he warned me to call you off the case, keep away from the authorities and wait. *Wait!*" thundered F.K. banging his fist on the desk.

"They come in all shapes and colors, these animals," I said.

Winthrop glared at me and dabs of red touched his cheeks. "Wale!" he suddenly barked. "Of course! With your contacts—a small man with a shaven head. One eye—his left—had no pupil! Completely white! He—"

"Get your bouncer in here," I snapped. "Chesty, the mug with the heater outside your door."

Winthrop flicked that key, barked: "Lucille, send Mr. Hogan in here at once."

Color was pouring back into Winthrop's face now. That was nothing to how ideas were pouring into mine.

Hogan stood in the doorway. "Want me, boss?"

"Over here," I said. He came over, then leaped away—but it was too late. His rod was out of its holster and in my fist. "I'm borrowing this," I said.

Winthrop nodded and Hogan backed out, his face a masterpiece of confusion.

It was a .38-caliber Police Special. A little heavy in my hand, a tight squeeze in my holster, but good enough.

I gave that thousand-buck check its last ride across the desk. "Pay off on results," I said. "Meantime, call off the dogs. I had to rough up a police inspector. Don't get virtuous on me!" I rapped as his board-of-directors voice began to sound. "Just call 'em off!"

"Wale!" he roared as I reached the door. "You've told me nothing! What happened to your face?"

"I tried shaving with an ice-pick," I said.

And left.

IT TOOK two nickels' worth of wait before the Sloan House clerk got "Mr. Kenneth Hammond" to the phone and, when that familiar voice grumbled; "Whosit?" I said: "Fan your tail to Bryant Park."

"I'm readin' a wunnerful story, Cash," came the Sailor's reply. "All about a shamus who scrambled a dozen crooks with gats and him with nothin' but his bare hands. And then—"

"Bryant Park, dope! Now!" I snapped and hung up.

He was there ahead of me, his eyes popping at the open page of a detective magazine. I sat next to him on the bench—at least he'd picked one under a tree—and waited for him to find out that the guy who was killed in the third paragraph wasn't really dead at all.

It was pleasant watching the fountains twinkle over the greenery. It gave me a chance to simmer down the half-dozen facts stewing in my mind.

The Maida Winthrop disappearance was coming to a head.

Nick, Tony Pappas' one-eyed bartender, was involved, and that was fact number one. Fact number two was that the two lame-brains who had attacked me hailed from Deever's Gym and I thought of Deever who was a mouse in dirty pants. The address Penny Gay sold me was another item. Hymie the Ham's offer to match Kid Apollo with the

Sailor was still another. Then there was Penny Gay's yarn about Lotta and a red-headed tramp and Lotta's husband.

I turned these items around in my head, fitting them one way and another and I began to get the glimmering of an idea.

Sailor had to pick that moment to bellow in my ear: "Wow! The dead lady's son turned out to be a midget. He was her husband an' the killer all the time!"

Walking along Fortieth, my hands were full keeping Sailor from shadow-boxing and mumbling the yarn back at me word for word, checking house numbers at the same time.

That was how we reached it without me realizing the set-up until the number Penny Gay had sold me was staring me in the face and old Tony Pappas was staring me in the face and one was right over the other—the number was *Pappas' Grill!*

He was on the sidewalk before the swinging doors, sunning himself. It was no time to back-peddle or try caution. Jump the other guy still held.

"I want words with you, Pappas," I said, pushing Sailor through the sidewalk crowd.

"I tella you how she is before, Wale," said Pappas without blinking or moving.

"It's about Nick, your bartender."

"You goes away now, Wale?"

"It's about Penny Gay."

"Scrams, Wale, huh? Mak' no trobbles, huh?"

"It's about Barbara and Lois and Lotta, three nice gals who knew too much."

It's funny about Greeks. Off and on I'd known Tony Pappas for over twelve years and had never seen his eyes express anything but stony nothing. Now I was throwing names at him out of a tangle and the ice suddenly melted from his eyes leaving deep, fiery pits.

"Eenside!" he hissed.

I glanced up and down the street. There was movement, heat and glare. Shipping clerks trundled hand-trucks through the crowds. The garment center tempo was in high. I nodded at Sailor, followed Pappas through the swinging doors.

A drone of talk faded to stares as I stood trying to adjust my eyes to the darkness. There was the usual rank odor of alcohol and stale smoke and something else—a sudden tension that swept through that room like a wave. Sailor felt it and moved close to me.

THE CENTER tables were now filled with the thickset men. They sipped coffee, dragged on foul cigarettes and regarded us silently.

I watched Pappas move towards the bar, called: "Not behind it, pal! Not this time!"

He turned to me slowly. "W'at ees it about Lotta, Wale?" he said.

"Nick comes first," I said.

"Nick!" shouted Pappas. "You come-a here!"

The stubby bartender emerged from the back, moving behind the bar. His white eye settled on me as if he could see through it.

"Nick," I said, "there is a certain blond female with very large eyes who had been missing for a week."

"I don't know what you're talking about, Mr. Wale," said Nick, one hand dropping behind the bar.

"Look in my hand, Nick!" I warned. The Police Special I held was centered on the middle of Tony Pappas' white apron.

"Look in my hand, Mr. Wale," said Nick bringing up his hand from behind the bar. It was a very large weapon, he held. Looked like a .45-caliber Frontier Model. It could make a hole large enough to see through that heater.

"So you drill me and I drill Pappas," I said.

"I'm just defending myself, Mr. Wale," said Nick.

"After I left here this morning you went down to Wall Street and threatened a friend of mine," I said. "I don't like that, Nick."

Pappas' voice rolled out in anguish: "You say t'ings about Lotta, Wale! W'at?"

"Ask Nick," I said.

The bartender's white eyes rolled between me and his agitated boss and I could have plugged Nick at that point. I could have drilled him very clean with the chance he wouldn't have the strength or inclination left to trigger that .45.

Instead, I repeated: "Ask Nick, Pappas. He knows all about dames who turn up missing. Maybe Nick'll tell you about Lotta's husband and a red-headed tramp on a jag."

Nick let out a sudden torrent of Greek—which was still Greek to me.

Sailor touched my shoulder. "Cash!"

It raised the hackles on my neck, how they did it. All twenty or more of the thick-set guys at the tables were getting slowly to their feet. I heard chairs scrape, watched cigarettes being carefully laid on the tables where they sent up faint trickles of smoke. They didn't utter a sound, just fastened me with expressionless eyes.

And reached into their pockets.

I didn't care about Tony Pappas and Nick spitting Greek at each other. I didn't care about anything but Cash Wale any more. Sailor and I backed.

It was like an action flicker on the screen coming to a sudden dead stop. Twenty hands froze in as many pockets as we backed. I had it then. It was an argument between Greeks. They wanted no outsiders. They wanted us out, that's all!

But I still moved that Police Special in a short arc from side to side as the swinging doors touched my back. They grazed my sides, then blotted Pappas' Grill from my sight. Sailor jerked me to one side.

Nothing happened.

Three factory girls passing by tittered at my crouch. I holstered the rod fast, looked around. That molten ball overhead still baked the pavement and the street still teemed with the life stream of the garment center.

That's when I noticed my gun hand was trembling and ice-water streamed down my face.

I've nothing against the Greeks, brother. They help each other out as few other races do. They mind their own business, keep out of trouble and do magic with edibles. A fine people.

Only, they are hard as hell to fathom.

CHAPTER FOUR

CASH ON THE LINE

SAILOR AND I zig-zagged in and around the Times Square district winding up over some telephone books in a cigar store across the way from an alley on Forty-first. We had just emerged from that alley and we watched its mouth through the plate glass until I was sure nobody had tailed us.

"Them guys meant business, Cash," rumbled the Sailor in my ear.

"I'd like to know why," I said.

"What we do now, Cash?"

"We go back."

Sailor's hand almost dislocated my shoulder. "Nah, nah, Cash! I seen you do plenty wit' a gat. But not against a army. Looked like a hunnerd of 'em, almost."

"Twenty. But we're not returning the same way we came out."

"Why go back anyhow, Cash?"

"Because they wanted us out, dope. They wanted us out because Pappas intended to ask Nick questions about Lotta and I want to find out how come."

"Who's Lotta?"

"One of the dames found in Central Park."

Sailor's mouth trembled a little. That news clipping must have struggled through the mush in his brain and struck a bell.

"We go back, Cash," he said.

It took some doing. As I mentioned earlier, Pappas' Grill had back rooms where skullduggery had a price. It stood to reason those rooms had an emergency exit in case of cop raids or to admit exclusive patrons who didn't want to be seen entering by the front.

I walked along Forty-first and narrowed the possibilities down to a darkened theater, two office buildings and a paper-box factory.

The theater proved a dud. An alley ended with a watch-man on a stump leg who yelled us back to the street. The office buildings resulted in blank walls, the box factory in an iron grating that was locked against union trouble.

On the street again, Sailor told me: "You don't work it right. You ain't got a system. Cash."

"Do better," I said, swabbing the sweat off my neck.

"Hokay!"

Sailor entered the nearest office building, then emerged and beckoned me over. "Got a buck?" he whispered. I gave him a dollar and he led me inside.

The colored elevator starter winked at me. I winked back. He took the bill from Sailor, looked around, then led us down a flight of stairs to the basement. There, he pointed to a dark passage leading between giant boilers and winked at me again.

The passage narrowed to a crude tunnel, widened after about fifty yards into another basement. It was smaller than the first with rickety wooden stairs leading up.

"O.K., dope," I whispered to Sailor. "What's your system?"

He almost cracked my ribs with his version of a playful nudge. "I just ast him where I c'd buy a good time, that's all, Cash."

I led the way up the stairs wondering why I didn't think of that!

At the top of the stairs a thick-set guy popped from behind a door, hissed: "Yess?"

Then he fell down and Sailor exhaled on his knuckles. The guard wasn't hurt bad, nothing that some raw beef-steak couldn't heal. There was a push-button on the wall near where he had been standing. I sliced one of the wires leading from it with my knife and moved on.

Ten paces brought us to another door. Beyond that, a hall that I knew led into Pappas' Grill. A wooden stairway leading down was just to our left and, past it, a row of doors opening on the hall—the back rooms of which I spoke earlier.

"Cover me," I whispered to Sailor, and opened the first door.

I walked in and closed it behind me.

Penny Gay looked up from the chair in which she sat and said: "Hello, hots!"

On a bed lay the sappy red-headed dame in the checked suit I had seen in Deever's Gym in the morning. She no longer wore those dark Hollywood sun glasses and I could see her eyes were huge pools of blood vessels.

She giggled: "Ooh, it's the little tough mans!"

A CLOUD of sweetish smoke filled the room, came from a hand-tailored fag the redhead was holding. I ignored her and turned to Penny Gay.

"I'm here for the rest of your story, babe. The last installment was without names. Now we'll get personal."

"Your face is different from the last time we met," she snickered.

I hit her on the mouth and the chair on which she sat tipped over on its back, Penny Gay with it.

Redhead giggled: "Ooh, goody! Do it again!"

I helped Penny to her feet. O.K., I'm a heel. She was a female and sitting and it is not cricket to smack a seated female with your fist. But this was trail's end. I had been nice to her once and gotten a first-degree brush-off for my pains. I didn't like it, hitting her, but all the answers I sought were under those waves of honey-colored hair.

Penny didn't like it either. Her eyes smoked and her lips twitched. Before she could talk, I said: "Names, baby, names!"

"You son of a ——!" she said.

I knocked her down again.

"Ooh, again! Ooh, *please* do it again, little tough mans!" squealed Redhead.

I ignored her and addressed Penny Gay who lay flat on her back not minding in the least how much of her black silk hose showed, and swearing noiselessly with her eyes.

"The last time," I told her, "you figured they were tougher than me and played it like that. Now I'm showing you you're wrong and you'll play it my way.

"You boozed me until you could lift my heater, then tipped those gorillas when I left your room. I didn't like that. But it's nothing to how I don't like the frame you're ringing on my pal. And how I don't like to find you sitting guard over this tramp on the bed."

"Whosatramp!" squeaked Redhead, sitting up.

I pushed her down again, snagged the reefer from her lips. "You're high and I'm making allowances," I said. "Keep out of it!" And I turned back to Penny who was crawling to her knees.

"Well, *hots?*" I said.

She had guts, Penny Gay. She came up off the floor swinging. Not clawing for my eyes with open hands as is the habit with dames, but swinging fists, like a man.

I ducked a wild hook and was about to put her down again when a voice spoke behind me and the play was out of my hands.

"That ees finish. Wale! No heet her more!"

Tony Pappas held that .45-caliber Frontier Model in one gnarled fist and he didn't look so good. His shock of dirty white hair was streaked with red and his eyes were the same color. From the corner of my eye, I watched Penny Gay back up, all of the fight drained out of her.

"Pappas," I said, "ask *her* about Lotta."

"Come, Wale!" said Pappas.

I went. I preceded that long barrel into the hall. The hall was empty. I wondered about Sailor who was supposed to be there covering me. I didn't wonder about Nick, the bartender. I was pretty sure Nick was past being wondered about.

It was coming clear in my mind now, Pappas' concern about Lotta, the first girl I had examined in the morgue. Loose ends were coming to a knot in my head.

Pappas motioned me down the wooden stairs next to the door where Sailor and I had entered and I descended to another door. The .45 prodded me through and all the starch went out of my knees.

This was a storeroom lined with sacks of potatoes and onions, boxes of canned stuff, shelves with bottles. One shelf was down and bottles were smashed on the floor under it making a puddle of ketchup, olive oil, spices and broken glass.

And, in the middle of this mess, lay Sailor Duffy, a whipped expression on his face, one eye already beginning to close.

KID APOLLO stood over him. Kid Apollo wore a bright green double-breaster. All his blond curls were in place. He brightened as we entered, chortled: "I got him for you cold, Tony!"

I reached inside my jacket and the .45 jabbed into my back.

"No do, Wales!" muttered Pappas from behind me.

I said: "Sailor, you all right?"

"Wale!" The .45 rammed into me. I let my hand come away, empty.

Sailor shook his head a little. "Sure, Cash. Me, I'm fine! I coulda took him easy. Only I forgot to roll with his right."

I said to Kid Apollo: "Punk, this is something you will regret until the minute you die—which is due."

"Wale!" growled Pappas from behind me. "You tal me about Lotta quick! Alla you know about Lotta or I break you to pieces wit' my hands!"

"Nick said what?" I said.

"Nick say other business—about screwballs rich woman. Nick die too fast to say more."

"Ask Apollo about Lotta," I said.

The .45 almost punched a hole in my spine. "I aska *you!*"

I said: "O.K., Apollo, do I tell him?"

The pug flushed crimson and waved his arm at Sailor who was getting to his feet and wiping sauces from his bald dome.

"Ask *him*, Tony!" yelled Apollo. "That's the Gorilla Man the papers been talkin' about. Hymie'll tell you. I was gonna explain it all to you now, Tony, when we came in and found Duffy in the hall—only things happened too fast. Duffy killed Lotta, Tony!"

"The Sailor had nothing to do with it," I said. "Lotta had a husband and the husband liked to play. He picked up a redhead in a Harlem binge, kept her hot with reefers and brought her here. That right so far, Apollo?"

"He's crazy, Tony!" pleaded Kid Apollo. "This is Wale, stoolie Wale. You know—Hymie told you about him. And that bum, Duffy, always botherin' girls!"

"Make more talk, Wale!" muttered Pappas.

I talked fast. The Police Special was still in my holster but, with Pappas at my back, it could have been in China for all the chance I had at it.

"Lotta was here when her husband brought in the redhead," I continued. "The dames scrapped. Redhead passed out. She was high on marihuana and she passed out. Lotta's husband discovered the redhead was a rich screwball in skirts. Somebody gave him ideas, painted a bright future. If he killed Lotta."

Kid Apollo lunged across the basement at me with a shout: "You talked enough, shrimp!"

Then he dove to his face with his fingers inches from my ankles and his feet wrapped in Sailor Duffy's arms. There was a glimmer of light in the Sailor's ugly face.

"That how it is, Cash?" rumbled Sailor.

"That's how it is, all right!"

Apollo kicked Sailor back across the floor, scrambled to his feet, whirled on Sailor with a sizzling left hook as Duffy came off the floor at him.

Sailor took it. Grunted. Unleashed a short right to Apollo's midsection. Followed up with a left under the heart and a whistling right hook that missed Apollo's jaw by a whisker.

Apollo's left whipped into the opening and I could see the Sailor's arms drop and a bright splotch of red under his closed eye. My .38 hopped into my fist. Instinct.

"*No!*" said Pappas.

I understood his attitude then, and re-holstered my weapon.

Apollo was following his advantage. On his side were youth, flash, legs. His arms worked like pistons. I watched Sailor try to dance back, his arms raised to ward off the barrage—but the spring had been out of his legs for years. He was stumbling.

Apollo primed Sailor with a stinging-left jab, his right cocked for a finisher—

"Rough him, Sailor!" I yelled.

KID APOLLO'S right was still cocked when he doubled with an agonized grunt and I saw the Sailor's knee come out of Apollo's groin. Sailor's massive right slammed the glamorous Kid into a row of potato sacks where he lay panting.

"Hold it, Sailor!" I cautioned, and stopped a massacre. My "Rough him!" had driven the gentlemanly Marquis of Queensberry from the Sailor's reflexes. It left them with the memory of a hundred barroom and dockyard brawls. "No holds barred," Sailor Duffy could lick anything on two feet. I wanted Apollo conscious.

I said: "To continue the story, punk, the guy who did the thinking for Lotta's husband figured a plan. Bump Lotta. Tell the rich redhead that she bumped Lotta during their scrap. Being in a marihuana fog, Redhead wouldn't know. Then offer her silence and protection for a price.

"It was foolproof, almost. It beat kidnaping or blackmail. Redhead would sign checks until the bank ran dry. She did sign one. Maybe, after that, this cute husband of Lotta's might even marry the redhead. She has a knack of wedding heels—"

Apollo was shaking his blond curls in a daze. "Don't listen to him, Tony, *please!*"

"So friend husband had to get rid of Lotta," I pressed on, "and, in the ride through Central Park, Lotta broke out of the car and started running. Or maybe the grass was to be her deathbed anyhow—but hubby's powerful hands strangled all but the last spark of life out of Lotta and she was able to gasp: *'Husband—the tramp was high— husband—'* before she died.

"You following me, Pappas?"

"I folla you, Wale. Talk!"

"The next day the papers all spoke of a 'Gorilla Man' attacker on the loose and that gave the guy who thought for Lotta's husband another brainstorm. It happened three women saw the fight between Lotta and the redhead and knew Lotta was alive *after* it. One could be bought—Penny Gay. The others—Lois and Barbara—had to be silenced if Redhead was to go on thinking she was a killer.

"So this smart cookie had friend husband bump these two in the same way he bumped Lotta and they dropped the bodies in Central Park on successive nights to make it look like an epidemic. The third witness—Penny Gay— was planted with a story that pointed to Sailor Duffy."

At this point Sailor had to slam Apollo back to the floor as the Kid tried to get up. This was not ethical, hitting a slug when he was down. But it was no time for ethics.

"You proof these talk, Wale?" whispered Pappas hoarsely.

"Sure I'll prove it!" I rapped. "Who told you to deny Sailor was here last night when I asked you—and the night before? How could Sailor have attacked those dames if he was in your place at the time, tell me that—*hagh?*"

The pressure eased off my spine. Pappas brushed by me with a terrible expression on his weather-beaten face. My hand darted for the .38—froze motionless.

It was becoming a habit! Something else had rammed into my back!

"Uh-uh, Wale!" cautioned a familiar voice.

"I'm only trying to save you a killer for the chair, Quinn," I growled over my shoulder at the inspector. "Listen. Pappas!" I yelled. "Was Lotta Mrs. Kid Apollo?"

The old Greek stood next to Sailor mumbling down at Apollo in his own tongue. Apollo didn't look good. A fear-crazed slob never looks good. I yelled my question again and Pappas nodded.

"What was Lotta to you?" I asked.

Pappas regarded me tiredly. "My girl Lotta Pappas, Wale. W'en she marry wit' Apollo, me, I'ma happy." Sheer hate emblazoned his features as he whirled on the cringing blond pug. "I t'ink you live too long mebbe!" whispered Pappas.

"Hold it," I said. "Was Sailor upstairs last night like he said? And the night before?"

Pappas nodded. "Hymie the Ham, he tal me say Duffy no here because you turning stoolpigeon."

"How about the redhead upstairs?"

"Hymie the Ham, he say she ees girl fran. Een trobbles."

Inspector Jack Quinn brushed past me and nodded his sharp face. "O.K., Wale. I was at the door a while before comin' in. I heard plenty. Enough to clear Duffy. Is that redhead upstairs?"

"She is," I said. "That how you tailed me?"

"When you pulled that screwball act, it was enough to get the commissioner to let me in on the pressure behind you. I hung around Winthrop's office until you showed. From then on I had you tailed until the score added. It adds."

"What got me more than anything," I said, "was Hymie the Ham siccing Kid Apollo on the Sailor to make him wackier than usual and cinch him to talk himself into the chair."

Quinn didn't hear me. He was halfway across the basement and that's when the shots rang out. Two. Spaced evenly. From upstairs.

"That's Sam!" yelled Quinn, his bushy gray brows hopping. "I left him upstairs to cover!"

IT WAS nip and tuck between Quinn and me up those stairs. A slug breezed between us as we reached the landing. I could see the inspector's beefy side-kick, Sam, crawling along the floor, a thin red trickle oozing from the shoulder of his gray serge. A Police Positive was about a yard in front of him and he was straining for it.

Just a glimpse of the others at the far end of the hall, then I elbowed Inspector Quinn aside. His shot sent echoes crashing and dug up a furrow along the floor.

This was *my* party!

I didn't have to aim. Hymie the Ham, was dragging the redhead in the checked suit out the door into Pappas' bar. Maybe he figured he still had a chance to squeeze dough out of her. I wasn't shooting at Hymie the Ham—then.

Two familiar gorillas in sweatshirts stood facing us, covering his retreat. They held rods in their fists and blinked nervously. I didn't have to aim, didn't even feel the .38 hop in my grip, just smelled the acrid wave of gas. One of them coughed as my slug took him in the chest and he stood swaying. The other closed his eyes and fired.

That was a mistake, closing his eyes. You get only one chance like that in a lifetime. His slug chipped plaster from the wall sending a fine spray in my face.

Then he dropped his rod and grabbed his neck. That's how he fell—holding his neck. The first stumble-bum from Deever's Gym still swayed on his feet but his eyes had turned to glass.

It all took less than a second. I was conscious of Inspector Quinn behind me swearing in white heat. I raced past the swaying corpse, crashed through the door.

It was a tableau for my memoirs. Believe it or not, those twenty-odd Greeks at the tables weren't even on their feet! Just sitting around like usual, sipping black coffee, puffing on smelly fags and muttering to each other in Greek.

Hymie the Ham was almost to the street. Redhead was babbling hysterically at his side, trying to wrench out of his grasp. She succeeded, as I appeared, and his fist came up with a small automatic.

I don't remember firing—just the way his nose suddenly bent in the middle leaving his face a caricature. He dove headfirst into the sawdust floor.

"You filthy ——!" screamed Redhead and began lashing her shoe at the head of Hymie the Ham.

Quinn swung me around by the shoulder. "You shoved me, Wale!" he panted. "It didn't have to be—all dead—you coulda just *stopped* 'em! My God, you—"

"I play it like that!" I snarled.

Sailor Duffy suddenly appeared behind us. Quinn and I stared at his expression, then at each other. I let him beat me back down the hall. It wasn't my party any more.

It wasn't Kid Apollo's, either. He still lay against the potato sacks in the basement storeroom but he would never get up on his own—not with that red splotch growing all over the middle of his bright green double-breaster.

The Frontier Model in Pappas' hand was smoking. Quinn took it away. Pappas didn't even notice him.

"You heard the story, Inspector," I said. "Apollo bumped Pappas' daughter for a chance at Maida Winthrop and the Winthrop millions. It would be very easy for you to report that one of the stiffs upstairs bumped Apollo in the confusion."

For a long time Inspector Quinn's eyes and mine battled. Then he said: "I don't like you, Wale, not one bit. But O.K. Apollo stopped a slug accidental. But Pappas gets booked for the kind of dive he's running."

"So he'll stand a fine," I said. I didn't worry about the cops finding Nick, the bartender.

Leaving through the upstairs hall, Penny Gay emerged from that room and stopped me with a hand on my arm. "You didn't have to take it out on me, hots," she reproached. "After all, it *was* my neck."

"I'll make it up to you, babe," I said. I turned to Quinn who was helping Sam off the floor. "Here's all the witness you need." To Penny, I said: "They'll just keep you long enough to get your testimony. Then you'll be clear, babe."

"I can look you up again, hots?" Her fingers still clung to my arm.

"It will be me after you, babe," I said. "Me after you!" and I entered the bar.

Maida Winthrop had her mouth under a beer spigot and the tap on full. I dragged her away, told Sailor to flag a hack. Quinn brought in Sam who was limping and pale around the beef, but healthy enough.

"What'd you do with our heaters, Wale?" demanded Quinn.

"You'll get 'em back," I said.

"O.K. I'm overlooking what happened, Wale. Take *that* home and steer clear of me in the future. I don't like you at all, Wale."

"I'm busting a tear duct," I said.

Those twenty-odd Greeks still sat around talking when Sailor and I bundled Maida Winthrop into the hack Sailor had flagged. A very unusual people. Greeks.

IT WAS only five when we reached Wall Street. The F.K. Winthrop anteroom was besieged by a new batch of Bigs. I recognized the police commissioner among them. He rose to speak to me—I brushed by. I didn't even wait for secretary number one to O.K. me. I winked at Hogan and banged the door until it ticked open.

Maida Winthrop was something out of a bad stomach when I thrust her in ahead of me—huge bleary eyes, her check suit awry, one stocking hanging around her heel. But papa liked.

F.K. scooted around that thousand-buck desk and grabbed his female no-good in his arms like she was a new corporation falling into his clutches.

"Her hair changed color and she needs an overhauling," I told him, "but it's her."

He reached under her arm and mitted me. He released her long enough to snag that thousand-dollar check from the draper and shove it at me. I took it.

I also took Maida Winthrop from his arms as he returned to the clinch.

"For finding her, I'm accepting this check," I said. "But there's one thing more. I'm gonna teach you what you should have done in the first place and saved a lot of citizens trouble. For free I'm gonna teach you."

I dragged Maida Winthrop to the five-hundred buck chair, laid her over my knee and, before I could be stopped, I was dealing with the softest part of her and creating strange noises.

"Me next, Cash, me next!" pleaded Sailor Duffy eagerly. "She done plenty trouble! I wanna crack at her next, Cash!"

I paused long enough to hear F.K. Winthrop yell into the office-to-office phone.

"Lucille! Make out another check to Mr. Cash Wale for the sum of one thousand dollars. I will sign it on the way out. In the meantime, I am not to be disturbed—no matter what sounds come from my office. *I am not to be disturbed!*"

Then he rolled up one sleeve and got on line.

WANTED: DEAD AND ALIVE!

ONE OF HIS CLIENTS WANTED
FELIX THE CHINLESS BUMPED IN
A HURRY—THE OTHER TO HAVE
HIM KEPT ALIVE AT ALL COSTS.
SO WHAT THE HELL COULD WALE
DO—FOR HE WOULDN'T COLLECT
A DIME UNLESS HE SATISFIED
BOTH.

CHAPTER ONE
KILL HIM DEAD,
MR. WALE!

A **FTER MAKING** sure he was permanently out
of breath, I crossed the small office to the front door,
the one with—*M. MATSON, REAL ESTATE*—reading
backward through frosted glass, and made certain nobody
prowled the corridor beyond. The door was locked from
the inside.

That sent me past Matson to the rear entrance which
had been unlocked when I arrived. This was solid oak
except for a metal peep-slot.

He'd been careful that way, Mushky Matson.

The slot framed a narrow vista of trampled snow and a
brick wall across the yard. Cold air jabbing into my eyes
made them water, sent me back to Matson cursing softly.
Not out of pity for the guy. He'd been a heel from way back.
And this was no more than he deserved.

A hairy heel. Now he slumped behind his walnut desk
and all the phoney real estate gimmicks that were his front
to the jeeps. Curly black hair ran wild from his brows to
the bottom of his neck, along the top of his hands. A meaty
pallid face that usually held the expression of a dirty pillow.

But not now. Not with his mouth hanging open and
blood-shot eyes half out of their sockets. There wasn't
much blood. Just a moist circle around the hole in his vest

pocket—practically no blood at all. Judging from Mush-ky's appearance, he must have died fast.

And fighting.

I could tell that. His right hand, clutching the top of his vest now, showed faint powder burns—the forefinger scraped raw. No visible stains on the vest where the slug had entered.

It was easy to figure. A rod had gone off in his fist—a big, leaky rod with old-time slugs, packed with black powder judging from the stain on his hand. Then someone had ripped the heater from Mushky's hand and used it on Mushky's vest.

He'd been fighting, all right. A heel, but he knew from nothing about gats and scraps.

I stood across the desk from him debating with myself whether to scram or frisk him, case the office and try for a line on the proposition he'd mentioned over the phone.

"A gilt edged set-up, right up your alley, shamus," he'd said. "Never mind the hour. Come in the back way. I'll be waiting—"

Matson's real-estating, as I mentioned, was a blind for the jeeps. The back door was for lamsters—for a price he steered wanted citizens to inns where questions rated coffins. He'd kicked a few deals my way in the past, muscling in on the take, of course.

So I had torn myself out of a warm bed at his summons at seven A.M. by the clock—midnight by my schedule—and hastened down to find him like this, slumped at his desk, blotted.

A fine thing before breakfast!

I was about to neglect the whole business and walk out, when this voice at my elbow spoke up brightly.

"If you had any manners," she said in a husky voice, "you
would have knocked first. Is that a watch charm?"

"Lousy job! The first lump, all right—and it cooked
him—but in the chest like that it didn't have to. It's a
wonder Mushky let it happen."

I turned very slowly on my heel and saw a pair of huge
eyes that seemed attached to a skeleton in clothes, standing just this side of a closet. I had overlooked the closet.

His hands were empty.

He must have sensed my thoughts because his next
words, in that sharp voice, were: "I ducked when you come
in the door." A bony finger indicated Matson. "He was like
that when I bust in. You, I didn't know—mebbe cops? But
then I seen you act like you can't figure, lam or no. So I
decide you are one of the boys. Lousy job, hunh?"

It got me, that voice coming from a face that belonged in a coffin—a thin, bony face that looked as white as the snow outside, and as cold.

"You know him?" I asked.

"He steered me once."

I took note of his pallor.

"But they got you back."

"I come out clean last week," he said briskly. "You?"

"I've always been clean," I said quietly. "I don't know about you, pal. Me, I'm exiting."

He made a faint gesture, as if he wasn't too pleased at this.

"You and me both, hunh?"

"Me first. Alone."

"Hunh?"

I didn't plan what happened then—instinct drew the .32 caliber Colt revolver from under my arm, aimed it— and it took will power to hold back my trigger finger. The Human Skeleton just looked at me and didn't even blink.

"Fast," he said professionally. "Spring?"

"No spring," I told him.

He said: "Look!"

It wasn't speed—I could have licked speed—it was sheer magic. Not a muscle on him moved, yet this little black automatic lay in his bony palm slanting up at me, dead center!

What he gripped was no more than a .25 caliber. The odds were still with my heavier rod—but not the percentage. My heater had been tagged so many times, the ballistics boys could spot my individual slug marks at fifty paces in moonlight. Anyhow, there was no point in gun-play.

All I wanted was out—before the sudden arrival of one of those inevitable innocent bystanders.

"Spring!" announced the Human Skeleton brightly. "Up the sleeve. Quick, hunh? Like this, we both go first. Good idea, hunh?"

We did.

I'd lost all taste for Mushky's proposition and Mushky's company. Side by side, we eased from the back door into a stinging gale that swept into us from a milky sky.

The yard opened on east Houston Street, alive now with crawling vehicles and early workers struggling through snow and wind. The Human Skeleton winked at me as his tiny rod leaped from view. My Colt revolver dropped back under my arm.

"Close shave, hunh?" he yelled over gale and traffic. I nodded. "He always had his mitt out, had it coming to him, hunh?" I nodded again. "Well, hope I never see you again, pal!" he concluded, heading east.

I nodded heartily and turned west, very glad to be alone again.

For the entire block as we plodded in opposite directions, our eyes kept meeting. No question about it, we were poison to each other—two wise guys who'd be cop-bait if they ever discovered either of us had seen Mushky Matson defunct and failed to report it. Cops are funny about things like that.

I boarded a hack on Seventh Avenue with no little relief. That ended it, I thought. I was only out a couple of hours' sleep and some awkward seconds. It was Mushky's funeral—Skeleton Face would keep his nose clean. It was all over. By the time I paid off the hackie on Riverside Drive, I'd practically forgotten the whole matter.

Like a damn fool!

THE GALE was cutting some fancy touches on the Drive. As the cab lurched away, a flurry of snow whipped off the ground, crawled into my collar. Distant blocks of ice jostled each other along the white Hudson. Past the river, the Palisades were ghostly through a fine mist.

In the foyer of the graystone room-factory I called home, I looked around for Sailor Duffy. He wasn't there, probably jogging through the snow around Central Park's reservoir on his usual morning work-out.

Our two-rooms-and-bath was on the second floor, rear. I keyed the door, found it unlocked. In my racket that could mean anything.

Warily, I kicked it open—then stared at this very cushy number unhitching herself from an old gaffer who belonged in moth-balls.

"Nice," I cracked. "You always do it like this, or are some tenants kind of particular?"

Her quick smile revealed an even set of mouth jewelry. A silver-fox jacket hung open in front, exposing a black satin dress inside, streamlining breasts and hips that were all of right.

A silver-fox cossack hat dropped a veil over the top half of features that had been furnished out of boxes, right down to eye-shadows. On her, it was wasted advertisement. Few eyes would rise above her neck-line.

"If you had any manners," she said in a husky voice, "you would have knocked first. What is that you've got there—a watch charm?"

I re-holstered my Colt. 32 which had appeared with the unlocked door and turned to the old gaffer who was making strangled noises in his throat, and trying to find his voice.

"The door—ah—was open. You must be—uh—Cash Wale?"

He said this, fiddling with a black ribbon which dangled from horn-rimmed specs.

His gray hair sprouted thick under his derby. His face was cramped, pinched, constipated-looking. Not what you'd call an attractive guy.

His black overcoat was cut to fit a low, round alderman. This made the lipstick daubed over his cheeks look positively silly.

"If I am—" I said.

His eyes wobbled to the dame.

"There's a thousand dollar job for Cash Wale," she said evenly.

I shrugged out of my rubbers, coat and fedora, then sat behind my desk and waved them to chairs. It was my office, this half of the apartment.

The city had me listed as the Cash Wale Investigation Service and had regretted issuing my license since. I didn't advertise because my grift and customers were strictly confidential. One guy told another—that was my advertising.

Also, editors had a knack of inflating the number of corpses I had promoted. This brought me clients. In brief, I wangled cases that were too hot for the big agencies.

I said: "Is this going to be legal?" The dame snickered.

"Does it matter—to Cash Wale?"

"You can bet your girdle on that, sister!"

The gaffer nodded hastily. "Certainly, Mr. Wale—entirely—um—legal." He glanced at the dame for support. "Ah—dangerous, but assuredly legal."

I said: "Who has the grand?"

"Does it make any difference?" bristled the dame.

"It does."

The gaffer ventilated his throat again.

"Er—I will remunerate you for—"

"That's enough!" I snapped. I pointed to the dame. "That eliminates you. I never deal in public."

The gaffer purpled but it didn't faze her a bit. Her carmine lips puckered speculatively. Then she said: "Homer, I think he is right. I also think he's cute—so little and brittle and quick!"

She was out the door before Homer had apoplexy and I said: "O.K., pal. Who steered you?"

"Did you—er—say—ah—*steered?*"

"Yeah. Who told you about me? I like to know these things."

"Well, I have, of course, read about your—heh—exploits in the—"

"Skip the press notice. Who do I smear?"

This time the color drained from his pinched face, leaving it pasty—except for the lip-rouge marks, brighter than ever.

"What makes you say that?" he whispered.

"You pegged me through the rags, you say. They generally tag me as a guncrazy shamus with my palm out. You come here with a yard—no peanuts, mister. It spells a bump."

This was putting it bluntly—I like the cards on the table facing up.

Homer wet his lips nervously. "I heard you were—heh, heh—unorthodox, Mr. Wale—"

"That's a word for it," I agreed.

"I am—uh—Homer Winslow."

"So?"

He took a breath, and a folded paper from his pocket and shoved the latter across the desk to me. It was a morning rag. I hadn't seen it.

A small headline on the bottom of page one stopped *my* breath—

BIG BILL VOSSOV OUT TODAY

It went on to describe how the former beer Czar's stretch for violating the Sullivan Law had terminated this very morning. It outlined a few highlights of his career, listed a few citizens who had died violently at, it was rumored, the hands of Big Bill Vossov.

I WAS suddenly alone with that item, seeing through it to a past I'd hoped was forever dead. I could have verified those rumors. I could see, in my mind's eye, each of the mentioned defuncts and a host of others the papers never got around to. I could remember how they died, each and every one of them.

Rats, the pack of them—I wasn't sorry. They invented the game and I just beat them at it—my draw was a little faster, I never fired before my target was lined in the sights. That was the margin between a dozen-odd graves in Woodlawn and Cash Wale.

No, I wasn't sorry. I was worried. I had been the hand of Big Bill Vossov—the gun hand.

Something plucked my sleeve and I looked up at Homer Winslow.

"Not that," he said. "I meant the other—ah—this." He indicated a three column banner under the war headline—

CONDEMNED MAN ESCAPES
ON EVE OF EXECUTION!

That was a neat trick. I forgot Big Bill Vossov and went through the rest of the report:

> One guard was slain this morning, two others wounded, when Felix Chase, condemned murderer, escaped from State Prison as he was being transferred to the death cell block. The prisoner, who was scheduled to be electrocuted exactly one week from this morning, somehow managed to secure a revolver, according to Warden Lewis, and forced the guards who were conducting him to the new cell to lead him instead through the prison laundry where a riot ensued.
>
> In the confusion, Chase managed to escape and Guard....

I looked up at Homer Winslow who was revolving his glasses in his fingers.

"You want *him?*" I said.

"Please, read it—uh—all," asked Winslow nervously.

The rest had to do with Felix Chase's original crime, a messy brush-off from the description. It was in a roadside sucker trap. Too much booze, two guys and only one dame. When the smoke cleared, Felix was atop the other guy, a fork in the other guy's throat and the handle in Felix Chase's fist. The dame was gone.

Chase never identified her. In fact, he never said anything through the entire trial except that his name was Felix Chase, and only that was on his word.

So twelve good men and true had lined him up for a squirt of juice by voting him guilty after thirty-two minutes' deliberation.

I looked up at Homer Winslow again and said: "Well?"

He leaned forward, said: "Mr. Wale, notice has already been issued that Felix Chase is wanted, dead or alive. I will—ah—give you one thousand dollars if, within forty-eight hours, Felix is—eh—dead."

"Why?"

"I—uh—prefer to keep that to myself, Mr. Wale."

He was looking deep into my eyes now. He was in dead earnest, Homer Winslow. I said: "And if Felix Chase is not dead in two days?"

Winslow's lips trembled.

"He must be dead, Mr. Wale! He must, do you understand?"

"No. And the whole thing is screwy as a barber pole. The guy's loose somewheres, making himself looser every second—and all you want me to do is find him out of a hundred and thirty million citizens in two days—"

"*Kill* him, Mr. Wale! Kill him dead!"

"You're bloodthirsty for such a mild-looking cuss, Homer," I remarked.

Winslow removed a snap cover watch from his pocket, said: "I am a businessman, Mr. Wale. The idea of your finding Stan—ah—Felix Chase with no clues is preposterous, certainly. The—er—point is, I expect him at my office within twenty-four hours, Mr. Wale. I am—ah—certain of that. I want you to be there. I want you to—listen, if he does not appear in the allotted time, I will still give you the thousand dollars. But if he does appear and you do not—hm—succeed. I will give you nothing. Is that—ha—satisfactory?"

I SIGHED and walked around the desk to the door. I hauled it open fast and caught the dame in my arms, as she stumbled across the threshold.

"Naughty, naughty," I said. "That isn't polite, kid."

"You're real cute," she smiled, making no move to stand on her own feet. Her fingers squeezed my arms. "And strong, for a little fella. Little Napoleon."

"O.K., Josephine," I told her, setting her erect. "Down the hall, please."

"And so masterful!" she called back, ankling down the hall slowly to give each satiny hip its full sway. I closed the door and returned to Winslow who was three shades redder than a beet.

"You mustn't mind Miss Joyce," he said. "My secretary is a trifle—uh—eccentric."

"I know another word for it," I told him, getting behind my desk again. "Wipe the lip-goo off your face." When his complexion settled back to the beet shade, I said: "So far, your proposition stinks. Wanted or no, it is not legal for me to cook somebody at a customer's behest. Furthermore, even if the grand induced me to overlook details like that, I'm not risking my neck on a blind date when I don't know from what.

"For instance, this rag has no picture of Felix Chase, or Stan something, as you were about to call him. A fine thing if you finger a guy and I rub him and it turns out not to be Felix but a sucker named Joe who makes faces at you in the subway.

"Another thing, collecting on an item like this couldn't be done legal. You'd have me on a spot and I wouldn't like that at all, see?"

Winslow nodded, his complexion now at normal, maybe a bit whiter where the lip-marks had been.

"You are by way of being a—hum—businessman yourself, Mr. Wale. Heh, heh, heh."

"I'd like to see the color of your dough, pal," I told him.

What he did then had me leaping across the desk but I was too late. All I saw was the face of Grover Cleveland peeking from a green bill he'd pulled from a wallet, then my fingers grabbed space and half of Grover Cleveland looked at me from each of his hands.

A grand in one note! And this hemming gaffer split it in half!

"Security, Mr. Wale! Heh, heh!" he beamed. "One half to you—the other, I keep. It will be yours also when Felix Chase is—hah—liquidated?"

"Hold it!" I rapped, trying to keep from crawling him for the other side of Grover Cleveland's face. Cash affects me like that, when it comes in large denominations. "Give with some details, pal."

"Ah," he said, thumbing his half of the bill back into his worn leather wallet. "As for the identity of Felix Chase, his—ah—picture, it will surely be in the afternoon papers. But that may be too late. In the meantime—"

He gave me a snapshot. It could have been made by a box camera. Three people in a boat. Winslow, his pot big as life, the Joyce dame in a bathing suit built from a handkerchief—the third subject was something.

A gawky kid with no chin and the eyes of a sick calf. A toothpick searching for its soul.

"Felix Chase!" hissed Winslow.

Something in my gut turned sour.

"Look, Homer," I offered, "this kid's slated to burn in a week anyhow. What's wrong with my turning him in? He'll be just as dead from juice as from my slug. Why?"

Winslow's expression turned bleak. Rising stiffly, he said: "You want the other half of the—ah—bill, Mr. Wale?" He gandered his turnip again, nodded, then laid a white card on my desk. "If you do," he went on, "be in my office in two hours. Everything will be, I am sure—harrumph—satisfactory."

I watched him wobble through the door, then his pinched features reappeared. "Miss Joyce is not—er—here, Mr. Wale—"

"Some pants must have floated past," I muttered, following him out.

I was right. We found her downstairs in the foyer, entangled in the arms of a massive leather windbreaker from the neck of which emerged a nude skull framing features that were swollen lumps and an expression that would make a dog crawl into a hole for shame.

"You're so strong, Mr. Duffy," came the Joyce dame's smothered voice as we hove in view.

"*Sailor!*" I barked.

He couldn't have dropped a hot potato quicker. Miss Joyce adjusted her assorted curves and took Winslow's arm as if this happened every day in the week and twice on Sunday.

"The midget master of men!" she snickered huskily.

The back of Winslow's neck as he dragged her out into the gale had all his other shades beat hollow. I looked at Sailor Duffy whose expression was out of this world.

"Ain't she a pip, Cash? Ain't she? She ast me fer a match, then if I was a slugger. I told her about stayin' fifteen heats with the champ and she says she allus feels weak around big, strong guys like me, so wouldn't I hold her up? So I hold her up. Ain't she—"

I told him what she was in about forty choice words. But they didn't register. Sailor Duffy, ex-heavyweight contender, was the other half of the Cash Wale Investigation Agency—a batch of muscle with marbles that rattled from too many left hooks.

I didn't know why I kept him around. He ate more than six of me, screwed up more cases with dumb shenanigans than I cared to remember.

Maybe it was just the fact that he hung around—that he wasn't ashamed to be seen in public with Cash Wale, the guy, for instance, a fruit like Homer Winslow would pay to erase a chinless mouse.

CHAPTER TWO
KEEP HIM ALIVE, CASH!

IN THE office again, I spread my half of Grover Cleveland on the desk together with the paper and card Winslow had left me. The card said he was the Winslow Scrap Metal Co. On the back, a Bronx address was scribbled in pencil.

I tried three numbers on my phone before reaching Scoop Hannigan, a tabloid leg-man with an itching palm.

"Is that you, heel?" his voice greeted. "Where's the corpse?"

"No corpse, Snoop. Ever hear of the Homer Winslow Scrap Metal Company?"

"That ——!"

"So he wasn't born legal—what about him?"

"He sells Japs what to civilize China with. Scrap iron, the ——! You launched on mass murder now, heel?"

I took this because getting chesty with Scoop Hannigan netted nothing.

I said: "This Felix Chase who bust out of State Prison this A.M. Anything new on him?"

"Don't switch the subject on me, you ——!"

"Same subject, Snoop."

A gust of sound emerged from the receiver.

"Hey, Cash, you mean there's an angle? No kiddin'?"

"They took boat rides together. You want to check this for me?"

"Do I collect?"

"Fifty, if it's right?"

"Make it a century, Cash. I'm hooked with this blonde tonight and she's nuts about caviar. I'm nuts about her, so—"

"Seventy-five," I compromised.

"O.K., heel!"

The phone clicked dead and Sailor grumbled into my ear: "That ain't gonna buy nothin', Cash." He referred to Grover Cleveland.

"You're gonna buy something, dummy!" I rapped at him. "Every rag on the stands. And breakfast. And make it snappy!"

"Sure, Cash. O.K." As Sailor shuffled to the door, he called back: "That Barbara Joyce, she's O.K., ain't she, Cash? Hunh, Cash?"

"Wipe that red ink off your puss!" I yelled at him as the door slammed.

I was in the middle of the column on the escape of Felix Chase when a bright, familiar voice said: "So we meet again, hunh, pal?"

He stood in the doorway—I hadn't heard it open—his face still bony and fleshless, his hands empty. It was my nemesis from Matson's, Skeleton Face!

"So you knew me," I said quietly.

"Naw. It's somethin' else this time." He jerked his head a bit. "C'mon in, fellas. Whaddya think, it's that little guy I told you about!"

I couldn't play for my rod, not after seeing him draw. I just sat there. The first two guys who walked in and ranged on either side of Skeleton Face were strangers to me, but both wore that same bighouse pallor. Two beetle-browed no-goods.

Then the third man entered and the bottom fell out of my pat little world. This was a round ball of fat with two unblinking eyes, the color of lead. He wore new clothes and the same pallor as the others.

He passed behind Skeleton Face, helped himself to a chair and grinned mirthlessly at me.

"You forget your old boss, Cash?" he rumbled in a voice like Edward Arnold's. "Ain't you glad to see me?" He turned to the others. "This is Wale, my gun in the old days, fellas. Not a grifter in the country had guts enough to play for me with little Cash Wale at my side. Big Bill's gun, they called him, and he could shoot the whiskers off 'n a fly without even tryin'! Ain't that right, Cash?"

I said: "What do you want, Vossov?"

HE WAVED a pudgy hand at the others. "I'm goin' in business again, Cash. They can't keep Big Bill down. A completely new graft and no kickback. You—"

"Count me out," I said quietly. "I'm legitimate now."

"Sure, boss," cut in Skeleton Face cheerily, "that's what he told me at Matson's. If you'da told me it was Cash Wale, I coulda told you that, boss."

"Shut up," said Big Bill Vossov without turning around. "As I was sayin', Cash. It's a new grift. We'll peddle patriotism. We'll sell protection against these fifth-column guys.

A lotta long hairs doin' it already without any idea what a take they could drag if they worked it right. You—"

"Count me out," I repeated.

"But I need a stake, Cash," went on Vossov as if I hadn't spoken. "There was a punk up the river with me, squat rap—I bunked with him awhile. A clam, but you know how clams open for Big Bill.

"He was nuts on a fluff on the outside. That bothered him more than fryin'—losin' her, I mean. It turns out this kid's no flash in the pan, get me? There's a policy on him—his old man's partner adopted him when the old man kicked off—so this partner insures him for—get this, Cash. The partner insures the kid for a quarter million! Get me?"

"He's way ahead of you!" popped Skeleton Face brightly. "Wasn't he at Matson's?"

"Shut up," admonished Big Bill mildly. "That was Matson tryin' to cross me. Now get this, Cash. When the kid fries, the partner collects. But the gimmick is, the partner doesn't even know the kid's on ice, see? The kid's goin' out on a phoney handle!"

"The partner's name wouldn't be Winslow?" I murmured.

Vossov turned to the others who watched me expressionlessly.

"See? I told you Cash Wale misses no bets. Already, he smells angles."

I didn't relish this, not one single bit. If it wasn't for the spring up Skeleton Face's sleeve, I would have put an end to it. As it was, I kept talking.

"It's clear and it stinks. The kid wanted to see his girl, you wanted the dough. So you dealed. You'd spring the kid and somehow collect on the insurance when and if, and you'd see to that. He agreed, you had him busted out—he was taken to Matson's for a steer—"

Vossov's grin was suddenly gone.

"Where's Felix Chase, Wale?"

"Ask Matson."

"See?" popped Skeleton Face. "He don't know. He come into Matson's joint after me. Mushky was already turnin' stiff."

"Shut up," said Vossov automatically. "Cash, I'm in business again. Mebbe you think your rod's got the last word like the old days. Skull here, he's pretty good, too."

Skull's hand was suddenly full of gun. I couldn't have even touched the butt of mine.

"The old spring!" popped Skull brightly.

"See?" spoke Vossov. "I'm in business again. How I see it, Matson figured to cross me and called you in to angle it and you bumped him to make it solo, then came back when Skull was there to make sure everything was right—you was always full of tricks. Where's the kid?"

"Ask Matson," I said.

VOSSOV SIGHED. "Maybe I should explain. He wrote a letter before breaking out to change the beneficiary to me, Cash. But he was smart. He sent it to a pal in Oakland and wrote the pal to mail it back to the insurance company."

"You're a sucker, Vossov," I said. "He could write another letter, after that, changing the beneficiary right back again."

"Sure, that's what I mean. I hadda spring him before he could do that. And I hadda keep an eye on him till the letter was on the way to the company—then it was all legal. If he's bumped, I'd collect the dough."

"And he'd be bumped," I said.

Vossov shrugged.

"You can still ask Mushky for him," I said.

"I'm askin' *you,* Cash—"

"I never saw the kid, Vossov, and that's straight. And you know my word's always level."

Vossov nodded. "Maybe. Anyhow, you got contacts, this shamus racket here—if the kid shows, you'll know it as quick as the cops. The letter's due to start back in forty-eight hours. I want him alive for that long, Cash, and I'm countin' on you to keep him alive. After that, I want the kid in my own hands, personal."

"You can go to hell, Vossov," I said.

I kicked back from the desk, reaching under my arm—but another hand beat me to it. One of the ex-cons had slipped up behind me. The rod was in his fist before I could help it—then I was over the desk and Big Bill Vossov slammed his blubbery hands into my face while the two ex-cons gripped my arms and Skull held his automatic slanted up, a very sharp expression on his face.

My kicks caught Vossov and a streak of blue pain shot through his eyes. But it was a weak try. Crazy. He calmly reached into a hip pocket and produced a sap and after that I was chewing sand and breathing fire—

Along about the middle of it, Vossov's lead-colored eyes were inches from mine and his voice was rumbling: *"Felix Chase. Stanley Burns, his real monicker. I want him alive, Cash—I want the kid alive forty-eight hours...."*

Then a fist blotted him from my vision and other fists sledged me into a crazy white-hot ball of hate. They could do this to me with their hands. I weighed under a hundred and fifty, stood around five feet two. The hate welled up in me until I could explode—

There was a let-off when a commotion at the door pulled the hands from my arms. But I couldn't lift a finger, couldn't move a muscle—

I glimpsed Sailor Duffy, his arms loaded with papers, barging in through a tangle of arms—until gun-steel twinkled over his bald head and the commotion at the door was suddenly over—

Vaguely, I remembered Skull's cheerful voice in the distance: *"No hard feelin's, Wale, hunh?"*

And a strange quiet peace stealing over me—until the phone jangling brought me to my knees. Sailor was prone on the rug with a blue lump forming on his skull. In the doorway peered curious faces.

The phone was somehow before me and Scoop Hannigan's voice pouring through it.

"Listen, you heel, I want no part of that seventy-five plunks! I want no part of Felix Chase! That's dynamite! You take my advice and lay off. That guy's wanted!"

I mumbled into the phone: "You're telling me something? Felix Chase is wanted, all right—*dead and alive!*"

With which I hung up. I slammed the door on the curious faces, then staggered into the kitchenette for a pitcher of water to drop on Sailor.

THE BRONX address scribbled on Homer Winslow's card belonged to one of those new apartment developments on a crag overlooking the Harlem, all corner windows and a liveried doorman. Civilizing China had done all right by Homer.

When I ducked from the wind into the gilt and chrome lobby, I glimpsed one of Vossov's no-brow playmates lumbering through the snow after me. I wasn't bothered, it sort of kept things in focus.

It was maybe an hour after Sailor and I had brushed off the effects of the brush-off. Sailor, sporting a brand new lump on his nude noggin, was downtown in the lobby of the Winslow Scrap Metal Co. as per instructions.

Everything was set. All that remained was for Felix (or Stanley) to show and be killed and kept alive.

Homer Winslow opened the door in person, goggled, mumbled: "Not *here*, Mr. Wale! In my office—uh—downtown!"

"That's what I thought," I told him, moving past him into a living-room packed with a couple of grand worth of streamlined knick-knacks. "Nice dump," I offered. "Always figured I was a piker burning down one punk at a time. You do it wholesale and collect accordingly. Neat."

"Mr. Wale!" cried Homer Winslow in agitation as I fingered the knob on the bedroom door. "That man will be at my—hah—office, perhaps now!"

"And you're worried he'll see Barbara Joyce and throw a curve?" I asked, passing into the bedroom. A swank sleepery, this. With gold tasseled bedspreads on low twin beds. A rug like three layers of sponge. Aside from the bureau, there was a vanity with perfume jars and such spread over it.

"You are—ha—shrewd, Mr. Wale," admitted Winslow from the door.

I opened the bureau drawer, lifted a pair of silk panties. "Why, Homer!" I grinned, turning to face him.

He couldn't speak. He tried. His mouth twisted and bits of sound choked out—I laughed and led him by the arm back into the living-room after returning the panties. It was almost pitiful, an old gaffer like him getting apoplectic over a few winter oats.

It would have seemed pitiful if some ideas weren't sickening my guts.

When we were seated and his horn-rims had made their final trip from his trembling fingers to the bridge of his nose.

I said: "Let's see the policy, pal. I'd like to gander a marker for a quarter of a million bucks."

The horn-rim specs began traveling again.

I said: "If we're dealing, I want to see all the cards. No hold-outs."

He showed it to me. It took some more persuading and a glimpse of what lay under my arm, but he showed it to me. Hell, it was laying on the mantel all the time, out of its envelope and spread open—as if that fact didn't give me ideas!

A recent policy that, taken out seven months earlier, one month before Stanley Burns, the insured, was indicted for homicide under the name of Felix Chase. And it was all there in black and white, beneficiary—Homer Winslow.

No wonder he wanted Felix dead!

I said: "O.K., pal. Now tell me how you found out Big Bill Vossov stood to ease you out of the picture if the kid lives another forty-eight hours?"

How his eyes bulged told me how close I was to home, but how his mouth pinched shut told me he was going to clam. Not that I thought it mattered. I had ideas.

I said: "O.K., pal. That's all I want to know. The rest will come. It generally does."

He choked. "Wale, you're going through with—ah—*it?*"

"There are wheels within wheels, as the guy said, Homer."

"But you promised!"

"Nothing, pal. Not one solitary promise."

"I—I—I'll make it five thousand—ulp—dollars, if you do, Wale!"

He didn't like money, Homer—the way he didn't like his right eye.

"Give me the halves," I said.

His Adam's apple batted away at the stiff white edge of his collar.

"Not here. I haven't—uh—got it now, Wale. But—"

"But after Chinless kicks in, you expect to collect," I said. And left.

CHAPTER THREE
THANKS FOR THE LIFT

V OSSOV'S GUNSEL must have been half icicle by the time I emerged from Winslow's deluxe igloo and made for the subway. That eased things in the train. He dove for a seat at the far end of the car, blowing on his gloved hands and I stepped back to the platform just as the doors shut.

He tried—I'll say that for him—but without heart. His bluish face pressed against the moving door pane expressed a mixture of vexation and relief. I tipped him a wink as the train bore his face past me, then went downstairs and invested a nickel in a drug store phone booth.

The insurance company voice trilled, after I'd had my say: "I will connect you with the legal department. Just a minute, please."

Another jit entered the kitty, then: "Hello? Legal department—"

"Listen!" I yelled, my voice climbing. "What kind of double-cross do you pull in that—"

It was a man's voice, silky and pompous.

"Will you state your business, please?"

"Sure, I'll squawk! My old man just kicked off, see? His policy named me as the guy to collect, see? Now a no-good son next door ups and says because I ain't in the butcher business like the old man wanted, my pop changed the guy who collects to him, this lickin' slob next door, see? He— my old man, I mean—sent a letter yesterday telling you guys about it, says this rat who'd keep a man's dough from the man's own son! What I want to know is—"

"Could you tell me your name, please?" came this voice.

"Listen, you're the legal department, you tell me what I want to know—do I or don't I collect?"

Some of the silk was fraying in that voice.

"If the letter was sent before your father died and has a postmark to that effect, in all probability it will be regarded as a will—providing it is established your father was in his right mind and there was no coercion. In that case, the name in the letter would probably be regarded as the real beneficiary. But this is a matter that can be determined positively only if all the facts are at hand. If you will tell—"

I hung up.

I rode a hack downtown to the building which housed the Winslow Metal Scrap Co. and scoured the lobby and hallways for Sailor Duffy. Not a bump of him was in evidence.

On a fifteenth floor door tucked away at the far end of the corridor was stenciled in gold:

WINSLOW SCRAP METAL CO.
Homer Winslow, Pres.

In reply to my knock came Barbara's husky voice. "Who is it?"

"*Stan!*" I whispered.

"Just a minute, Stan, darling, I'll be right with you." The keyhole was blocked from the inside, but by pressing my ear close to the glass, I heard a door close softly, then a very distant-sounding voice, then someone breathing tensely just beyond the glass partition. Then the door swung up and I stepped in.

I said: "Hiya, kid—"

Barbara Joyce no longer advertised her geometry, but the alterations were recent. Her face was scrubbed white where the paint job had been, revealing tight little creases around her eyes and mouth which had been effectively concealed before. She wore a green office smock over the satiny curves that had stirred my senses earlier.

This prim, genteel front had been enhanced by a sticky, soulful expression as the door opened, which changed to an involuntary snarl when I registered in her vision instead of "Stan, darling."

"What's the gag, Shorty?" she demanded in harsh tones.

"Napoleon, remember? No gag, kid. I'm just checking some inside wheels. Everything's O.K."

Something entered her eyes then which should be banned from every female's winkers.

"*You did it!*" she whispered, casting an apprehensive glance behind.

A DOOR was behind, tagged: *OFFICE*. I skirted a wooden rail which cut this ante-room in half, entered the door. Nothing but the usual office jib-dads here—desk, chairs, filing cabinet. I noticed the long wire hanging from the desk phone coming to the end of a sway.

"You did it?" breathed Barbara Joyce, sidling in after me.

I looked into the wastepaper basket where some crumpled Kleenex showed smears of rouge, lip-grease and powder. "Didn't they recently bar scrap from the Japs?" I asked.

"Didn't they—*what!*"

"You know, kid. Unborn bullets. Roosevelt's proclamation to that effect must have pinched Homer a bit, hey?"

There was no more primness in Barbara, not when her open palm struck air where my cheek had been. She gasped from the effort, then reached into a lurid past for words.

Some were new, others, standbys—she used them all, took my ancestry apart down to my earliest lecherous forbears, returned to the present and called me every kind of perverted what-not in the book.

It was not pretty. Not pretty at all.

Me, I was admiring the flow with only half my attention. The other half was on my hands, probing through the drawers of that desk. I found bills, more bills and still more bills and a couple of strong letters asking how come there was no remittance in their mails and such.

I had the idea and was becoming alarmed at Barbara inhaling for round two when the door slammed open and I looked past her hip at half a dozen gun muzzles backed by grim jaws and blue uniforms.

Then Inspector Quinn of Manhattan's Homicide detail swept through the artillery with a look in his intense eyes that didn't like me.

"Just like you are, Wale!" he rapped, prowling the little office with a grimly determined look on his face.

"You missed an education by five minutes, pal," I told him.

Quinn, satisfied that only the two of us were present besides Barbara and his stooges, barked at them: "Spread around, cover this layout. Every office, hall, elevator. Go on, snap to it!"

When the jaws and gun-muzzles in the door evaporated, Quinn whirled on Barbara Joyce: "Well, sister, where is he?"

"Felix?" I said.

"It was a—uh—mistake, officer," whispered Barbara Joyce, taking a leaf from Homer. Her face was greenish, she tried covering with a seductive glimpse of her dentals. But, lacking the other accessories, they failed to register.

I yawned elaborately. "Maybe you two want to be alone," I suggested.

"Stick around, Wale!" rapped Quinn. A hardboiled dick of the old school, he made a point of despising my guts. He featured bushy eyebrows and a jaw that could hammer nails. "I'll come to you later, Wales. Just stick around!"

Back to Barbara who still exhibited her mouth furniture: "Listen, sister, you claimed Chase was here. You'd hold him here. He was armed and desperate and we should come in shooting. You can't phone headquarters with a yarn like that and then say it's a mistake!"

"She's doing it, pal," I contradicted. "Me, I know from a hole in the ground about this. I'm interested in scrap metal. Also, I'm interested in leaving. Will it be peaceful?"

It was a point. Quinn, of course, could hold me forty-eight hours without reporting it—but right now he was playing God to a deceitfully meek Barbara Joyce.

He growled at me: "Just be handy in case, Wale—"

SAILOR DUFFY was not in evidence when I pushed through office workers and cops enroute to the street, but that was O.K. That, in fact, was fine.

If Sailor's rattling marbles had not prevented him from carrying through my simple instructions, it meant I held the only wild deuce in this impending murder game—I hoped!

The next hour passed in the newspaper room of the Forty-second Street library where I scanned old news copy that dealt with the crime of Felix Chase.

Pretty much as I already knew, he'd been hauled off a shady character in a roadside tavern with the handle of a fork in his grip and its prongs in this shady character's jugular.

The bartender and a few patrons dimly remembered a woman, their collective description making her a short, fat, tall, skinny dame with red, blond, brunette and no hair and a wardrobe on her person that read like a Hearn's ad.

On one point there was a sort of uniformity. This dame had whirled her curves and eyes at practically every male in the house and, with a few drinks, she made a violent attempt to undrape those curves.

A number of pictures showed Felix—or Stanley Burns—to be the same chinless punk of Winslow's snapshot. He'd offered no defense and got as much from the shyster appointed by the court.

Result: one squat rap. Pretty severe for a roadhouse brawl, but there it was in black and white—a little out-of-the-way kangaroo ride that never graduated from page three.

I spent the last part of the hour examining more recent issues, their financial pages. Came across one interesting item, a gossip rumor that Winslow Scrap Metal Company was angling for a U.S. contract in the armaments drive.

Homer certainly had his palm out!

It was noon when I emerged from the library. The gale was abetted now by a light fall of snow. I lunched in an automat, entered a downtown subway at Grand Central, then stepped out again.

Skull took his hand from my arm as we reached the platform. His palms were opened—I couldn't, for a moment, figure how it happened.

"We keep meetin', hunh?" he shouted in my ear.

"In the screwiest places," I agreed drily. "What now? Bill getting fidgety?"

"Uh-uh." Skull let one eyelid drop. "*Me,* pal. Let's check, hunh?" He led me into the men's room. Too crowded. We tried the street. Too cold. I finally signaled a hack.

"The punk," whispered Skull as the cab rolled up Lexington, "I want him."

"You and the marines," I cracked. "Crossing Vossov?"

"You don't catch on," whispered Skull. "I want the kid." He was nudging my side and not with a finger. His arms crossed to do it, nothing off-color for the hackie to see through his rear-vision mirror.

The skeleton face was in dead earnest at my side.

"What makes you think I tagged him?" I asked.

He shook his head slowly. "Don't be a wrong guy, Wale. I been with you since Winslow's, seen the cops and all—"

"That was Barbara. For a gag, I said through the door I was Stan. She called 'em. She wanted 'em to burn Felix down, the ——!"

"I figured that," nodded Skull, "But it didn't bother you, all them cops, and you stood to lose a grand if they picked him up alive, hunh? So—"

"You're Homer's pipe-line," I cut in.

"So you, a dough-crazy gunsel, not gettin' sore set me thinkin'," went on Skull. "You come outa there with a wise look on your puss, gandered around a little, then went to that book warehouse. So you got the punk, hunh?"

"Maybe."

"I'm my own pipe-line, Wale. This figures more'n a grand for me—enough more to cut you in for a slice if we play this right. You're my kinda guy, Wale, but if you crossed me, I'd—"

"Use springs?"

Skull swallowed hard and looked past my chin at Lexington Avenue slipping by. "Yeah. You seen me, hunh?"

"And you, me."

"Springs is faster."

I watched a traffic light turn green, said: "How about Matson, pal?"

Skull winked again. "The punk there when you burned Mushky?" he leered.

I said: "Let's start all over again, we're not talking the same lingo. To know that Winslow offered me a grand to rub Chinless—"

"Chinless? Ha! That's good, Wale!"

"To know that," I went on, "you have to be the guy who tipped Winslow that Vossov was muscling in on the policy—" We were passing Fifty-seventh Street. I called to the driver: "Swing over to Park," then whispered to Skull: "So it adds you're crossing Vossov and angling by your lonesome—"

Skull almost cracked my ribs with his automatic. "I wanna talk about Felix, pal, hunh?"

The cab was turning left on Sixtieth, heading into a pocket. A red light on Park with a pair of delivery trucks ahead of us and more cabs crowding behind.

This time my ribs did crack a little but the cop on the sidewalk who'd seen me wave was on his way, flapping his arms against the cold.

"It's curtains!" rasped Skull in my ear.

"Be your age. You couldn't lam out of here with a ouija board!" I whispered in reply, then opened the door at the cop. "Fifth Avenue buses running in this weather, officer?" I yelled at him.

He nodded with an expression that could have struck me dead, started turning away. I was at his side, calling back: "I'll walk to the bus, Mr. Zap. Thanks for the lift!"

Skull looked more like one than ever as his mouth hung open, his arms still crossed mandarin fashion. The lights on Park Avenue turned green and the cab had whisked him down the one-way street before he could scramble out— leaving only a fervent curse in the wind.

"Think I'll take the subway on Lexington instead," I yelled at the cop. "Some weather!"

"A——!" he agreed, stamping on, still flapping his arms.

CHAPTER FOUR
WHEELS WITHIN WHEELS

GILLEY'S SQUALID flop-house on the Bowery had been one of Mushky Matson's pet inns for lamsters. There was a dummy register for the cops and Gilley's memory for the "boys."

Gilley, himself, a slob of a man with drooling lips, was perched high on a stool where he could overlook the hall in back which boasted two-bit flops.

He said, without looking at me: "Top, front, Cash."

I mounted rickety wooden steps past mounds of rubbish and waves of body odor to the top floor. My knuckles elicited Sailor Duffy's cautious query, at the top of his lungs: " 'At you, Cash?"

"Me, dope!" I growled.

The door swung open and I sped through, swiftly shutting it behind. A contrast to the flopperies below, this room. Not elegant, but neat. Two windows, well over the El tracks, offered a view of Manhattan Bridge spanning a snow-fluffed sky in the distance. Flakes brushed the panes like feathers.

Sailor grinned proudly.

"I got him, Cash! It was easy, a pushover!"

"Him" was a shivering young punk in leather windbreaker and gray golfing knickers sprawled listlessly on the lone cot, a chinless young punk with dull, hurt eyes and the pallor of prison—and a freshly shaven skull.

He didn't look like a quarter of a million dollars. He did look like the pictures of Felix Chase, alias Stanley Burns.

"He walked into my hands like that!" chortled Sailor. "At the freight elevator like you said he would, Cash. With my arm around him, he couldn't hardly breathe, couldya, fish?"

The dull eyes flicked pain. Sailor's arm was like a steel press.

I asked the kid gently: "When'd you eat last, kid?"

That dull stare. Sailor's palm jerked the shaven head.

"S'matter, fish? Cash's talkin' to ya!"

I kicked Sailor's shin and tried again: "Barbara Joyce wants to know why you haven't seen her, kid. She's worried sick."

Felix spoke in a tone that belonged in a coffin: "Did she tell you that?"

"Not exactly. She asked me to look you up. She was afraid you'd make a dumb play like walking in on her at the office—cops staked all around the dump—so she asked me to bring you here where you'd be safe—"

"You are lying," said the kid dully. "You're Cash Wale, a gunman for Big Bill Vossov. I heard all about you in the"— that flicker of pain again—"jail. You are after the money also. Not that I blame you.

"I learned much that I had never known about people before. I learned what people do for money, I understand how greed can degrade a person now—"

"It talks, Cash!" bellowed Sailor, exhausting his supply of wit in one breath.

I kicked Sailor's shin again, hard.

Felix Chase said: "You tell Vossov if he wants to speak with me to come in person. And, if not, assure him I retain my honor in spite of his intentions. My beneficiary will not be changed again. My promise holds good."

He rose to his feet unsteadily. My toe on Sailor's shin prevented Felix from landing on the bed, bottom-side up. He said: "Now may I go, please?"

I said: "How long do you expect to live, kid?"

"Not very long."

He smiled faintly, saying this. It got me, his attitude. With no chin to start with, something had been squeezed out of Felix. He was all mush—but not afraid of dying. I wasn't used to this.

"Suppose I fix it for you to live out a natural life," I offered. "Suppose I arrange to stash you away with a new front, what then?"

He shook his head, still wearing that smile. "May I go now, please?"

"Suppose," I continued, "if you refuse my offer, you will suddenly drop dead—what then?"

"Does it matter very much?"

What could you do with a guy like that?

I said: "But you went to all the trouble of getting Vossov to spring you. You took a desperate chance, burned a guard and singed two others—what the hell for, if you don't give a damn? I don't get it!"

His narrow shoulders lifted, dropped.

I said: "Does it hinge on Barbara Joyce? A sympathetic line, a warm breast for your weary brow and stuff—"

A palm exploded on my cheek. "Don't foul her name, you scum!" screamed Felix, suddenly out of his coma.

"Well, *lookit!*" exclaimed Sailor Duffy, amazed. "He's gone on that hipper-dipper I wrestled in the hall, Cash! Can ya tie that?"

My own palm sent Felix reeling back to the cot. "Don't try that again, Chinless. Nobody pushes me around," I warned him. "I'm trying to steer you out of a two-way frame and don't you forget it. I could turn you loose in the street and you'd be morgue-meat in jig time. Or I could burn you right here and collect a cool grand—"

"*Why dontcha, pal, hunh?*" inquired a taut, bright voice from the door behind me.

SAILOR JERKED around, his fists balled, turned rigid. I noticed the kid was back in his trance, then looked around slowly to face the huge unwinking eyes of Skull.

This time his hand was not empty.

At his side stood the other pale-face who'd been with Vossov in my brush-off. I'd forgotten about him. Behind them stood Gilley, his drooling lips crawling with apology.

"I can't stand no noise here, Cash," he pleaded. "I couldn't help it. I tried but he"—Gilley jerked a thumb at Pale-Face—"saw ya come in."

"Fade, leaky!" snapped Skull. "No noise. Everything's gonna be nice an' peaceful. Nobody hears shootin' here when the El passes outside, hunh?"

Gilley was blotted out by the slamming door and Skull nodded to Pale-Face who snagged my own Colt .32 from my holster. My heel on Sailor's toe stopped his hands from dragging us both into trouble.

"That's smart, Wale," approved Skull. "But you're thick, for a guy with your rep. While I tagged you, Risko, here, stuck to the palooka. After you shook me, I checked by phone, found out Felix came here. You're pretty dumb, in fact."

Skull could talk like that, with his trick sleeve-rod slanted up at me from his fist.

"Who's a palooka!" growled Sailor at my side.

"Can it," I said wearily. "O.K., Skull. Who are you working for, Big Bill or Homer?"

"I'm workin' for Skull, sucker. You're a dope, angling this for Winslow and that tramp secretary he beds. Me, I know about insurance. You can change the beneficiary every night in the week and it's the *last* change counts, Wale!

"Me and Felix, we're gonna cook a little writin' before Homer catches wise and misses a payment." Skull looked past me at the cot where the kid lay sprawled with a peculiar expression smouldering in his dull eyes. He was getting life in hard doses, that kid.

"O.K., rabbit. We go, hunh?" prodded Skull.

Felix uncoiled himself slowly from the cot and when he was on his feet, something inside of my head clicked. But my eyes were too occupied for me to check.

Felix was on his feet and in his fist, pointed shakily at Skull was a huge black revolver, a .45 at least. From out of his jacket, I thought.

"*I* go," he corrected.

Skull's mouth sagged limp. His trick automatic was on me. Risko, his silent pal, held my revolver by the barrel. No good to anybody, holding a rod like that.

"Rabbit!" whispered Skull. "Don't shake that thing—"

"He shook it at Mushky Matson this morning after taking it from Mushky's hand," I said drily. "That's how he got away."

Felix said, in a high squeaky voice: "The villain left the paths of ease, to walk in perilous paths, and drive the just man into barren climes. Now the sneaking serpent walks in mild humility. And the just man rages in the wilds where lions roam—"

He said this with a slow flush creeping into his cheeks.

"Nutty as a fruit cake!" muttered Skull.

"Poetry," I told him.

Felix was holding the hammer back with his thumb, always a risky habit.

"Drop your gun, Skull," he said.

"I can't!" Skull choked. "It's on a spring!"

"Turn around."

Skull did.

"Kid," I said, "write the insurance company another letter, change the beneficiary to the Red Cross and you'll live longer."

His cropped head shook slowly. "No need for letters, and there will be no beneficiary. And I will not live long. But thank you. Now kindly step back." He lined that .45 on my chest and I backed, Sailor and Risko likewise.

At the door, Felix said: "I will remain outside the door for an indefinite time. If, while I am there, any of you attempt to leave, I will not hesitate to shoot."

The door slammed and Skull whirled around, his face crimson, his automatic leaping up. I slapped it down.

"Go after him if you want, but no wild gun-play!"

He nodded curtly, took a step forward, then halted. The door was suddenly a very serious proposition. Risko went up to it, but was careful not to finger the knob. Skull looked back at me. I laughed.

"It's a gag!" Risko snarled and jerked the door open. His right leg shot from under him as a revolver exploded from beyond and the rest of us dove for the wall.

A wave of gas fumes drifted gently through the doorway.

"Got ya?" Skull whispered.

Risko dragged himself by his hands to the wall without replying, but I saw two holes in the fabric of his trouser leg. Skull passed a sleeve over the moisture on his brow.

"Cripes," he whispered reverently. "Alla time in stir, we pegged him for a rabbit. Wale, that punk's *screwy!*"

"Probably a more technical name for it," I agreed.

AFTER A while, Gilley's wet chin poked in the door. He looked around, said:

"He's gone, Cash. Out the back and wavin' that cannon like in the movies."

I nodded, said to Skull: "My roscoe, pal. I feel naked."

"Like hell!" swore Risko from the floor.

"Give it to him!" snarled Skull. "We ain't buckin' Wale no more. That's why you'll always be a punk, a one-track nut. Me'n Wale, we're smart. With us, it's business. It hurt?"

"I feel nuttin'," said Risko blankly.

"Shock," I told him. "It'll wear off, then you'll feel plenty. Gilley, patch him up."

The flop-house boss looked at me dubiously. "If you say, Cash. Only they'd no call chestin' in here like they did—"

"Shut that fat yap!" clipped Skull. "And patch up Risko. And you, Wale, don't cross me no more, hunh? Me, for a whole month in stir, I been figurin' this proposition. Vossov braced me to gun for him when we got out. Still figured he packed weight, that bum.

"I strung along for laughs until this Felix business came out. So my heart's in it. A real big-time stake. You're O.K. in that shamus grift. Me, I want Felix. So it'll be like that, hunh?"

"Wheels within wheels," I muttered, snagging my Colt from Risko's lax fingers and holstering it.

"Hunh? I didn't catch that."

"Poetry," I said, leading Sailor past Gilley's apologies and Risko's curses and Skull's questioning features.

The gale had died when we hit the street, but snow fell thick enough to obscure the El structure a few yards before us.

When Sailor Duffy and I reached home, we had two fifths of good Scotch between us.

After a while, Sailor said: "This turned out bad hunh, Cash? All 'at runnin' around and all we got's that torn hunk of dough. It's all over now, ain't it, Cash?"

"We'll land the rest of Grover Cleveland," I promised him. Then muttered: "Poetry with his thumb on the hammer—that's for the book!"

"Punchy. Hunh, Cash?"

"If he wore a chin, I'd have taken him," I went on. "He's figured it all out and it'll wind up like something out of Shakespeare, mark my words. None but the lonely heart and such." I spilled half a tumbler of Scotch into my throat and slammed the glass down hard. I was thinking of Felix's crack: *There will be no beneficiary....*

I growled: "Why'd they let a rabbit like that loose!"

"Punchy as a bag," nodded Sailor.

After a while the office phone rang and I went out to answer it—

"Cash Wale? This is Barbara Joyce. I called to explain—"

"You did, kid—"

"O.K., Napoleon, don't freeze up on me. We all make mistakes. Can't you let your hair down? What there is of it," she giggled.

"So?"

"Nothing. I merely thought we could compare notes. I like smart boys, Cash. You're smart. Even that hard case cop had respect for you. But you shouldn't have run out on poor little me."

"Poor little me!" I mimicked. "In the pig's rump!"

Her giggle was real this time. "Cash, sweet, won't you play on my side? I can make it worth your while, I really can—"

"And freeze Homer?"

"You can't freeze an empty bag. He's with his lawyer now,"—that giggle again—"he can't take it in the clinches, he's practically laying eggs. Come over, sweet, we'll really make something out of this."

"You in the Bronx?"

Her voice careened to high C. "Will you come, darling?"

"Just control yourself till I get there," I growled, and then I broke the connection abruptly.

Sailor was gazing moodily at the bottom of his glass as I came in. "I figgered it, Cash," he said. "The punk's punchy, 'at's what!"

"Put on your shoes," I said. "We're going out."

"Where?"

"We're going to play house with your hipper-dipper."

"I'd *like* that, Cash!"

I removed two slugs from my revolver and worked over them with a knife before returning them to the cylinder. "We're also going to be measured for oaken kimonos," I added. Sailor winked, contradicted: "Naw! Not with you around, they ain't nobody measurin' us fer nuttin', Cash! I seen you wid a heater plenty, don't forget!"

"Wait'll you see Skull," I muttered, re-holstering my rod.

SNOW NO longer came down but the gale was back, with a knife edge and howling like a sick banshee. The snow, packed hard underfoot, sparkled from street lamps and crawling headlights. It was almost midnight—we'd been a long time over the two fifths of Scotch, Sailor and I.

But that trembling in my gut was still there as we rode the subway to the Bronx and it kept me sober. I didn't like what was in the cards, nor the fact that I hadn't warned Felix off the Joyce tramp.

But the cards were falling like this: That chair up the river was still wired for the kid, nothing could alter that, not after he burned down a guard and I was under no delusions on that score. The escape plan had been Vossov's, and the riot which helped it, but it had been Stanley Burns, alias Felix Chase, who killed one and winged two screws.

Probably quoting poetry as he did it!

So this was the best way, all things considered, Grover Cleveland in particular. Only I felt like a double-barreled heel.

We made the walk from the Yankee Stadium to Homer's beddery in silence. The doorman wasn't visible, probably sneaking a bracer against the cold. Up the street, the night's silence was jarred by a guy kicking the starter of a motorcycle.

"No muffler on that, Cash!" Sailor yelled in my ear. "That monkey's due for a ticket!"

I thumbed Winslow's bell in the foyer and the Joyce tramp's husky accents issued from the speaking tube. "Who is it?"

"Napoleon, kid. You provided up there, or should I collect a couple of pints first?"

"Enough provisions here to keep you under for a week, sweet."

"O.K., kid."

A buzzer ticked us through the door into the gilt and chrome lobby. I told Sailor: "Stick here about ten minutes, dope. If that guy on the noisy bike outside happens to follow us in, stop him."

"O.K., Cash. Only I'd like to meet that Barbara lush once more, hunh?"

"You will," I promised. And added: "In ten minutes come up. Apartment 7D. Don't finger the bell, just walk in. The door'll be open. Got that?"

Sailor nodded and settled himself in a purple plush chair facing the lobby door. I rode a self-service elevator up seven flights, then unfastened the collar of my trenchcoat and made sure no flaps stood between my fingers and the butt of my Colt .32. I removed the glove from my right hand.

Then I fingered the bell with my left.

From the street burst the faulty exhaust of that unmuffled bike, but I didn't hear the bell inside. They came soundproof, these apartments. I waited patiently for the door to open.

It didn't. Just that clatter outside and me waiting in the hall.

Instead of ringing again, I felt the knob, turned it, pushed gently. The door was already open.

That was lovely. If it wasn't for the other half of Grover Cleveland, I would have turned away from there, collected Sailor and marked the whole filthy deal down to profit and loss.

But Cleveland called.

I went through that door.

Not as one usually goes through doors. I hit this with my shoulder on about the level of my knees, went diving into a pitch-black foyer—inside, a radio was giving out swing at full volume. The racket, blending with that exhaust outside almost drowned out the sound of the shot.

But the flash was there, a tongue of flame licked over me from the other side of the foyer—licking over where I *should* have been, I mean!

My foot hooked on the door, slammed it shut. I pegged two quick shots into the darkness, blinked to the sting of cordite fumes, then scrambled to the side wall.

A second tongue of flame pointed like an index finger to where I'd lain—not over this time—and I heard the slug tear into wood, followed by a terrific muzzle-blast. The radio switched off.

Then silence.

CHAPTER FIVE
NOBODY LAUGHED

WITH THE door shut, not even the motorcycle exhaust outside was audible. I held my breath, waited—

Until a *click* showered the foyer with light and I was staring at Felix Chase standing at the foyer's end and Homer Winslow's pinched face peering at me from behind the wall.

Felix now lacked a nose as well as a chin. Instead, there was a hole, strangely blackish against the pallor of his cheeks. His eyes were shut. I wondered vaguely what held him erect.

Homer's jaw hung slack. From the ends of his fingers dangled a very large black revolver, the .45 I'd last seen with Felix. Homer was trying to speak but only a hissing sound came from his lips.

"Drop it," I said. He did.

I scrambled off the floor, keeping my revolver in line with Homer's pot, and lifted the .45 from the floor, smelled the muzzle, sneezed from the acrid stink of gas.

This brought me into the living-room where Barbara Joyce, once again highlighting her landscape, goggled at me. The landscape was pressed against the mahogany panel of a radio, her fingers were still on the switch.

"Surprise, surprise," I said drily.

A chair held Felix up, a chair from the kitchen tilted into the small of his back.

"I—uh—took the—gun from him when you—arrr—shot him, Wale," stammered Homer Winslow.

"Sure," I said and looked at the Joyce tramp. "I came like the marines, hey?"

She said, very slowly: "I knew nothing about this when I phoned you, Wale. Right after you spoke to me, they came in, Stanley holding the gun on Hom— Mr. Winslow. He was desperate because"—green satin shoulders shrugged delicately—"he'd wanted to play with me in the old days. He was queer, Wale. I couldn't. He must have let it work on him in prison—"

"A psychopathic case, Wale," put in Homer eagerly. "Not evident—ah—ordinarily, Wale. No institution would commit him but—heh—I knew about it, Barb—uh—Miss Joyce knew all about it too."

"Shut up, Homer," I said quietly, "you make me nervous."

He said: "—ulp!"

The slug which did for Felix had blasted his entire nose away, passed through the back of his neck. I retched. Not at the weird effect no nose had given the chinless face. I'd seen worse. But at the memory of his crack: *"I will not live long. But thank you—"*

I didn't look around for the slug. I told Winslow: "You'd better phone the cops. But first, I want the rest of Grover Cleveland."

"Er—yes, certainly—uh—*who?*"

"The other half of that bill, Homer," spoke Barbara Joyce quietly. "Give it to him."

He fumbled the green strip a full minute before getting it from his wallet, his face a pale shade of green. It was like giving me his right hand. But then he glanced owlishly at Felix, still propped against the chair, and actually licked his lips!

"We should—er—move him?" he asked.

"The cops'll do that. You'll tell 'em what you told me? And that I came in the door and he shot at me and I plugged him dead?"

Barbara swept across the room and snake-hipped between me and the door, her breasts heaving.

"Why do you say it like that?" she whispered, facing me.

The muzzle of my Colt .32 touched her where she bulged the most, sent her leaping to one side.

"I don't have to answer that," I said grimly. "I'm finished here. I'm paid off."

I started for the door.

And stopped as it slammed open with Sailor Duffy, his features twisted into an agonized knot, stepping through and the bright voice of Bones chirping from behind him.

"You ain't paid off yet, Wale. Not by a long shot you ain't paid off!"

From under Sailor's arm poked Skull's little black automatic. Sailor's eyes were pleading with me.

"I waited for that bike guy like you said, Cash. An' when he walks in, I see it's one o' the lugs who jumped us this mornin'. So I'm reachin' for him when they show, Cash. An' they're heeled. You allus told me my dukes ain't beans against rods, Cash."

"You did your best," I told him, watching Big Bill Vossov appear beside Sailor. The fat, lead-eyed former big shot took in the set-up, called over his shoulder: "It's all in hand. Shut the door, Chink." Vossov pursed thick lips at Felix who was propped inches from those lips.

"You shouldn't a tried crossin' me, Cash," spoke Vossov. "A good thing I picked a smart boy like Skull. He tailed you all day, he tells me. He was stashed outside when I come along to give this Winslow jeep a talk. Skull tells me you're ahead of me, Cash. You with Winslow means a cross."

A stubby gloved finger indicated Felix. "Now that ain't gonna do me no good, Cash. The letter ain't gonna be in the mails for a good day yet. Now I gotta play it rough. With long hairs in city hall, it's gonna come risks, Cash."

I shrugged and Skull prodded Sailor into the room. They had to squeeze past Felix. Vossov came next. Then the other pale-faced beetle-brow of the morning's brush-off. Risko, I guessed, was still at Gilley's nursing his leg.

I noticed Homer Winslow's horn-rims aimed at Skull whose eyes were riveted to me. Barbara Joyce was on a rust-colored lounge gnawing one crimson fingernail, very unladylike.

I could almost hear the wheels in their heads turning.

THE COLT .32 was still in my right hand, pointing at the rug, in spite of Skull's heater. The black .45 was hanging by the trigger-guard on the index finger of my left hand, top-side down.

I cleared my throat and told Vossov: "If you had the brains of a peanut, you'd see the show's over where you're concerned. You and these stir-birds can't afford to mix in a kill, not just out of stir you can't. I told you this morning I'm legit. I'll tell you something else now that Felix's burned and it doesn't matter any more. You—"

Skull appeared from behind Sailor, the tiny automatic centered unwaveringly on my nose. An unpleasant sensation, that.

"Naw, Cash! I got it all figgered!" he chirped brightly. "Bill, how's this? As it stands, Winslow collects, hunh? Suppose we rig the stiff for the cops to find, mebbe a couple of months from now when they can't say he croaked today or two days from now—"

"Shut up," said Big Bill Vossov automatically. "That stinks."

"I ain't finished," objected Skull. "It's air-tight because it's got a check. Wale an' his palooka gotta be rubbed because they'll hold us up if they're not, mebbe even spill. Wale ain't playin' ball because he's gone legit like he says.

"So mebbe in the end Winslow gets the dough anyhow. So we cut ourselves in by framin' him for the kill of Wale an' the palooka! We make him cut up the stiffs and stash the pieces in one of his own trunks with his prints all over it. Then we bury the trunk someplace. Anytime he thinks of yappin', all we need's to tip off the cops about the trunk an' he's cooked—so he'll play. Neat, hunh?

"All I gotta do is rub 'em here an' now! Look, Wale's gotta rod in each hand, but they ain't pointed right. Me, I got—"

Homer Winslow croaked like a sick bullfrog: "My God! You can't—*agh!*" He lapsed into a fit of coughing.

Skull's eyes deflected an instant. Not enough for me to chance a shot, but enough for words to come.

I snapped: "He can because your offer to split your take on the insurance with Skull isn't enough! He wants all the candy, that guy!"

Something moved in the side pocket of Big Bill Vossov's gray overcoat.

"What offer?" he rumbled.

I whirled on him, letting my Colt sag even lower. A tension easer that—to give Skull the idea he could cover Vossov's pocket as well as my hands.

"You damn fool!" I rapped at Big Bill. "You're a wash-out and you don't know it! Where in hell'd you get the idea a gang of wisies like Skull, Risko and Chink would back your play just on your old rep, hah? They played you for laughs until this Felix gag came to light, then it was strictly business—*ask Homer what offer!*"

Homer's green complexion was answer enough!

It became deathly still. You couldn't hear them, but the wheels within wheels were going round and round, enough crosses to give even Adolph Hitler a happy hour.

Skull's eyes jerked back to me as he realized his mistake in letting me talk. But it was too late to get Vossov's guard down now, the fat ex-big shot was about to explode, I could *feel* it!

Dimly, I was conscious of Chink's hand moving behind Vossov and Sailor Duffy turning slowly towards Skull and Homer Winslow standing rooted, like a gnarled petrified tree. He couldn't answer to his own name at that moment, Homer!

We were a roomful of smoothies waiting for an accident to happen—except Felix. He'd had his.

Then Skull whispered, without removing his eyes from me: "O.K., Bill, that's it. But we can return to the old line. It'll still work—"

"Cross *me!*" screamed Big Bill Vossov, his ego aflame. "*Me,* you penny-ante crook! Chink, burn him! *Burn Skull!*"

There was a movement behind Vossov and Chink spoke. "Like this, big pants?"

And poured a slug flush into Vossov's side!

BARBARA JOYCE screamed as if her lungs were tearing apart. Vaguely, I was aware of Sailor Duffy lunging at Skull and Skull's bead on my head not wavering an inch as he side-stepped neatly and Sailor plunged sickeningly into the wall.

Vaguely, because at the explosion of Chink's rod, I was twisting to the floor, my Colt jerking a little in my right hand.

Skull wore a tight smile on his gaunt face. A crazy gesture, I couldn't jerk that muzzle up faster than he could press that trigger in a month of Sundays. His eyes fixed brightly on my rising Colt.

He laughed a little as his automatic winked flame—and the laughter terminated in a painful grunt that jack-knifed him to the rug, his slug tearing wildly to his right.

My left wrist seemed cracked from the recoil of the big .45 I'd fired upside down with my thumb on the trigger, the gun Skull neglected while he watched my Colt. Over-powering fumes swept that room in waves.

"*Cash!*" bellowed Sailor from the wall.

But my Colt was already turning on Chink whose prison pallor had given way to an even whiter shade.

He fired at me—sure! Twice! He was no gunman, Chink, he saw the black curtains in my eyes. He was shooting from reflex—from *fear!*

The Joyce tramp's scream cracked into a hoarse gasp as my first slug took Chink in the throat and blood spouted a yard from his lips.

Big Bill Vossov was on the floor, struggling weakly to pull the rod out of his pocket. I pulled it for him, growled: "You know better, pal!"

He whispered: "Get me a doc, Cash—*please!*"

Big Bill learning manners!

Behind me came sounds of a scuffle. I whirled to see Sailor Duffy tear the little automatic off a spring that extended a good foot out of Skull's sleeve.

I went over to Homer Winslow prone on the rug, began feeling his pulse, then changed my mind. There's no heartbeat in a man with his forehead split by lead—one of Chink's wild shots!

Barbara Joyce wasn't screaming any more, just moaning faintly. I asked Sailor if he was hurt.

"Me, Cash? Naw! I landed on my head. 'At can't hurt!"

Skull's fists clenched at his belt. He stared at me. I couldn't help him, not with a belly wound. I said: "No hard feelings, pal—"

His cadaverous head shook slightly. "Even faster than—springs!" he whispered.

And died.

I couldn't blame the Joyce tramp's moans. She lay half on the rust-colored lounge, half off, her palms clapped to her face, her right leg at an odd angle.

There was a hole in her sheer silk stocking, right below the knee. I pulled the hands from her face—a slug had raised hell with the bridge of her nose. Not serious, but painful, and no help to her male-bait at all.

"They couldn't touch me when you was my gun," whispered Big Bill. He was struggling to his knees. He'd torn open his coat, jacket, vest. Two holes showed on his shirt front. Not serious either, a chest crease. He couldn't have hit himself with a surveyor lining his sights for him, Chink!

"I played it wrong from the start," whispered Vossov.

"You never had a chance," I told him. "Felix held the joker all the way and cashed it in the end."

Barbara Joyce suddenly began to laugh in loud jerks. She was pointing a bloodstained hand at Winslow on the floor.

"I came out on top!" she cackled. "Now it all comes to me, *me!* I get every last red cent!" Her eyes blazed in my direction. Over her mangled nose, the effect was weird. She cried: "Napoleon, ha! Everything that was Homer Winslow's becomes mine! *Mine,* you little runt, do you hear? I'm his common-law wife! I—"

"You're common, all right," I muttered, sickened, "but what you'll get, you've got—together with all those unpaid bills in the office. Not one cent of insurance. That policy on Felix is less than a year old—"

"But you shot him dead!" she screamed in triumph.

I said quietly: "The hell I did."

I SAID: "I fired two home-made blanks in the darkness. When you phoned me, I figured the set-up pretty close. Calling me up to play on a mattress with you was as phoney as a Hitler promise—after that little scene this afternoon.

"Felix was killed by the same rod he shot Mushky Matson with, after taking it from Mushky—this forty-five. The cops'll go through this dive and find the slug where it came out of his neck.

"How I figure it, you were the dame in the brawl that sent Felix to the deathhouse in the first place. The papers mentioned she was a nymphomaniac.

"It all came from Winslow's scrap business going bad after the embargo. He needed a stake until America began using scrap in the armaments drive. He was due for a contract. I saw that in the papers also. But he needed a stake until then.

"So he insured Felix who, being an impressionable and slightly queer squirt, happened to be sold on your bedside manner. You framed him into that roadhouse brawl. Nothing I can prove in court—it just fits. Let the kid burn and Winslow collects. And you, being Winslow's common wife, you'd collect.

"But then Vossov entered the picture. Felix was queer to start with, prison loosened a few more screws—and when Vossov propositioned him, he took Vossov up. What'd he have to lose?

"But Vossov couldn't figure to what extent Felix was still gone on you. Felix suspected nothing, being double-dyed green. He knew he couldn't go on living and he'd been fed too much Shakespeare. With no chin, that counted.

"He burned Matson and broke away with the screwy idea of earning your undying love by a supreme gesture. How'd he know you've a tin bank for a heart?

"I can prove he came up here tonight and used the only joker in this whole rotten deal. The policy is less than a year old and it features a suicide clause. He came here to die tragically at your feet and, at the same time, cross Vossov.

"Felix, himself, told me there'd be no beneficiary and, remembering that, when you called, I cut the lead from two slugs, just in case. The cops'll find nitre in the skin of his hand and powder grains in the pores around the wound. I know you washed it, but you can't wash dead skin *that* well.

"I'm willing to bet my shirt they'll peg Felix for a suicide and the policy will fall through!"

IT WAS no bet. The way her fists clenched and she allowed blood from her nose to trickle down her cheek showed me how right I was.

I licked my lips and went on: "So you and Winslow cooked up a phoney kill. Maybe Skull, also. Chink raising hell with that motorbike in the street to compete with gunfire was no coincidence.

"I was to enter, have a slug miss me—fired by Winslow hiding behind the wall. Then Felix, propped ahead of me, was to get my slug in his chest. Then I was to drop dead from a second slug. I was getting too close all around and everybody'd feel safer with me out.

"You'd tell the coppers I burned Felix just as he burned me and then you'd collect. Except the cops would have figured it was suicide anyhow."

The Joyce tramp's palms were covering her nose again. She was sobbing tears and blood into them, moaning: "What will become of me now? What—"

I could have told her that she would never walk again without a limp, that her face couldn't be repaired without the kind of dough that a chipped-nosed floozie like her would never get, that she was due for street work.

It was justice come home with a vengeance! Vossov would go through life the bum that he always was at heart. Only Sailor and I came out with anything—Grover Cleveland!

I wondered what Felix would have said to that.

Vossov whispered: "Cash, we can still work it. The letter's still good. Go ahead like Skull said—we'd split three ways. Duffy won't talk, the dame'll take a split, and there's nobody else. What do you say?"

Barbara Joyce looked up eagerly.

I went to the phone and lifted the receiver. I said: "Operator, I want a policeman." When I'd given the address and hung up, I noticed my hand trembled a little. I said: "That's a laugh. Me, Cash Wale, the gun-crazy shamus, calling copper! Isn't that a laugh?"

But nobody laughed.

THE BULLET FROM NOWHERE

PINT-SIZED CASH WALE,
TOUGHEST PRIVATE PEEP ON THE
MAIN STEM, PROVES HE CAN BE
A SOFTIE TOO WHEN HE HOPS
A MERRY-GO-ROUND TO GET
WHIRLED BACK EIGHTEEN YEARS
INTO THE CASE OF THE CRIB-
SWITCHED BABES, THEN BACK
AGAIN TO CLOSE A $20,000,000
LOVE MERGER THAT LEAVES ONLY
A LOUSY TWO GRAND STICKING
TO HIS OWN DIGITS.

CHAPTER ONE
MURDER IN THE MIRROR

PHILLIP, **SINGING** waiter of Dorgan's Dump, was serving drinks off his tray to the Murray party at ringside. His little finger held a folded note to the bottom of the cocktail glass he set before Ruth St. John. But her attention was away, her ivory-doll face turned expectantly toward the entrance, and she lifted her drink without seeing the note.

Phillip served Gilbert T. Murray, the tall, tanned blond whose legal designs on the girl were blue book chatter. But Murray was gazing with an expression of disgust at nothing and also missed seeing the note.

Phillip set the third and last drink before Egbert St. John, pimply-panned young cousin to Ruth. A character around the Stem, Egbert, with constant hunger for a loose buck or broad, and a pair of long, tapering hands.

One of these slid over the note.

I watched this tableau through the mirror slanted over Dorgan's bar. In fact, I watched the Murray party in the line of business. Their table was at ringside, jammed amid other tables packed with blue-bleeders, and visible through a sort of murky haze due to indistinct lighting—but the action had been clear.

His chin jerked east and west as
my gun-muzzle connected twice.

In the mirror, I watched Phillip make his way back, pass behind me on his way to the kitchen which was to my left—but my eyes stopped at Vivian Day before he got there. I had not noticed her climb the stool at my elbow. Our eyes met in the mirror.

"That's none of yours," throbbed her voice in that husky manner that packed Dorgan's Dump nightly.

"Yours?" I said.

"I didn't say that," she said.

"Which makes it old home week," I said.

She kicked my shin.

"That Murray crowd's nice people, Cash Wale, and you're a heel. Don't mix with our customers."

I stared without expression at Harry Dorgan across the bar until his eyes dropped.

"Don't let it throw you," I told Vivian.

THROUGH THE mirror I watched her nose wrinkle in distaste. The rest of her helped that deep-river voice keep Dorgan's at capacity. It was not a matter of bumps. She had them, and in formation. It was her face that registered.

It wore clean brown eyes flecked with gold. The same brown and gold swam through her hair. Her complexion made society dolls bite their lips and streak for the lounge to manufacture competition. This, despite her close-to-forty age and a clip-house pedigree from when. But now her expression was taut from worry.

She said: "You couldn't throw me, heel. You couldn't play any tune that hasn't already worn a groove in my piano. So that makes two of us—"

Harry Dorgan leaned over and touched the stem of her glass which showed evidence of use. *"Vivian—"* he said. She clung to the glass.

"I know what I'm doing, Harry. Cash and I speak the same slum, is all. I'm doing fine, Harry—"

Dorgan shrugged and dropped his eyes from mine again. Most citizens around the shady fringe of Broadway dropped their eyes from mine. The bulge under the left side of my jacket did that—and its history.

A beefy, darkish, always scowling character, this Harry Dorgan. The Dump was his without strings, but he chose to work the bar and leave ceremony to the hirelings.

Dorgan moved down the bar as the mirror showed me Phillip emerge from the kitchen with a tray of free lunch and bring it between Vivian and me with a wise grin.

"It's for free, sports!"

"I hear someone polished your corners, Phillip," I said, without turning.

His face couldn't turn paler than normal. It was a long, rubbery face with a coal-black mop topping it off, and wide blue eyes that gave him a baby's expression, and a loose mouth which earned him side jobs at mimicry and off-shade crooning. The twitch of his lip corners betrayed him now.

"Those things happen, sport," he said.

"I'd like to know," I said. "Maybe I'll even buy to know."

Phillip shook his black mop and moved off. That was something, I thought. He generally broke his arm reaching for odd change. He was, aside from waiting and entertaining, a one-man supply depot for cops, columnists and anyone who wanted to know enough to pay.

I watched him leave through the mirror until Vivian pushed her empty glass at Dorgan and said: "You only see things in reverse through the glass, heel. A corner table has the same view, and it's a straight one."

"Easier to move from a stool than a table," I said.

"They'll get you anyhow," said Vivian.

I said: "That's right. What do you want, Vivian?"

Vivian frowned at Dorgan who was clearing his throat to butt in.

"I said we talked the same slum," she told him. "Cash knows I'm angling."

"Walk down the bar, Dorgan," I said. And, to Vivian: "I'm listening—"

She turned from Dorgan's retreating back to scowl at me. Something afire between those two from way back, but that was none of mine. Vivian opened her mouth to speak, then closed it as her eyes widened at the mirror.

It was Barney Kane. A fleshy character in tails with a chin dimpled in half and the idea that dolls were manufactured for Barney Kane—which generally was the case. He stood before the check-room, surveying the Dump like some conquering hero.

The man with him surveyed the floor. This character wore an oversized red schnozz in the middle of his face. Dirty red stubble covered the rest of it. His pants bagged, his jacket was three sizes too large and patched. He surveyed the floor because his face was halfway to it. Kane supported him by one arm, holding him like a rag doll.

"He's doing it again!" whispered Vivian Day.

"Sure," I said. "Like that guy O. Henry wrote about, Kane brings in a bum off the street every night. It's a build-up for chatter columns."

Vivian's eyes crinkled when Barney Kane waved and she turned to wave back.

"You in his parade?" I asked.

"Barney's all right," murmured Vivian without conviction. "But why—"

"I told you. He's hipped on O. Henry."

"Not about this mooch, heel. It's the third night in a row for this tramp. *Why?*"

I DIDN'T reply because Kane and his derelict were passing the Murray table and a second tableau showed in reverse through the mirror. Ruth St. John's small, exact, ivory face had been on Barney Kane from the moment he appeared. Before that, it had been on the entrance.

And two deuces still made four in my book.

Now, as he supported the tramp past her table with his right hand, he leaned over, whispered in Ruth St. John's ear and patted her bare shoulder with his pudgy left.

Vivian at my side gasped, "*Oh!*"

Gilbert T. Murray whipped half out of his seat—dropped back at a gestured command from his white-faced fiancée. I caught the expression on Egbert St. John, an unholy satisfaction that showed in every line of his pimpled face—and I thought of the note.

Then Barney Kane was being bowed by Phillip into a seat at a corner table. His derelict slumped into another and conversation, which had died at Kane's appearance, picked up to normal again.

Vivian was struggling to compose her face in the mirror.

"Green-eyed?" I grinned at her.

"She's engaged to Murray!" snapped Vivian.

"I'm not referring to Kane," I said. "Murray used to play in your garden—"

Her shoe nicked my shin again.

"Lay off, heel. This is business."

"What's business?"

"Working for me."

"I'm expensive, kid—"

Vivian fingered my arm. There was pain added to the worry in her expression.

"This is serious, heel. I'm willing to pay you one hundred dollars to investigate something for me. That's not high, as your rates go, but it's not peanuts—and it's for me, heel."

"I'm listening," I said.

Vivian's bosom was rising and falling rapidly. Dorgan was close again, glaring down at the peel he was draping around a Horse's Neck.

"I want you to find out why Barney Kane brought that mooch here for the third time," said Vivian breathlessly. "I want you to find out what hold Barney has on Ruth St. John—and why her wedding to Murray has been delayed. And for learning these, heel, I will give you one hundred—"

"No," I said.

Vivian's face was suddenly all lines and anguish.

"But why, heel? *Why?*"

"I'm on a case now."

"I'm not asking you to drop that. Just to learn these—"

"One case is enough," I said.

Vivian Day's teeth bared at me. "I've heard of you handling two—"

"Two cases? Yes," I said. "But not opposite sides of the same case."

The Horse's Neck dropped from Harry Dorgan's fingers and smashed on the floor. Vivian Day's eyes were luminous on mine.

"*I'll—kill—you—heel!*" she breathed.

"It's been tried," I said. "That's why I'm sitting at the bar in front of a mirror instead of at a table. It's been tried and I'm still pitching shutouts. You skip all this. It's over your head anyhow.

"And stop following Ruth St. John around the streets. She didn't know who you were and it made her jittery as hell. Good-bye for now, Vivian Day," I said and slid off the stool, leaving her to stare at Harry Dorgan who stared back at her in a manner that made me dwell on the bulge under my jacket.

THE HAT-CHECK girl, a pert little blonde in a red turtle-neck sweater—"atmosphere" in the Dump—pushed the front of her sweater expectantly my way as I came up. But I passed her, looked in the first of three phone booths that lined the wall alongside the check-room, read the number and entered the third booth.

I dialed the number of the first. Phillip, passing with his tray, answered it.

"Gilbert Murray there?" I asked through my handkerchief. "Tell him it's Frank."

"O.K., sport!" came through the receiver. I watched Phillip zig-zag to the Murray table and lean over. There was some talk, then Murray rose and came my way. It had taken a dozen generations of moneyed swank to produce him, and every line of Murray's clothes, easy bearing and face showed it. His face, in particular—tanned, lean-jawed, wide gray eyes and a blond wave that had dented many a chorus line until the St. John doll got under his skin and he returned to his ship-building family fold.

He didn't look into my booth, but went into the first.

"Wale," I said, without benefit of handkerchief.

"Did you learn why she is following Ruth?" came his cultured tones.

"It's got to do with Barney Kane and that stiff Barney dragged in tonight."

Murray uttered a word they'd have booted him out of the social register for. Then: "Listen, Wale, is that all you have learned?"

"It's a start—"

"That will hardly do, Wale. I employed you to discover why Ruth changed her mind about marrying me. But remember, according to our little agreement, you either produce results before tomorrow morning—before Ruth announces our broken engagement to the press—or you will not be—"

"The payoff is my headache," I said.

"Listen, Wale. I know Kane has something to do with it. She doesn't love that tinhorn—she loves me. She told me that, when our engagement was broken. It smacked of muck, which was why I hired you. You have the reputation of—"

"You hired me. That's enough!" I clipped.

"Wale, if you are attempting one of your reputed deals—if you are in league with the person influencing Ruth—or if you are holding out for more money—I will—"

"I'm one-priced. Don't threaten me, and hang up."

There was a pause during which I saw Egbert bow away from Ruth St. John and head for the lounge. Then: "Hold on a minute, Wale, I forgot to tell you something. Ruth's cousin, Egbert, has been acting very—"

"I know that," I said. "Good-bye for now." I broke the connection and watched Gilbert T. Murray stalk past my booth without a glance. His ancestors and my rep saw to that.

Blue-bleeding citizens hesitated about knowing me in public because recent history—pre-repeal history—had me peddling my gun to a parade of mobsters who are now mainly dead or in Alcatraz.

Now I was legitimate, I was the Cash Wale Investigation Service—in demand when impolite shenanigans were in order. Which meant my gun was still for hire. Also my savvy of the ins and outs of this and that. But all in a nice legal, cash-on-the-line way.

Gilbert T. Murray depended on me to smear any scandal keeping him from his intended. He'd reached me via another blue-bleeder who had sampled my services, and found it good. Murray's price was good, but he would rather have lost his right hand than been seen with it in mine.

Which was his loss, I figured.

PHILLIP WAS carrying by a new trayful of free lunch as I emerged from the booth. I stopped him.

"You passed a note to the St. John doll before. From who and what?"

Phillip held the tray as if offering me a sandwich.

"Two," he said.

"One," I said.

He nodded and I passed a dollar bill under the napkin which draped over his tray. That was Phillip's bank. His rubbery face leaned close.

"Barney Kane gave it, sport. At the door, outside. I didn't look. O.K.?" he said quietly.

"You slipped her the note before Kane arrived."

"He was outside waitin' to pick up the stiff. O.K.?"

"How about that stiff?" I said. "You ever feed him in back?"

Phillip nodded.

"I never turn no one away, sport. This one was out back about three days ago. O.K.?"

"O.K.," I said, letting Phillip move on with my dollar. I walked through the kitchen into the alley that ran alongside Dorgan's Dump. A crap game was going on in the light from the open doorway. High blank walls and an iron grille-work fence out of sight around a bend in the alley hemmed it in.

It was one of those early spring nights with balmy currents thawing out the air.

Sailor Duffy held the dice. His battered, naked head glistened with moisture. Before him lay five dimes which the others covered without comment. Although among themselves, they bet a ten buck minimum. Some of them spotted me, nodded.

Sailor crapped out with a grunt from his heart. He saw me, pleaded: "Lemme have a tenner, Cash. Hagh?"

"You broke?"

"I on'y got a buck, sixty-five. Cash. How'm I gonna roll a streak wit' a buck, sixty-five, hagh?"

"You figure that out," I said and started back inside.

Someone snickered and someone else shushed him with a whispered: *"That's Wale, you dope!"*

I liked it—sure, I liked it! That was the lifeblood of my grift. That guy's whisper floated on my reputation—which was nine-tenths hot air. But the other tenth kept it alive and I knew that whisper in a high-flying bone game was better than a full page ad in the *Times.*

Sailor Duffy was the muscle in my grift. They let him play dimes alongside of their real stakes on my rep. Not that Sailor couldn't have as much dough as they flashed—and more—if he needed it. We shared even. Only Sailor had "spells." He listened to noises that weren't there.

It had been like that since he dropped a fifteen round slug-fest to the heavyweight champ of the world. When I picked him up, it was on a Hoover breadline and since then it had been the two of us, up or down—and don't crack!

Back in the Dump, I made my way to Barney Kane's table. The stiff was half on and half off the table. Barney Kane's usual grin became cautious.

"H'lo, Wale. Drink rye?"

234 THE COMPLETE CASES OF CASH WALE

There was a chair and a fifth of Seagram's with glasses but I ignored both.

"Want you to do something for me, Kane," I said.

His caution gave way to a cold mask that froze the meat on his face white. He carried a bulge under his arm also, Barney Kane.

"That's out, Wale," he said.

"I haven't told it yet," I said. "I want you to lay off Ruth St. John. No notes, phone calls, or words—in public or private."

BARNEY KANE'S breath sucked in as he scrambled to his feet. The table wabbled, making the red-stubbled tramp sit up and glare at me from swollen eyes. Conversation around us stopped in mid-air.

Barney Kane's chubby fingers fluttered between suicide and wisdom—

Then Harry Dorgan pushed his scowling hulk between us—I still can't figure how he made it from the bar that fast. He was facing Kane. He said: "Telephone for you, Barney. Important—"

Barney Kane's breath wheezed again and he blinked rapidly, backing off. "I'm gonna call you on that, Wale!" he shouted.

"The booth nearest the check-room," said Harry Dorgan. He pushed Barney Kane away with one hand, gripped my arm with the other. I shrugged it off. "You'll take a drink now, Wale," Dorgan mumbled. His eyes were unfriendly.

I led the way back to the bar between rows of silent, upturned faces. Ruth St. John's expression as I passed marked me three times lower than bottom. Gilbert T. Murray avoided my eyes and cousin Egbert leered. Kane was entering the booth as I occupied the stool next to

Vivian Day. She kicked me, began to speak, but Dorgan whispered to her: "Start Phillip's act."

"He's busy now, Harry."

"Then go on yourself."

She called me the same thing Murray had mentioned on the phone and made for the platform.

I watched her through the mirror until her song was launched in that low, throbbing voice—a song about what bedsheets could tell. But somehow it left her clean. I looked around.

They were arguing at the Murray table in whispers. Kane's tramp was gulping rye out of the bottle. Phillip moved smoothly around with his tray. Kane, in the booth, was motionless, not talking. Suddenly he flung open the door, yelled over Vivian's song: "Hey, Dorgan, this lines dead!"

"Long-distance," replied Dorgan in a hoarse whisper. Kane slammed the door and shook a chubby finger at me through the glass.

Dorgan scowled at his hands and said: "Why don't you get out of here now, Wale?"

I said: "Ask Kane. I fight for what I get. He's a tout, and a pimp. Ask him, Dorgan, and don't ever crack like that to me again!"

"Whenever you show, it's a headache," muttered Dorgan, edging down the bar.

Through the mirror, I watched Ruth St. John shake her head angrily at Gilbert T. Murray, then rise and make for the entrance. She passed the check-room and stopped, facing Kane in his booth. He didn't see her. His attention was on the phone. I could see he was listening, not talking.

Ruth St. John stamped a foot impatiently, turned to look at her table where cousin Egbert was having words with Murray. She turned back and rapped on the door of Barney Kane's booth.

Then she screamed!

Vivian's song faltered on a high note, leaving dead silence. I streaked to the booth, Harry Dorgan at my heels—he'd vaulted the bar. Ruth St. John lay crumpled on the floor. The hat-check girl was stooping over her.

I didn't open the booth. I didn't have to. Dorgan tried, and I knocked his hand away.

"Get the law," I said. "Block the exits and get the law."

"You outa your head?" he growled. "A dame faints an—" He reached for the booth's door again, but stopped as the muzzle of my automatic sank deep into his chest.

Vivian Day, just coming up, yelped.

"Get the law!" I rapped at Dorgan. "Someone shot Kane's Adam's apple away! The guy's dead! It's murder—"

Vivian Day joined Ruth St. John on the floor.

CHAPTER TWO

THE QUICK KILLER

I T TOOK half an hour for me to get out of there. Inspector Jack Quinn, of Homicide, saw to that. It was one of those anybody-could-have-done-it and it-ain't-possible kills. Quinn took it out on me. That was one of his favorite pastimes. The other two consisted of wagging his shaggy eyebrows and growing livid as a red-hot coal. All three were in operation as his stooges—print men, photogs, questioning dicks and the like—built up a picture of the case.

And now Quinn's finger jabbed my chest as if the secret somehow lay buried there.

"You was lookin' in the mirror and you saw Kane shut the door," Quinn said, jabbing. "He waved at you after closing the door and you saw nobody around his booth from then until the frill screamed."

"That's right."

Quinn's eyes became flinty.

"Kane's got a thirty-two slug in his neck which he didn't put there himself because his own rod's unfired—" Quinn jabbed.

"You asking or telling?" I said.

Quinn ignored that, continued: "There's no bullet hole in the booth and no gimmick in the phone or anything like that. Nobody heard a shot. Although he was in view of forty, fifty people, nobody was near him at the time. He couldn't have walked in there shot because that slug killed him immediate—" Quinn jabbed.

"So what does that make me?" I said.

"Nobody called him long-distance," Quinn continued, "but there was a call. It came from the next booth. The killer put through the call from one booth to the next. Dorgan heard a woman's voice and clicks like it was long-distance—" Quinn jabbed.

"That makes me what?" I repeated.

"A damn liar!" snarled Quinn, jabbing. "*Someone* opened that door, shot Kane with a silenced automatic and walked on. Maybe that goon stooge of yours, Duffy, maybe a hired punk, maybe someone not connected with you. But, whichever it was, you had strong words with Kane just before he went to the booth. You've been chiselin' in each other's grifts from way back. And, whichever it was, you saw the killer in that mirror!"

"I wasn't watching Kane all the time," I said quietly. "Sailor was out back and you know I don't hire gunsels. Furthermore," I said, "touch me again and, so help me, I'll clip you!"

He didn't and I didn't.

There was a moment in which Quinn's eyebrows debated about me—he topped me by six inches and maybe fifty pounds—but then he turned away without another word and started on the hat-check girl, the blond dish in the turtle-neck sweater whose name, it developed, was Sadie.

This was in one of the Dump's upstairs rooms. Dorgan, the Murray party, Kane's tramp and a few others were assembled.

The room dated from the time Dorgan's Dump was strictly clip, before Vivian's smile and songs attracted customers who could afford to be robbed honest. It was a "creep" room—that is, a room with a hidden closet from which a dip could emerge at the right moment and empty the wallet from trousers belonging to a gent otherwise occupied.

I went downstairs without interference. Kane's body had long since been removed. Drinks were on the house to hold the crowd—most of which "held"—listening to Phillip's impersonation of Laughton impersonating Mickey Rooney. The crowd ate it up.

Vivian stared moodily at me from the mirror as I entered the kitchen and found Sailor Duffy watching a pearl diver set cans of garbage into the alley.

"What happened to the game?" I asked.

Sailor shrugged. "I'm down to fifty cents, Cash. That ain't right, Cash. Suppose I wanna drink an' play also, hagh?"

I gave him a five dollar bill.

"Drink cokes," I said. "Stick around. I'll be back later."

He brightened at the bill, frowned at my words.

"*Cokes*, Cash?"

"Anything else and I'll slug you!"

"O.K., Cash, O.K.! I just asked—"

The pearl diver, a little Filipino, grinned. Sailor packed two hundred odd pounds in six feet three. I managed a hundred and forty in five feet two. People generally laughed when I ordered the big palooka around. Sailor wiped the grin off the Filipino's face with a backhand slap.

The check-room was deserted. I crawled the counter for my fedora and top-coat. Phillip's tray of free lunch, minus the overhanging napkin, was on the counter. I helped myself to a tuna, left two quarters—one on the tray, the other on the counter—and went out.

Vivian's voice followed me—something about what happened when papa turned off the light. It still left her clean.

THE DUMP was off Eighth Avenue in the Fifties. From outside, it resembled a huge tilted garbage pail through which citizens entered. The doorman, Andy, was rigged in patches and beard.

"H'lo, Cash," he mumbled. "Hot stuff inside, huh?"

I looked at the prowl buggies angled to the curb and nodded. "You here when Kane walked in, Andy?"

"Sure. Wasn't he with me ten minutes waitin' for that stiff to show?"

"It was a date?"

"Looked like."

"They say inside he gave you a note to deliver."

Andy bristled.

"Not me, Cash. I ain't seen no note. Mebbe Phillip, that guy. He talked with Phillip. Right there—" Andy pointed.

"Then I heard it wrong," I said indifferently.

We both turned as the Murray party emerged. Ruth St. John's ivory face was nose-deep in the ermine collar of her evening jacket. Murray's gray eyes passed over me without a flicker. Egbert eyed me, frankly curious.

Andy whistled through two fingers and a chauffeured Packard drew up outside the prowl buggies. Egbert St. John patted Murray's back as the latter helped Ruth inside.

"See you tomorrow, Gil?" spoke Egbert.

Murray nodded, entered, and the limousine purred into the night. Egbert hesitated a few moments, then began walking toward Ninth Avenue.

"Be seeing you, Andy," I told the doorman, and moved off on Egbert's tail. I wanted a look at that note. Quinn's interrogation had failed to arouse mention of it. It was just among Vivian, Egbert and myself—only Egbert thought it was exclusive.

He threw a few nervous glances over his shoulder, but I was across the street by then. Anyhow, it was black as pitch—one of those moonless, motionless nights.

We turned a block north on Ninth, then went left and continued toward Tenth, an even darker block of warehouses, closed machine shops and no traffic.

Egbert stepped into a parked cab.

It was so unexpected, I had gone on. But, when he didn't emerge past the cab, I withdrew into a shadow. The cab stood without lights. I could make out the driver's bulk in front. He sat motionless, made no effort to get the cab going.

About a minute passed like that, then I loosened my automatic in its holster and walked deliberately across the street toward the cab, my feet echoing hollowly on the pavement.

I came up from behind and peered inside—at Egbert's pimply face. The driver still didn't move. I opened the rear door, stared at Egbert a moment, then at the other rear door which hung open.

My automatic was out when I stepped through that door to the sidewalk. As far as I could see there was no activity, just night-blackened houses and silence.

Before me yawned the black maw of a yard. I found the wall, guided myself with my fingers edging into the blackness. The wall led me to a five-foot wooden fence which blocked the yard. Peering over it, I made out a flurry of motion as a shadow sped from the yard beyond the fence and swerved into the next street.

When I reached this street, more silence confronted me, more blackened house fronts and fathomless shadows. It would have taken a squad of men half an hour to probe them all. And I had no squad.

I returned to the parked cab.

The driver's hands were on the wheel although both legs were on the right side of the steering shaft. Someone had propped him up like that. Blackish lines ran down his cheek from under the cap. He was very still. Egbert must have entered the cab without noticing the driver's condition.

Egbert should have run like hell.

It was under Egbert's jaw—like the quick killer's signature—a small, blackish hole. Thirty-two, possibly. Egbert's head lay back, his eyes open, mouth wide. He was still warm, but dead. Egbert would never be deader.

My foot struck something as I moved about. I found it—a hollowed metal cylinder. I wrapped a handkerchief around it. It was also warm. I knew about that, also.

The cab's interior smelled from gas fumes—the smell was strongest inside the cylinder.

It was a silencer.

The killer had fired once, then removed it. He had to remove it. A silencer jams the mechanism of an automatic and you have to remove it, let the gases escape before screwing it back on for a second shot.

The killer must have been doing this when I crossed the street. In his haste, he dropped it. In his fear of facing a pitched gun fight, he left it.

I wondered about the quick killer as I emptied Egbert St. John's pockets into mine. Quinn said a woman lured Kane to the phone and the shadowy figure I saw could have been a woman. But no woman had stopped before Kane's booth while I watched in the mirror. Unless—it just struck me—unless it happened while Dorgan held my attention.

Before leaving, I felt the driver's pulse. There was no pulse, just a tire iron on the floorboard. I began to dislike the quick killer. He could have just sapped the driver—all he wanted was the cab. He didn't have to kill the driver.

I CARRIED a mug of beer to a small booth in a bar off Columbus Circle and went through what came from Egbert's pockets. The wallet held exactly one dollar bill aside from cards to a few swank clubs. There was an address book which would have done the Vice Squad proud. A pair of gray suede gloves, a handkerchief, two key rings, a pocket knife, pen, two cigars and the folded note comprised the remainder of the haul.

I read the note carefully, then took everything to the men's room and flushed all but the dollar, cigars and metal objects down the bowl. The cigars landed in my pocket, the dollar paid for the beer, the metal objects were slated for the first sewer and the words of the note remained in my head.

> When you leave here, walk from Ninth Avenue to Tenth Avenue along the south side of Fifty——— Street and step into the first parked taxicab you see for the pay-off.

It was unsigned and printed in pencil. Riding the subway downtown, I wondered if Egbert caught the "payoff" intended for Ruth St. John—or whether it was she who was to pay off and Egbert's recognition of the cab's occupant earned him a slug in the throat.

In either case, Egbert asked for what he got.

And, in either case, Barney Kane had pushed one of his fat fingers into the pie. And one of Vivian Day's slender digits was angled at the same pastry, Harry Dorgan's not far behind. And another pie-involved finger belonged to the red-headed stiff Kane had carried into Dorgan's Dump. And, plumb in the center of this pie, sat the quick killer—minus his silencer now.

But most of all, I wanted to learn about Barney Kane. The subway carried me to Fourth Street where I got off and walked to his Village hide-away.

KANE LIVED in a three-story brownstone, on the second floor. The vestibule door was open. Kane's door was locked. A trapdoor in the roof and the rear fire-escape led me to a bedroom window which happened to be open. The balmy air currents had seen to that.

Closing Venetian blinds all around, I switched on a reading lamp in the library-office from which Kane had bossed his grifts. The place was neat and modern—no bulges in the furniture, everything streamlined into everything else—all in a sort of gray shade.

I spent ten minutes opening and closing drawers, riffling the pages of books, searching under the gray broadloom rug, inside chairs, behind vases—and found not one solitary word of writing, not a single letter, not even a rent receipt.

It was a three-room apartment and ten minutes were enough. No wall safe or anything like that—it pointed to a safe deposit box. And that would be Quinn's department. He'd been very careful, Barney Kane—except in the pinch.

I switched off the light, started for the door, stopped as a fist rapped on the panel.

"Someone's in there, Flannagan—I saw a light!" came a low voice that was vaguely like Quinn's. The knocking was repeated. Then a hand touched the doorknob—

I was on the fire-escape when the door swung open, and in the yard below by the time a light appeared in the windows of Kane's apartment. The back door of the building was open. I entered a dimly lighted hall, walked to the vestibule and peered into the street—

Dark and empty. That was wrong—Quinn never walked. Manhattan's Homicide Squad was strictly motorized. But the street was empty.

I was leaning against the vestibule wall, peering out to make sure of this, when my shoulder dislodged something and I caught it halfway to the floor—a black letter box that had been on a nail. I caught the box, but two letters spilled to the floor and the name, *Barney Kane,* stared up at me from both of them!

Scrawled in pencil over one was: *Mr. Shane thout these was for him. He dident open them. Mrs. Downes.*

I dropped both letters in my pocket.

I remounted the stairs slowly, and loudly, with my automatic drawn.

Barney Kane's door stood open. The lights were on inside. The library was empty, but a picture of confusion. Someone had duplicated my search without putting things back in place. I followed the lights to the bedroom where the window I had closed stood wide open. I turned off the bedroom light and looked out.

A figure was dropping from the bottom rung of the fire-escape to the yard below. Definitely, a man. I could not make him out in the darkness, he was out of sight too fast. But I was getting the idea—it was just the two of us on a merry-go-round.

A merry-go-round to yesterday, as I learned on reading the letters back in the library.

The first letter contained a glossy photostat of a baby's footprint, together with a receipt for two dollars made out to Barney Kane and a typewritten note with the letterhead of the Buffalo Maternity Hospital.

> Enclosed find receipt and reproduction of the footprint of Mary Delaney, as requested. Mary Delaney was born in our hospital on June ninth, 1922, daughter of Mrs. Violet Delaney, of this city.

The second letter was from Abe Schulman, Barney Kane's mouthpiece.

> Barney:
> The St. John estate consists mainly of metal plants in Buffalo, New York, also an estate nearby, also other assets amounting to

about twelve million dollars. Mrs. St. John died in childbirth—in 1922. The old man died about five years ago.

His will leaves the entire estate to his daughter, Ruth, with the provision that if she dies before her twenty-first birthday, the estate goes to her cousin, Egbert St. John. (Incidentally, Gilwater, Egbert St. John's attorney, was checking this will in probate records last week) And, if Egbert also passes away, the administrator, Gilbert T. Murray, is instructed to give the estate to various named charities.

I can get a list of these for you, but don't think you want one. Is there anything to this?

Abe.

BOTH LETTERS became little pieces in my hands and I started them toward the ocean through Kane's bowl. Partly to cover Ruth St. John, partly because I was developing an idea.

Once more I switched off the lights. This time I walked out the door. I walked into the fist of Harry Dorgan!

He'd been standing before the door, listening, the scowl on his face etched in blue. There was no word spoken, no change of expression. I just opened the door—then gasped wind as the floor came up behind to jar every tooth in my head. Dorgan leaped as I jerked the butt of my automatic. I jerked it through a haze, in slow motion—he tore my hand away, snapped my wrist up until I was swaying on my feet, then his fist exploded on my temple and the floor hammered my back again—

I remember air whistling in through my teeth and how I couldn't get enough of it. And Dorgan's bitter scowl looming at me through a blood fog—and then another expression smoothing the lines of his face.

I was struggling off the floor—I'd forgotten my heater. I was coming off the floor with my fists when that expression of wary caution chased the scowl from his face.

Dorgan's knee caught my teeth as he leaped over me. I whirled dizzily until floor polish burned my lips. I wanted to stay there and close my eyes and sleep—but, vaguely, I heard a low growl from the street below—the last turn of a prowl car siren!

A door slammed downstairs—voices—Inspector Jack Quinn's voice, no mistaking it now!

Somehow, I was on my feet and staggering back through Kane's apartment. When I leaned out the bedroom window and cool, dark air swept over me, I almost passed out from the reaction.

But I made the fire-escape. I was touching the roof when Inspector Quinn's head poked out of the window below. He didn't look up. With Harry Dorgan leaping to the yard from the bottom landing, all Quinn's attention was focused.

"Hey, *you!*" he called.

I didn't see what happened. I was over the next two roofs, down carpeted stairs and out in the street, moving off in the shadows. I didn't know if Quinn had captured Dorgan—I hoped he hadn't. Not before I did.

At least I was off the merry-go-round.

CHAPTER THREE
THE STIFF AND THE GOON

A **PROFESSIONAL** crowd was at Dorgan's Dump now—show people, musicians, grifters and wise guys, and the rubbernecks who always manage to bask in reflected gossip-column glory. And the tale of the bullet from nowhere, that had done for Barney Kane, was on every lip.

A druggist had made me presentable with some tape, where Dorgan's knee split my lip. I drew a few nods and no comment, approaching Vivian Day at the bar. She was on straight Scotch now. Her only greeting was a grimace of dislike.

"Harry around?" I asked, meeting her brooding glance in the mirror.

"Nobody's around," she murmured in that husky throb. "Coppers put Sadie through hoops—but she don't know from me and I'm blank. Phillip takes two hours' relief and Dorgan's mutterin' threats." Vivian's expression brightened as she turned from the mirror to me. "He's going to kill you, heel, Dorgan is—you know that?" She noticed the tape on my lip and said, *"Well!"*

I said: "You want to tell me why you followed Ruth St. John around?"

Vivian said: "Why don't you—" It did not sound pleasant, coming from her. Particularly, since she meant every curse of it.

"It's coming dawn," I murmured, and I retreated to the kitchen. The Filipino pearl diver nodded at the alley and I walked out to find the bone game resumed. Sailor once again held the dice. This time, with nickels before him.

I stood in a shadow, half watching and marshaling some facts together when a draft of second-hand alcohol washed over me and someone mumbled: "Two cribs—*two*, see?"

He leaned on me and I didn't shove him off. It was Kane's tramp, complete to the beet-like nose amid red stubble. Under that, he looked fortyish and a long time kicked. I stood there and took the fumes and said: "Yeah. "It's funny about cribs—"

The tramp swung around to peer down at me, his eyes swollen out of focus.

"*Funny!* Shorty, if you knowed th' half of it!"

"You tell me half of it," I said, "and let me guess the rest."

A wise grin spread through his red stubble.

"Nah, nah," he mumbled thickly. "Evr'body paysh an' paysh t'hear good ol' Charley Delaney tell about th' cribs. Evr'body—paysh an' paysh an' paysh an' paysh an'—"

HE LEANED heavily on my arm, began sagging. I jerked him against the wall. We were a few yards from the crapshooters and they were occupied.

"Delaney?" I prompted. "You ever hear of Mary and Violet Delaney—from Buffalo?"

"M'own flesh 'n blood—" he mumbled. "Paysh an' paysh—" He sagged from my grip to the concrete and began snoring.

Sailor loomed over me. "He botherin' ya, Cash?"

"How'd you make out?" I said.

"Me? I'm rollin' good for once, Cash—"

"Then why play for jits?"

"Aw, Cash!" Sailor explained earnestly, "that way I hold on to the winnin's longer—" Sailor winced from my expression, changed the subject. "The lush botherin' ya, Cash?"

"You're taking him home," I told him. "You'll let him sleep a couple of hours in *your* bed." My watch showed it was two-thirty. "You'll let him sleep until five, then put him through hot and cold showers. Give him hot black coffee and bromo. I want him sober by five thirty."

"Aw, Cash!" protested Sailor, his lumpy features aghast. "In my bed. Cash? Mebbe he's got bugs an' I'll catch 'em!"

"It won't be the first time," I said.

"Aw, Cash!"

"Take him in a cab," I said.

I followed as Sailor reluctantly carried Charles Delaney to the grille fence at the end of the alley. None of the players glanced up.

Phillip was in the kitchen filling a tray with more free lunch. He grinned at me. "That was you took the tuna?"

"Me," I said.

Phillip's grin broadened.

"You have a Scotch rep, sport—but not by me. Damn few chiselers around here'd leave a tip on a loose tray."

"Maybe you'll give me Dorgan's address," I said.

Phillip assumed his business look and extended the tray. A dollar passed from my hand under the napkin draping it.

"Right across the street," grinned Phillip. "Apartment 3B. Thanks, sport—"

I watched until the swinging doors closed behind his black mop. The Filipino was out of sight. The row of garbage pails alongside the door caught my attention. The lid of one was slightly to one side and, beneath, I could make out something white. Absently, I kicked the lid more to the side. I stood looking down into the pail all of five seconds.

Then I stooped and lifted the automatic from inside. It was folded inside a powder-stained napkin. Under the napkin, the muzzle wore shiny nicks. The silencer from my pocket fitted snugly—it belonged.

The gun was a Colt, thirty-two caliber, with a dull, blue-steel finish and a powder-darkened bore. I worked the slide and a bullet hopped out. Rapidly, I dug the lead from the pellet with a fork, then returned the empty cartridge-case to the top of the magazine clip and closed the slide.

Pocketing the silencer, I re-wrapped the gun in the napkin, set it back in the garbage can with the lid askew as I had found it.

Vivian was singing about bedrooms when I left. Somehow, the Scotch seemed to have made her more intimate with the song than I liked.

THE DOORMAN, Andy, was leaning against the wall, cupping a lighted cigarette inside his palm. Smoke dribbled from his nostrils when he saw who I was.

"Everybody's hoppin' in and out tonight," he said.

"Who?"

"You, for one—"

"Who else?"

Andy squinted thoughtfully.

"Well, there's that Murray guy—he's been around twice since you left, lookin' for somebody. I don't know who. Then Vivian's been comin' in and out. And the boss—"

"Where's Dorgan now?"

The doorman angled a stubbled chin across the street at a renovated tenement house that loomed darkly in the night.

"He lives there."

"O.K., Andy," I said. "Who else has been around?"

"That chippy St. John doll. She come in a taxi, stayed in it for about ten minutes, then rode away again. I saw her face lookin' out the cab's winder, like she expected to see somethin'. Everybody's lookin' for somethin'. You, Mr. Wale?"

"Dorgan," I said.

"Like I told you, he's across the street. Apartment 3B."

"Suppose he's needed here?"

Andy stared at me uncertainly, then shifted his attention to his feet.

"You mean how do I call him?"

"That's it, Andy."

"I knock on his door three times," said the doorman, not meeting my eyes. "Then I get back here and he always comes. Even if he's grabbin' a nod, he gets outa bed and comes—"

I felt Andy's eyes on my back as I crossed the dark street. 3B was in back, at the end of a long gloomy corridor flanked by peeling green wallpaper—it was that kind of house. I had no trouble. My three knocks drew footsteps from inside. The door swung open and I said: "Surprise, surprise—"

Harry Dorgan said nothing. He was in shirtsleeves and suspenders, a black tie hanging loosely over his shoulders. He didn't look surprised, just white. His scowl was so white it was almost blue.

He backed inside. With the muzzle of my automatic boring into his chest, he *had* to back inside. I kicked shut the door in passing and we came to a stop against the far wall of his living-room.

"Going some place, Harry?" I said.

This because a suitcase lay open on the cheap studio couch with shirts, underwear, and such piled around.

Dorgan's eyes, now that I saw them close, were yellowish and foggy. They were motionless on me. The rest of him was also motionless—except his nostrils. They quivered in spasms the way I had once seen a cornered rat's belly quiver in spasms.

I said: "What brought you to Kane's, Harry?"

He spat down into my face.

Then his chin jerked east and west as my automatic's muzzle connected twice and Dorgan crumpled to his imitation oriental rug. I wiped the saliva from my face with a sleeve and checked through the suitcase.

Snapshots and studio portraits filled a good quarter of it. I riffled through them and got the idea. They were all of Vivian Day. Vivian smiling, gazing soulfully down—up—right—left, before a mike, in cheesecake—a fine collection if you liked Vivian. I sometimes mistook pillows for Vivian nights—

Under everything else in the suitcase lay a Buffalo marriage certificate made out to Charles Delaney and Violet Conroy. It was dated June, 1923.

I muddled over this a few seconds, then put it out of my mind. Charles Delaney, in person, would talk when he sobered. He would tell me, among other items, why the certificate was in possession of Harry Dorgan and Delaney would also tell me why it was dated in 1923 when his daughter Mary's birth certificate was dated in 1922.

I RETURNED to Harry Dorgan who was crawling slowly to his knees. I put my heel on his left shoulder and propped him back against the wall. He reached for my ankle, then snapped his hands away with a grunt—but not fast enough. A red welt ran along the back of one hand, continued along the back of the other.

An automatic cuts everybody down to one size—used right.

I said: "What brought you to Kane's, Harry?"

He didn't spit this time—he'd caught the idea. But he didn't talk, either. He lay against the wall and wished I was dead with every part of his face.

A peculiar egg all around. Harry Dorgan—what with bartending in the joint he owned, carrying the torch for a streamlined smoothie like Vivian Day and living in this dive notwithstanding a five-figure income.

I said: "Harry, suppose I go to the cops and tell them Barney Kane was bumped because of a payoff involving Ruth St. John and a tramp named Charles Delaney, and a couple of females named Violet and Mary respectively, and a matter of two cribs about which various citizens have paid and paid—"

I got no farther. The hate washed out of Dorgan's face, leaving it haggard and old.

"*No!*" he whispered hoarsely.

I said: "Harry, what brought you to Kane's?"

"To cover for someone," he whispered.

"Ruth St. John," I said.

He stared dumbly at me.

"O.K., you went to cover for Ruth St. John," I said. "Why?"

Dorgan's eyes dropped to the welts on the backs of his palms. He muttered: "You were at Kane's, Wale—"

"To cover for Ruth St. John," I said. "Only me, I get paid for it."

His eyes shot up to my face again, as if to force the truth from me by the intensity of his stare.

"That a fact?" he whispered.

I said: "You've got it all wrong, Harry. I'm asking you—"

He said: "I was the St. John's chauffeur around eighteen years ago. Up near Buffalo, that was."

I waxed sarcastic. "That's a real good reason for racing the cops to Barney Kane's—and chesting me. You know what it means, using hands on me. You've been around long enough to know what happens. You know my grift floats on reputation and I'm not going to let a pair of loose fists spoil it. You know it so well it's probably why you're fixing to lam. So now tell me why you covered for Ruth St. John."

"I told you, Wale."

"Then tell me about Violet Conroy who married Charles Delaney," I said.

Harry Dorgan was sweating now. There was business with his tongue and Adam's apple getting mixed before his next words came.

"Lay off her, Wale. I don't care how fast you can shoot, Wale. If you mess into this and smash a lot of people's lives, I'll smash you, Wale. I'll say this much. Violet Conroy was the maid with the St. Johns. Delaney was the gardener—"

"And you were the chauffeur," I said, ignoring the threat. "And baby Mary Delaney happened in, a year before she was legal. I got that much, Harry. Also, about that time, Ruth St. John likewise hatched, her mother dying in the process. Who nursed and took care of Ruth?"

A rivulet of sweat ran down Harry Dorgan's cheek.

"Violet," he said.

"And she took care of her own kid at the same time?" I kept hammering at him.

Dorgan nodded imperceptibly.

"That would make two cribs," I said. Then, as hate began to inflame Dorgan's yellow eyes, I asked: "And what became of Delaney?"

"He drifted."

"And Violet?"

"She drifted."

"With Mary Delaney?"

"Mary Delaney fell accidentally from her crib and died when she was three weeks old," said Dorgan.

"That left one crib," I said.

Dorgan's scowl could have been engraved in ivory—wet, streaming ivory.

"So that's it," I said, taking my heel from his shoulder. "Unpack that grip, Harry," I added. "You're not going anyplace. Not unless you want Ruth St. John in the gutter, you're not going any place. Just across the street, Harry. I want you there with Vivian Day in about an hour."

At the door, I said: "Good-bye for now, Harry Dorgan—"

CHAPTER FOUR
TWO CRIBS
AND TWO GRAND

SOME CHILL air left over from winter sifted through the night as I once more stood before Dorgan's Dump. Andy, the doorman, was not in sight. I hesitated about entering, then thought about the gun in the garbage pail and walked to the grille-work fencing the alley.

The gate was unlatched—beyond it, heavy shadows—beyond them, around the bend in the wall, a hazy shaft of light from the kitchen window. I was almost to the bend when the rod jammed painfully into my spine. A hand snaked under my arm, withdrew my heater from its holster. Then warm breath lingered on my neck and Inspector Jack Quinn's growl mocked: "I figured you'd show sooner or later, and waited in the yard to catch you in the club—and you walk right into my arms!"

He stood alone, must have been deep in the shadows when I peered in the gate. He stood with his positive covering my middle as I turned to face him. He was between me and the street.

"Very funny," I said.

I couldn't see his eyebrows. I could have imagined them writhing from sheer joy. The joy was in his voice: "Funny, shrimp? It goes like this: you're under arrest, Wale, and I'm warning you that anything you say may be used against—"

"The charge," I cut in. "Give with the makings for a nice legal suit."

Quinn chuckled. "Just a technicality, shrimp. I'm charging you with homicide!"

"Kane?"

"No, shrimp, not Kane. We'll maybe ring that one in on you later. For the time being, there's Egbert St. John, found shot and another guy found sapped two blocks from here—with your prints all over the coupé—"

I was supposed to blurt: "You mean the *cab!*" I didn't. I said: "You arresting me for the murder of Egbert St. John?"

"No," drawled Inspector Quinn, "not for that either. Although I think you'll do fine when ballistics is through. No, shrimp, you're under arrest for murdering a tramp named Charles Delaney!

"I found his remains in your flat when I went there to ask more questions about you and Kane. I have witnesses who will avoid a gambling rap by testifying they saw your goon, Duffy, carrying Delaney out of here. Other witnesses to show Delaney was the only person in hearing distance when you scrapped with Kane—a possible motive.

"Delaney may have listened to something that would have connected you up to the neck with the murder of Kane and you rubbed him. Or had that goon, Duffy—"

Inspector Jack Quinn stopped talking then. He stopped talking because an arm the size of a log had wound under his chin from behind. Another arm of the same dimensions was generating pressure on Quinn's diaphragm—

Quinn may have had ideas of shooting. Not that he saw me or where his rod pointed—his eyes were swollen white in their sockets and pointing up. His tongue bulged out.

Lifting the rod from his fist was like lifting it from a cushion for all the resistance he offered. As I found my own automatic in his coat pocket, his breath whooshed out and Sailor Duffy's misshapen face peered over Quinn's shoulder.

"What's a goon, Cash?" growled Duffy. "That's what I wanna know—what's a goon, *hagh?*"

"Leggo his throat before he croaks!" I snapped. Sailor's arms loosened their hold and Inspector Quinn sagged a foot, his breath coming in jerks. I told Sailor: "Hold him against the wall until I get back."

"Aw, Cash, suppose he comes outa—"

"Keep holding him!" I flung over my shoulder.

THE FILIPINO was not in the kitchen. The automatic still was, still wrapped in its napkin. I worked the slide twice and caught my hand-made blank as it hopped out. I pondered over it awhile, then pressed it back into the magazine and closed the slide.

That this was the quick killer's rod, I was certain. That it wasn't used to bump Delaney was equally certain. I was faced with two answers. Either a second killer was on the prowl, or the original quick killer had used another weapon on Delaney which could frame me. Both questions led to others which I didn't have time to brood over.

The automatic was back in the napkin and in the pail again when I returned to where Sailor held Quinn's limp form in the shadows. "I can't do this all night, Cash," pleaded Sailor.

"You couldn't stay with that tramp either," I said softly. *"Or did you?"*

"Me, Cash? Hagh! I figgered I'd get back to the bone game an' win us a little stake, Cash. Alla time it's you bringin' home the berries. Me, I—"

I stopped him impatiently.

"How about the lush?"

"He was in dreamland, Cash. He snored to beat sixty an' I kept turnin' him over but he'd turn back an' then I got sick o' listenin' so I come over for another chance at the bones, on'y they ain't no game. On'y this flatty with a heater on you. So I—"

"Shut up," I said. "Let me think. I wish I knew how Delaney was rubbed—"

Sailor brightened.

"Ask *him*, Cash!" He shook Quinn like a rag doll.

"Can't wait, Sailor." I regarded my slap-nutty partner thoughtfully, then said: "Look, if he was handcuffed, think you could hold him quiet but conscious for about half an hour?"

"Aw, Cash—"

"It would mean getting him upstairs without being seen," I said.

"I could fix that," said Sailor, without enthusiasm. "There's a winder in the kitchen goes to the back yard an' back stairs. But let him wake up an' keep him quiet alla that time, Cash?"

"If it doesn't work, you'll only get around ten years," I said.

"Aw, Cash—"

It took five minutes to maneuver Quinn through the kitchen and out the window, Sailor after him. Neither the Filipino nor anyone else interfered. The kitchen was deserted because it was after three and what customers remained had no interest in grub.

Through the swinging doors, I saw the Filipino mopping a distant corner of the floor. A sprinkling of customers were occupied with drinks and confidential talk. Harry Dorgan stood behind the bar in his overcoat and Vivian Day spoke to him from a bar stool—their heads were close, their expressions drawn.

Back at the window, I saw Inspector Quinn's number twelves sail by. They swung around to be replaced by Sailor's assortment of facial bumps.

"Cash—" he hissed.

"What?"

"I wanna know, Cash. What's a goon, hagh?"

I closed the window.

GILBERT T. MURRAY'S voice was nervous on the phone: "Listen, Wale, I didn't expect you to go that far—"

"How far?"

"Well—Kane." Murray's voice grew angry. "It will only serve to embarrass Ruth. She was seen talking with that son of a ——"

"You're speaking of the dead, pal," I said. "And pull in your horns about Kane. I don't work like that—not for this kind of dough. And that brings me to the point. Have that dough on ice, as agreed."

Murray forgot his ancestors to gush familiarly: *"Cash! Do you mean you—"*

I mean I don't take checks," I said.

And hung up.

I walked three blocks to another drug store and phoned Ruth St. John. It took her seconds to answer. Nobody was sleeping this night.

"This is the man you didn't meet at the Dump tonight," I said through my handkerchief. "How about that payoff?"

For a moment I thought I was talking into blank space. Then, tense words filled the blank: "You have found them?"

"I told you about that."

"May I see them?"

"Uh-uh. Not till my palm is crossed with shekels, babe—"

Again the line seemed to go dead. Then: "You sound— uh—different."

I growled: "You wanna play, or do I peddle 'em elsewhere?"

"Now?"

"Maybe."

"Oh, I have the money! I had it all night as I promised but never received a sign as *you* promised. I even drove back to the club later. Won't you *please* let me see them?"

"I'm coming up to your place, babe. Tell the doorman to admit Mr. Frank."

"Why, last time you were Mr. Jones—"

"I'm ambidextrous," I said, breaking the connection.

IT WAS one of those super-de luxe apartment palaces with twin towers overlooking Central Park from the west. In spite of the hour, the name of Frank whisked me through a plush and palm lobby, up a cage of streamlined gilt to a narrow foyer with one door. A penthouse, this.

Ruth St. John answered my ring herself. Recognition stamped her eyes, as if they were saying, *You!* but her lips didn't move.

She was a trim slip of a doll in a light blue robe that flared to the rug.

She backed a little as I entered. She spoke when I closed the door behind me.

"Where are they?"

"We alone?"

"Where are they?"

"That was a device to crash in, Miss St. John," I said, gently. "Me, I'm playing on your side—"

For a moment she stood poised, taut—like a bird about to take wing. Then every trim line of her face wrinkled and a sob broke past her lips. The back of her wrist flew to her mouth. She spun through eggshell drapes which blocked the foyer.

I followed into half a million dollars worth of living-room—all done up in low, smooth curves and eggshell colors.

She had flung herself on a curved lounge, face down. Her shoulders heaved—but it was soundless.

I felt like a fish out of water and kept my eyes on a painting that looked like scrambled eggs gone wrong.

After awhile she sat up and found my eyes on her.

"Why don't you go away?" she pleaded.

"Because I want to tell you it's no use looking for your parents," I said.

Her eyes went to a pair of oil paintings which hung over the fireplace, a young couple with chins out of the blue book—the late Mr. and Mrs. St. John.

"Not them," I cut in as she was about to speak. "I mean your *real* parents, Mary Delaney—"

She began to say, "You don't understand—" then my words clicked. *"You know?"* she whispered.

"But you didn't?" I said.

"No," she whispered, "not until that man phoned. He said it could be proven from my footprints—"

"And he wanted dough to stay clammed," I said. "He threatened to expose you. It would mean losing the St. John inheritance because the will gives the estate to cousin Egbert if Ruth St. John died before she was twenty-one, and the *real* Ruth St. John had died at the age of three weeks—as Mary Delaney."

The girl's chin went up.

"Believe me, it was not the money—it was my own father and mother, do you understand what that means? My own parents! I wanted to—"

"I know," I said. "And, learning this, you broke with Murray because it might cramp his position, maybe even douse the torch he carried for you. How about Barney Kane? He was once overboard for you, probably still was, from habit. You get him into it—to check for you?"

"Oh, he *did!*" cried the girl, flushing. "Tonight Barney said he had learned the identity of the man who phoned me. He told me he had thrashed that man and that I would not be bothered any longer."

"And when Kane was plugged, you knew you would," I concluded. "That's why you let me in. But I'm here with Barney's tune—you're not going to be bothered again—and I don't plug easy."

She went to the window as mixed feelings began chasing across her ivory face.

"Don't worry about the man who called you," I said quietly. "And forget about the woman who's been following you around lately. As for Charles and Violet Delaney—believe me, babe, they're past your help. Or anyone's help—"

The girl whirled.

"*They are*—"

"Yes," I lied solemnly. "These many years, babe. It's tough on you. It makes you a two-time orphan."

"You know," she whispered, "you know, I *thought* it would be like that—"

"Answer it," I said, as the door chimes sounded.

GILBERT T. MURRAY'S agitated voice sounded from the foyer: "Ruth, dear, please steady yourself for a shock. It is about Egbert. I've just learned that he was—*Ruth, you're crying!*"

I couldn't make out what she said, but Murray burst through the eggshell drapes, the tan on his face turned ashen, and his fists knotted. "What have you been saying to her?" he demanded hoarsely. "Who gave you a right to come here in the first place? Get out, Wale!"

"You ready to pay off?" I said.

The girl appeared behind Murray, her eyes swimming. "Pay off—for *what?*"

"Everybody's asking questions," I said. "The boy-friend hired me to learn why you were freezing him out—that's why I told you I was on your side. I learned why you turned him down and now I intend to collect, as agreed."

Murray's strained face turned to the girl, her wet face turned to him, and everything became so quiet that I was able to hear late traffic moving in the street twenty floors down.

Then Murray turned back to me with an expression that feared what he had seen.

"That's off, Wale," he barely managed. "I'll pay you—but no more snooping."

"The investigation came through," I told him.

"Damn you, I don't want to hear it!"

"You want to marry the girl?"

Both of them stared at me now. Both wore the same frightened expression.

"Miss St. John was being blackmailed," I said, emphasizing the *Miss St. John* with a sidelong glance at her. The back of her wrist was to her mouth and her eyes stared.

"Don't say it, Wale," Murray pleaded.

"O.K., I won't," I said. "The blackmail was a phoney anyhow, one of those things. But Miss St. John, figuring the kind of snobs you both hatched from, knew what damage even a faked scandal could do to your marriage. So—"

The girl's ivory cheeks grew spots of red as Murray swept her into his arms.

"Sweet," he whispered, "I don't care anything about your past, true or false. I don't even want to know about it. All I want is for you to—"

I tapped his shoulder.

"That stuff bores me even in the movies where it's done with practice," I said. "You ready to pay off?"

He let her go long enough to pass me an envelope with four bills, each worth five centuries.

"That closes the deal," I said. "Tonight wipes out every trace of the blackmail—but complete. And you'll never find out, pal."

"That's how I want it," whispered Gilbert T. Murray happily.

Passing through the eggshell drapes, I looked back, said: "Well, good-bye for now—" But they were in a strangle hold.

The doll was gushing: "Oh, yes, darling, *yes!*"

I slammed out the door feeling like a piker. There I was, wanted by the cops for four unsolved kills. I was due to be wanted for attacking and snatching a cop inspector. I had been slugged, chased, pushed around and marked lousy by Vivian Day, one of the few Manhattan she-jobs who affected my pulse—and all for a lousy two grand.

While, due to my work, that crib-hopping babe inside was able to gush, "Yes!"—and close a twenty million dollar merger!

CHAPTER FIVE
THE BULLET TO NOWHERE

VIVIAN DAY questioned me in that husky throb: "You want to see me upstairs, heel?"

"Harry also," I said. "This will be a lecture on a bullet from nowhere and two cribs. Interested?"

They stared helplessly at me, Vivian from my side of the bar, Harry Dorgan from behind the bar—still in his black overcoat.

The swinging kitchen doors were propped open now. I called through them to Phillip who sat hunched over a cup of coffee and a tabloid: "Bring two quarts of Haig and Haig in pinch-bottles to that creep room at the end of the corridor upstairs. I don't mean refills, guy. O.K.?"

"O.K., sport!" grinned Phillip. The only other sign of life in Dorgan's Dump was the Filipino. He'd piled the tables in a remote corner. Now, with the enthusiasm of a robot, he plied a mop.

"We'll go upstairs and listen, Wale," said Harry Dorgan.

"Fine," I said.

Vivian shrugged bare shoulders and eased off her stool with great deliberation. Even the slight waver as she crossed the room took nothing from her. Harry Dorgan came around the bar and helped her with an arm to the stairs.

Halfway up, all three of us froze as my hand emerged from Dorgan's coat pocket with a revolver that thought it was a cannon. Aside from size, the bore was rusted and the hammer waggled.

"You'll spend years combing this out of your face if you ever try firing it, Harry," I said, wedging the long barrel under my belt.

Dorgan's yellow-fog eyes turned helplessly to Vivian, then he urged her upstairs. I followed after a backward glance. Phillip was behind the bar, assembling bottles and glasses on a tray.

THE CREEP room at the end of the corridor was done up in red leather, red upholstery, red carpet, red-shaded lamp and pictures that would have reddened any high school girl's cheeks. Vivian and Dorgan sat side by side on the couch while I seated myself facing them. I pointed to the paneled wall at the foot of the couch.

"Ought to seal that creep door before some wise cop spots it."

"Get to the point, Wale," muttered Dorgan.

"That's right, heel," echoed Vivian. "The quicker I don't have to see your ratty little face, the quicker my digestion will return to normal."

Phillip entered with his napkin-draped tray supporting two bottles and three brandy glasses. He set the tray on the table and began tearing the seal off one of the bottles.

"The point," I said, facing Dorgan, "is that somebody got next to that tramp, Delaney's yarn about two cribs. A rich little doll occupied one and the kid hatched by the housemaid occupied the other. The maid's doll was a little accident due to the gardener who also happened to be the tramp, Delaney—"

Dorgan's scowl was blue again. His fingers made convulsive stabs at his coat pocket, then he remembered I carried the baby cannon.

I continued: "It seems there was a switch in the cribs. I think it came about when the rich little doll fell out of hers and landed dead. That was at the age of three weeks. Most kids look alike at that age, except to their mamas—and the rich kid's mama was dead.

"That left the maid. Maybe it was the idea of giving her own girl a break in life. Maybe this maid wanted to feel her oats—she was young, healthy, and ambitious. Maybe it was both—giving the kid and herself a break.

"So the record has it that the maid's kid died—that was the switch. The maid ran both cribs. It was a simple matter to change clothes from the rich little corpse to her own daughter. And now she was, as they say, a bereaved mother—"

"Wale, do you *have* to go on?" whispered Dorgan hoarsely.

"If I want to avoid a bum rap, I have to go on, Harry," I said. "To cut it short, the maid's kid has now grown up—an heiress. Not only has she a mint, but she is engaged to wed another mint. When the guy who heard the tramp, Delaney, get this far, he angled for a slice of the girl's mint. In short, he blackmailed the girl—and that brings me to Barney Kane—"

"*Barney?*" choked Vivian Day.

"Did the one clean thing in his life," I said. "Or maybe he was angling for the squeeze himself. He got next to Delaney—probably by accident, through his habit of feeding tramps off the street here—and Delaney talked. Delaney also mentioned talking to others and, in that manner, Kane learned about the blackmailer.

"Kane beat the blackmailer with his fists and warned the guy to muscle out as of then. What happened, you know. The blackmailer muscled Kane out instead—"

"*How?*" whispered Dorgan. "Do you know that, Wale? You watched Kane in the mirror—I watched him across the bar. Vivian's act held the customers at their tables. We would have seen anybody at Kane's booth—"

"We could have seen and not realized."

"What do you mean?"

"How about a waiter passing by?" I asked, turning in my seat to watch Phillip who stood across the table from me, the tray in his hands.

"A waiter could have done it with both of us watching him," I said. "Using a silenced rod hidden by the napkin under his tray. He could have motioned Kane to open the booth's door, then plugged Kane in the throat, kicked the door shut and moved off. This could have taken maybe five seconds."

I saw Phillip's tray was in his left hand now. His right was somewhere under it, hidden from view by the over-hanging napkin.

"*You're framing me, sport,*" he whispered carefully.

"Phillip's been with me three years," spoke Dorgan from the couch.

"And always hungry for a buck."

"You sure of this, heel?" asked Vivian unsteadily from the couch.

"Phillip was dusted about the time Kane used fists on the blackmailer," I said. "Phillip admitted to me he fed Delaney in back, and Delaney must have talked from grat-itude. Phillip was on a two-hour relief when somebody bumped young Egbert and when someone bulled me out of Kane's apartment by imitating Inspector Quinn's voice—and Phillip's a mimic. Which could also account for the female voice that lured Kane to the phone.

"Also, right after the Kane bump, I found Phillip's tray in the check-room minus its napkin—powder stains, proba-bly. And finally, to make the case legal, ballistics will show Kane and young Egbert were done in with slugs from Phillip's rod—"

"What rod?" came from Dorgan.

"The one he's holding under that napkin now," I said.

TEARS WERE forming in Phillip's eyes now from the intensity of his stare, but his thick lips pursed speculatively. There was no movement in the room. There was a pause that built up tension until Phillip said: "How you set this up, you're pretty much of a dope, Wale."

"Am I right about your heater under the napkin?" I said.

"Now it's got to be three more," he said, flicking his eyes to the others.

"That's what killing does," I said. "It becomes an epidemic, once the fever gets in you."

"I always figured you for a smoothie," Phillip said.

"I'm a smoothie," I said. "Inspector Quinn's in that creep door behind you."

"The hell he is," Phillip said. "Quinn hasn't been around for hours. Anyhow, he wouldn't work with you, not after wanting you for strangling Delaney—"

"So you know Delaney was strangled," I said. "You were in the kitchen when I told Sailor to carry Delaney home. Probably took another relief—"

"He took a second relief!" spat Vivian hoarsely.

Phillip said: "That's enough for stalling. I'll get a medal for this—"

The napkin around his tray suddenly flamed to a crackling explosion. I watched his eyes blink out the tears that had formed. He flung off the tray, revealing the smoking blue-steel muzzle of his automatic. He turned it on Dorgan, who was lunging from the couch—then his face snapped back, grew an expression of astonishment that I wasn't dead—

I winked at him and shot him through the neck.

I said: "Bring him out, Sailor."

The creep door at the foot of the couch swung open, revealing Inspector Jack Quinn in cuffs, his mouth lost in Sailor's ham-like left hand, his arms pinioned by Sailor's telephone-pole right arm.

He wore puffed, blue circles under both shaggy brows.

I scowled. "What's that for, Sailor? I didn't tell you to slug him!"

"Aw, Cash," pleaded Sailor from behind Quinn. "I asked him an' he tol' me. He tol' me what is a goon."

I said: "Inspector, before I remove the bracelets and return your rod and tell Sailor to ungag you, let's get this straight. You heard what went on.

"For the rest, unless you want to be laughed to your grave for being held in a creep closet while your prize suspect solved a batch of kills for you, my advice is to forget Sailor's and my part in it and take credit for that—"

I nodded at the remains of Phillip, then told Sailor: "Let him go."

Quinn, when he calmed down to yelling, yelled: "You didn't have to kill him, Wale, not how you can shoot, you didn't!"

"Self-defense, Inspector," I said. "I was in a hurry—"

"Not how those shots were spaced, you weren't!"

"They came one on top of the other," I said. "I've got witnesses. We mustn't forget the witnesses, Inspector."

Quinn glared around at Harry Dorgan who stood motionless with an arm around Vivian, then at Sailor— who nodded: "Me, I'm a witness!"

Quinn looked at Phillip on the table, then at the floor beyond where I'd been sitting. "If he stood where he fell and he missed you, why don't the slug show in the floor there—" He pointed. One hand followed the other with a metallic clank. "Get these off!" he yelled.

As Sailor went to work on the cuffs, I said: "I never look to make sure if a slug comes with the shot before shooting back—"

"How about that maid's kid who's inherited a fortune illegal?"

I pulled the silencer out of my pocket, still in my handkerchief, gave it to him.

"Be satisfied with that," I said. "Maybe it's got Phillip's prints on it. I found it in the cab where Egbert and the hackie were bumped. As for what you mentioned, I don't know what you're batting about. My advice is to leave blackmail to professional blackmailers and stick to homicide."

Quinn's face was hot enough to fry eggs on. "Get out of here, Wale," he choked. "*Get out!*"

SO IT was Vivian, Dorgan and myself on the stairs again, with Sailor behind us and the Filipino still dreaming over his mop below. I gave Dorgan his baby cannon and told Vivian: "What you wanted to hire me for is cleared, babe. The doll will hook the mint, thinking both Delaneys are dead. But it would have been a lot easier all around if you had told me that you're Violet Delaney—"

Vivian shrank into Dorgan's arms and he turned a white face to me.

"Let it hang there, Wale," he pleaded. "She's suffered eighteen years for one mistake. I tried patching things by marrying her in Delaney's name but the kids had been switched around then. And now, after all these years, Delaney had to show three nights running with Kane. And Kane had public words with Mary—Ruth—and it's been hell for Vivian, Wale."

"The kid has Vivian's eyes," I said.

"So you—we had you all wrong in this, Wale," pleaded Dorgan.

"At least the kid gets a break," I said.

Vivian suddenly broke from Dorgan's arms and faced me. "You're still a heel, Wale! I know what you want—"

"I want to get out of here now," I said, thickly.

"You're such a wise-angled, dough-angled little heel," she giggled, "and all this night you've been working for me for free! For *nothing,* Cash Wale—" her words drowned in a sob and then she was back in Dorgan's arms, letting it all out against his shoulder.

Dorgan's face framed a wide-eyed plea: "Not any more, Wale—"

But Sailor bristled: "Whaddya mean Cash comes outa this night for free? Cash an' me shares alike an' I come outa the bone game a winner by two bucks an' eighty-five cents! Howya like them apples?"

I patted the two grand in my vest pocket and, forcing a grin in the face of Vivian in Dorgan's arms, whispered: "Yeah! Howya like them apples?"

www.ingramcontent.com/pod-product-compliance
Lightning Source LLC
Chambersburg PA
CBHW031208020726

47499CB00002B/532